A NOTE ON THE AUTHOR

RAFFAELLA BARKER, daughter of the poet George Barker, was born and brought up in the Norfolk countryside. She is the author of seven acclaimed novels: *Come and Tell Me Some Lies*; *The Hook*; *Hens Dancing*; *Summertime*; *Green Grass*; *Poppyland*; and *A Perfect Life*. She has also written a novel for young adults, *Phosphorescence*. She is a regular contributor to *Country Life* and the *Sunday Telegraph*, and teaches on the Literature and Creative Writing BA at the University of East Anglia and the *Guardian* UEA Novel Writing Masterclass. Raffaella Barker lives by the sea in north Norfolk.

www.raffaellabarker.co.uk

@raffaellabarker

BY THE SAME AUTHOR

RAFFAELLA BARKER

FROM A DISTANCE

BLOOMSBURY

LONDON · NEW DELHI · NEW YORK · SYDNEY

Bloomsbury Paperbacks
An imprint of Bloomsbury Publishing Plc

50 Bedford Square
London
WC1B 3DP
UK

1385 Broadway
New York
NY 10018
USA

www.bloomsbury.com

BLOOMSBURY and the Diana logo are trademarks of Bloomsbury Publishing Plc

First published in Great Britain 2014
This paperback edition first published in 2015

British Library Cataloguing-in-Publication Data
A catalogue record for this book is available from the British Library.

ISBN: HB: 978-1-4088-3373-5
TPB: 978-1-4088-0808-5
PB: 978-1-4088-5415-0
ePub: 978-1-4088-3374-2

2 4 6 8 10 9 7 5 3 1

Typeset by Hewer Text UK Ltd, Edinburgh
Printed and bound in Great Britain by CPI Group (UK) Ltd, Croydon CR0 4YY

To find out more about our authors and books visit www.bloomsbury.com.
Here you will find extracts, author interviews, details of forthcoming events
and the option to sign up for our newsletters.

For Sam Banks, in loving memory

CHAPTER 1

The HMS *Stanley Livingstone* sailed into Southampton harbour on a spring day in April 1946 to be greeted by sunshine and a flutter of smiling faces. It was a Sunday and on the quay the Salvation Army brass band was conducting a popular weekly service. Gleaming instruments reflected pomp and ceremony into the skies, trumpeting a welcome to the returning soldiers. Today's congregation was restless and excitable. Troop ships had been arriving for months, docking at Southampton to disembark men, back in their thousands from the war. They were demobbed and sent on their way across the British Isles to their families, returning to life as civilians in a changed country. Peace was no longer news, and Southampton's residents had lost the edge of jubilation that had fuelled earlier celebrations, previous homecomings. The end of the war had turned out to be a murky, fractured process, full of dashed expectations and uneasy silences. Once home, no soldier eased into the role of hero. Happy ever after remained a dream to chase.

Today, though, the soldiers on board the *Livingstone* were unaware of what lay ahead or that the band would have been there today anyway, the welcome a coincidence. Water glinted and slid beyond the churning docks, the breeze was unusually warm for April, and the congregation was a throng of Sunday morning citizens enjoying a spring day. Along the quay where the ship loomed like a cliff a small boy with a flag, his blue sailor coat buttoned to his chin, a scruffy dog at his heels, ran to and fro. A soldier at a porthole waved his red spotted handkerchief, and the child laughed and swung his little flag above his head. Higher, above the tiers of men lining the three decks of *Stanley Livingstone* and up on top of the gun tower, another flag danced and waved. The brass band began to play:

> *And did those feet in ancient time*
> *Walk upon England's mountains green*

A girl walking past the band had stopped to listen. Smiling, she twirled on her heel, her head tilted back to stare up at the ship and her throat flashed. Her skirt fluttered up the curve of her thigh with another glimpse of pale flesh. The little boy ran up and put his hand in hers. A wolf whistle shrilled through the thrum of waves against the bow, and a cheer shivered across the decks. The brass band pumped out the tune, and over the roar of the engines came a ribbon of melody, the soldiers' song plangent on the breeze.

> *Bring me my spear, Oh clouds unfold,*
> *Bring me my chariot of fire.*

On board, hats wheeled in the air, the verve of the hymn, the proximity of land, a tonic to the soldiers lining the decks. Pressing forward for their welcome, trying not to see the rubble and the broken windows, the dereliction beyond the harbour, silence fell. Facing a group of friendly people was out of kilter for them. Excitement coursed beneath filthy uniforms. No one spoke. They had been waiting to come home for months, gathered from outposts all the way from Burma back to Europe, stopping and starting as if on a never-ending bus journey.

Jokes were the shorthand for the future as the boat made its passage home:

'Lucky we're on rations, or we'd sink her,' an officer, whip thin, his hands big like hams had observed, when the ship stopped in Ankara and another five hundred men embarked. Now, he leaned on the railings as the ship docked, and remarked to his second in command, 'You could weigh the whole British Army against this old tank and we'd bounce against her like a rubber ball.'

A couple of artillerymen standing on the quarter deck reread letters from home.

'Bet your girl didn't wait for you, mate,' one nudged the other. 'You should've sent those nylons when you had the chance.'

'Nah,' the other chewed gum, spat, and swaggered as he hitched his belt up a notch, 'she'll have me when she sees me, just you wait and see.'

The big ideas thrown about over card games had evaporated with the approach of land. Last night's talk had been expansive: 'I'll take over a munitions factory and put it to building cars.'

'I'll bring some of those Arab horses home and breed them on a stud farm.'

'Forget all that, mate. I'm for the quiet life, thinking of opening a little guest house by the sea and running it with the missis.'

Today they were quiet.

On the middle of the three decks, standing apart as was his habit, Lance Corporal Michael Marker of the Royal Norfolk Regiment absorbed the approach of his homeland and the prospect of post-war life with equal measures of excitement and apprehension. He'd been set to go to university to read English Literature and become a teacher. He looked around him today. At twenty-five, he was among the older men. Sometimes he felt that he inhabited a different skin from the Michael Marker he was in 1942 when he joined up in the spirit of bravado and excitement, encouraged by the swagger of his brother Johnnie, back on leave in a smart new uniform that made the girls jostle and giggle. Michael queued for his own uniform and army number with Ned Baxter and Charlie Denham, the boys he'd gone to school with, lads from his home village he'd shared his childhood with. He looked along the row of men beside him. New friends made on the journey home. Scriven, patting his pocket to check his tobacco tin was where he'd put it, was a nervy guy. He twitched now, pulled out a pair of dice and rolled them on his palm. Back to Birmingham he would go, and a job on a car production line. Michael wondered if he would ever see him again.

Ned Baxter had died in Normandy. Michael had been with him at Sourdeval. Saw him shot clean through the head and fall like a suit of clothes with no one in it. The bullethole was no bigger than the end of a pool cue. D-Day they called it. That was a joke. The next time he was home on leave, Michael had visited Baxter's parents at the pub they owned. His dad, Eliot Baxter, had a wooden leg and a medal from Passchendaele, 1917. He'd taught Ned and Michael to tie flies for fishing when they were boys. Michael remembered the moment he stepped into the familiar darkness of the pub bar and Eliot Baxter looked up. For a fraction of a second, a wild fleck of hope had glinted like a spun sixpence in his eyes, extinguished the moment he remembered his son was dead.

Charlie Denham, red-haired and flame-fast on his feet with his pockets always full of things to trade, up for every spree and then some more, had joined the Northamptonshire because it was his mother's county. He died after twelve months of fighting, drowned in the Rhine among the chaos and floating bodies.

Nor shall my sword sleep in my hand
Till we have built Jerusalem
In England's green and pleasant land.

Michael walked to the port side of the boat, and shaded his eyes to the glittering horizon. The deck was deserted. Every man on board was facing land, ready to dock and walk free. *England's green and pleasant land*. Where was the green? Michael gazed across at Southampton. Buildings had collapsed in heaps, a wall lay like a wafer on top of a mound of rubble and in front of it a grey delivery van was buried up to the driver's door, dirty and abandoned. Two buses were parked on what would have been the kerb if it had not crumbled to brown sugar. A ringing sound became louder inside Michael's head. He closed his eyes. Within, everything turned red.

Michael had seen tears haunt soldiers' faces. He'd never seen an adult cry before the war. They dreamed and spoke of peace, but none of them really knew what it was or would be. Among the older men was a new anxiety, impossible to share in a few words over a cigarette. What now?

The ragged welcome at Southampton, small though it was, was overwhelming. Michael heard the liquid sound of faith swelling from the tuba, the trumpets and the clear voices of the civilian congregation and he felt unequal. Chain and anchor hissed as the winch spooled iron into the sea, and everything suddenly looked like newsreel footage, separate and ethereal. Servicemen waited, united for the last time. They inhaled the salt in the air and tasted expectation spiked with fear. Michael braced himself for another version of the unknown.

The *Stanley Livingstone* dropped anchor, its wake churning the busy harbour yellow while seagulls complained and wailed, their cries mingled with the brass melody on shore. Michael realised that in between the two extremes of his happiness and his fear, he felt nothing. Panic played a rhythm in his heart. He hissed an oath and returned to his place. He knew the price a soldier paid. On his last leave his father had sat down opposite him at the kitchen table and clasped both hands together. Michael was reading, but he closed his book. Johnnie said Dad had got serious with him one day; it had to be Michael's turn now.

'I never imagined my sons would go through this.' He cleared his throat and his eyes flickered over Michael's uniform, not meeting his gaze. 'We thought we were fighting so this could never happen to you and Johnnie.' Michael flinched. His father stood up, walked round the back of his chair and shrugged his shoulders. 'Peace. It matters more than victory you know.'

Michael opened his mouth to say something back. He wanted to reassure his father, but he'd walked out of the room.

Disembarkation began. More of a crowd had gathered now, and people jostled, wanting to be first to meet someone off the ship. Who would not want to be waiting with open arms? Michael shrank back, alarm still locked in him from the smoke and guns, the mud and noise of war. Steadily the troops began to surge down the narrow walkways. Michael watched some shake hands, others embracing each other in a bear hug. Into the crowd they walked, and became invisible, a beat in the rush of escape. No longer an element of the huge grey mass of the boat, no longer a rank and an army number, the soldiers were home, desperate to become nothing more than ordinary people in a crowd. For a moment, Michael truly understood the war had finished. It couldn't touch him.

Smoking had become his comfort, the only act in his soldier's daily life he felt he chose for himself. He was on land. What did he do now? He lit a fag and angled his leg to the wall, his shoulders warm against the brick, comfort in the contact. He was on home ground. He watched through narrowed eyes as army units dispersed. Private Williams over there was wrapped around a blonde in a blue coat, her hat perched like a small nest over her ear. Williams's beret had fallen off, his hair waxed to a sharp ridge above his face. He kissed the girl. Who was she? Michael was momentarily embarrassed by his own ignorance. He threw down the cigarette, a wry twist in his face. Knowing Williams, she was probably the first woman he had run into, a kiss as random as a bullet.

As if in a dance, figures came forward cautiously, until the whole Salvation Army and all their congregation had someone to hug from the troop ship. Embraces and kisses, versions of Private Williams and his welcome chimed along the quay. Laughter bubbled and burst in the crowd as the band crashed cymbals and began a Dixieland jazz tune that didn't quite work. A pause followed, then 'We'll Meet Again' swooned out of the big shiny tuba. Michael knew he should feel euphoria, hysteria or excitement of some sort, but he felt nothing. He was empty. He drifted above the scene like smoke, he had no point of reference, no one was coming to meet him. No one knew he was back.

In his last letter he had told Janey he would be home 'before too long'. His fiancée. His sweetheart, at home in Acle with her parents, waiting for him. A whole lifetime lay ahead for him and Janey. Somehow, what that might mean to them both after the war had never surfaced in their three short weeks together. Three weeks. Why could he not have just left it at that?

Michael rolled his head against the wall and the rough brick was solid and comforting. He'd been wired when he met her, biting his nails, smoking even more than now, if that were possible. Unable to be still. Extraordinary, really, that Janey looked twice at him. She was kind. When she laughed, the sound soothed him, gave him respite from the tension running through his body. With her, the clatter of his nerves, which felt like the ceaseless rattle of marbles in a tin, was stilled. He traced a hand across her cheek in wonder at the soft bloom. His response to Janey was visceral. He wanted to touch her, to feel the pulse beneath her skin. Physical contact, resting his arm along her shoulders, sitting beside her, thighs touching, refreshed him. She reminded him that he was alive, and he needed to know what that felt like to go back to the front. When he asked her to marry him so soon after they met, he meant it with all his heart. For ever was so temporary, yet promises were vital in wartime. Now he was not so sure. To be honest, he could scarcely remember what she really looked like. The photograph he had was unreal somehow without her scent, her voice, the touch of her hand. He'd looked at it a hundred times, but it was hard to believe she existed, that her life was running on in some distant parallel universe to his own. It wasn't that he had anything better in mind, it was more that he could see now how little he had to offer her. They would have got married on his next leave. Sherry with her father and into a suit and off to the Registry Office in Norwich. No fuss, no church wedding, just a quiet exchange of vows. Perhaps that was a sign in itself, he thought. It would have been another memory, a colourful day, happy and hopeful. A year after they met, Normandy came instead. That was two years ago and Michael hadn't been home since.

Michael left the harbour. Exhaustion and confusion coursed through him, chasing out any sense of purpose or decision-making ability. A pub door swung open, a pair of soldiers, arms around one another, stumbled out grinning. Michael went in. The dark interior was a surprise, he blinked and sat down. He didn't want a drink, he wanted peace. He pulled out his wallet to look at the photograph of Janey. He'd commissioned it from a photographer in Norwich to mark their engagement. There she was, her lashes feathering on her cheek, a serene gaze, her fair hair shiny and bouncy, lips pinkly pretty in the hand-tinted picture. Charming, but flat. He wished it evoked a memory, a spark of conversation, but it didn't look real. The studio setting was false and distancing but it was all he had. Tucking the picture back into his wallet, he closed his eyes. If he tried hard enough, could he conjure up Janey's scent, floral and delicate like her? Could he bring any part of her to life? Her soft skin, her kindness, her warmth? He craved the sweetness that surrounded her, it had intoxicated him. He didn't know if he loved her when he asked her to marry him, he'd just known she could make him forget. She was a beacon to live for through Normandy and the rest.

In the pub, a wood-tinged aroma of cigarettes and a yeasty blast from the beer muffled the senses. Michael bought a whisky and took it outside. He pulled out the last cigarette from the last pack he'd had on the boat, and stopped a passing couple for a light. The soldier had his kitbag over one shoulder, his arm around his girl, shrugging her to him with a grin like the Cheshire Cat on his face. He flung down the kitbag but kept holding on to the girl, who wriggled closer and let her hair fall over one eye. Michael noticed a dust of freckles across her cheek, and a tiny scar at the edge of her eye which disappeared when she smiled.

The soldier flicked open his lighter for Michael. 'There you are, sir, best of luck to you, sir.' He saluted and they swung off down the road, the girl's mouse-brown curls bouncing on her shoulders, his arm around her waist, their step in perfect time with one another.

Janey's father was the rector of Oby, a tiny village near Acle, about twenty miles from Kings Sloley. The day after he had proposed to Janey, Michael had been anxious, waiting for her father to return from church. Was there a right time of day, or a correct day of the week to ask a vicar if you could marry his daughter? If there was, surely it was after the morning service, in the Sunday hiatus before lunch, where the smell of boiled cabbage mingled with the fresh fragrance of lilac in the hall, and the grandfather clock ticked, reassuring and regular as a heartbeat.

Michael could still see the painted glass paper-weight on the desk, and taste the coat of anxiety dry on his tongue as he waited for Reverend Thompson to pour him a glass of sherry. The vicar's hand, when he passed the glass to Michael, shook a little, but his gaze was steady. Michael wished Janey was in the room with him, and knocked back the sherry in one. It was sweet, unexpectedly sickly, and potent. He spluttered into his handkerchief, then wiped his eyes.

'I hope you don't mind me asking, but I wonder if you, if I, if we— I've asked Janey to marry me and I hope you will give us your blessing.'

God. Was that right? Should he have put it differently? Had he been impertinent?

Reverend Thompson looked grave. He was nodding, his mouth folded neat as a napkin in his flat pale face. It seemed to Michael that he might never answer, and his mind raced ahead with the difficulties of protocol that this would bring. Should he ask again? Is silence a yes? He coughed. The room was stifling. He found his gaze swerving towards the door no matter how hard he tried to keep it on the Reverend.

Finally the utterance came: 'If she's chosen you, you're a lucky young man.'

For a split second Michael had no idea what he meant, then relief shot through him. They shook hands. What was supposed to happen next? Michael looked uncertainly around the room, and in that moment, the Reverend took advantage of his lack of concentration and vanished noiselessly into the garden through the floor length sash window. Dazed, Michael went to find Janey.

A lifetime away from that moment, he imagined more than could recall her presence, laughter spreading between the two of them as he held her in the chilly tiled hall of the rectory. She was wearing the flowered dress she'd had on the day he met her, pale blue with pansies scattered across it.

The pansy freaked with jet

The line from Lycidas, about a youth killed in his prime, leapt into his head in the pub bar, with Southampton noisy and harsh around him. Tears scorched his eyelids, a veil across his memory. Poems were scant comfort, but they were something. Michael clung to lines and verses, turning them over in his head when he didn't want to think of anything else. Whisky burned, licking a path down into his empty stomach. He hadn't eaten today, no one had, the ship had run out of rations before it left Italy, and the only food on board was black market chocolate and dry bread stolen by soldiers from Italian farms. He couldn't imagine what men looked like with more than an ounce of flesh on their bones any more. The pub shelves behind the bar were stacked with a few tins of tobacco, and a jar of pickled onions.

Now he was back, he would eat regular meals. Michael imagined days spooling endlessly by marked by plates of sandwiches like the ones at his cousin Angela's wedding. Fish paste or corned beef. Not egg mayonnaise, Angela had explained to him, laughing, the eggs had been saved for the cake.

Angela's mother with a slash of orange lipstick and a long pheasant feather in her hat, 'Would anyone like a top up? There's another pot brewing.' A future full of cups of tea and rationed slices of fruitcake over which people would politely nod as they passed the plate. He swirled his whisky in the glass and knocked it back. Rationed cake and tea. Was that what this had all been for?

Angela married an RAF pilot in 1942, the Christmas before Michael met Janey. Soon after, he was called back to his unit and sent into the sky. Had he known, like Yeats's airman, what was to come?

I know that I shall meet my fate
Somewhere among the clouds above

Angela hadn't had a lot of time to become a wife. She lost a husband she scarcely knew, and was stricken, bereft of something she'd never had. Their time together measured in slices of wedding cake and sandwiches.

A waste of breath the years behind
In balance with this life, this death

The same story echoed everywhere. Janey's unfaltering smile, and her kindness steadied Michael. He'd met her then, home on sick leave, a flare up of malaria. His nerves had grated like steel on ice when he woke with a start every night. In the lanes of his childhood, where he strolled with Janey, Michael had listened to her identify honeysuckle and heartsease, pansies again, and ragged robin and love-in-a-mist, she knew all the flowers of the hedgerows. He was soothed. Janey taught piano to the infant class at her local primary school. Michael felt the joy of fluttering impulse, and was led on by the indomitable essence of spring, the rousing cheeriness of blackbirds singing, and Janey's uncritical friendliness.

No one could imagine the future during the war. Michael looked around Southampton's broken streets, dusty and gaping, a filmset unreality for the servicemen milling about, these thin ghosts, free to go anywhere, do anything. Maybe he should have married Janey there and then, on that first leave when he met her. Michael had known he was looking for solace when he asked her to come and spend the last nights he had at home at a pub near Angela's parents' farm in Suffolk. That short time was an oasis, though, in truth, he could only remember fleeting images. They went to see Angela, the visit to his cousin the excuse for visiting the Suffolk coast. She welcomed them to the farm but her smile was dull. She sighed in the pretty sitting room with its sea view and the vase of sweet williams gay and colourful among the family photographs on the mantelpiece. She waved them off from the door and retreated back into her grief.

The air was sweet, a cloud of gnats hung above the duck pond, and swallows dived and swooped across the water, turning on sharp wing blades. Their spirits flying, Michael and Janey hurried to the sea, played tag on the beach and fell breathless against one another.

'Shall we swim?' Her challenge. How could he say no?

'After you.' Smooth calves, a flash of skin and she was in the sea. He dived under the first wave beside her, turned to see what she was looking at and a wave towered over them. It hurtled down as his hand caught the jut of her hip and he pulled her deep under him, holding her closely, safely beneath the wave.

At night Michael smoked and paced, he stretched a yawn and brushed against the ceiling of the bedroom. He didn't fit in the chalky pink room, with its windows hung in sweet frills patterned with grey feathers. He pushed the window wide and leaned out into the velvet night, the damp scent of leaves and soil lingering about him. Janey slept, her skin like petals, so soft he thought it might tear when he touched her. Back in the bed he curled himself around her, reaching for her, face pressed to her shoulder, craving her peaceful sleep. Both nights they stayed, he lay awake, afraid that she might stir and become aware of how much he wished this time would never end.

He returned to the ruined French beaches, and their idyll became fragmented memories, blown from time to time across his thoughts like the wind-tossed apple blossom that had once existed in Normandy's orchards. Almost two years on, no feeling was attached to his thoughts of Janey except anxiety. They hardly knew one another. He forgot her birthday, she remembered his, and sent a card that smelled of her scent. He loved the waft of sweetness curling out of the envelope, but he couldn't bring her to life in his mind. She remained a studio image and a crumpled photograph. He hadn't written much after that, though she sent frequent cards and letters. He kept them, but he didn't reread them, like the others did. He wasn't sure if he was different from everyone else. Did he care enough? He couldn't say. All he knew was that Janey had no idea he was in Southampton today, she didn't even know he was alive.

Skirting the harbour, Michael began to walk up through the side streets away from the sea. He needed to go somewhere, or at least to look as though he was going somewhere. The town shops were diminished by war but, nonetheless, many of them had taken to exhibiting threads of joy among their usual wares. Faded flags and paper streamers looped along the half-empty shelves, suggesting a victory party to come. Michael suddenly felt insanely tired. A dog sniffed at the base of a wall, then lay down and rolled on the pavement, rising to wag his tail as a group of children advanced from a side street with a ball. The tallest among them glanced across at the ship, and in his face Michael recognised the pinched look of hunger he'd seen throughout Europe.

Someone around the corner was playing 'Land of Hope and Glory' on a mouth organ. A young girl, aged about nineteen, sauntered past him and down a side street towards a propped bicycle. She smiled at Michael, put the mouth organ into her pocket and lifting the bicycle away from the wall, swung onto it and pedalled away. The sun glanced off her hair as she vanished round a corner. Michael rubbed his eyes. He had a sudden memory of Janey jumping off her bicycle to greet him, flushed, bright-eyed, laughing, on the night he asked her to marry him. She had been setting races and fielding teams of school children in their sports day that afternoon. She was lit up and proud, happy to be leading her life. Michael wanted to lose himself in her vigour and her uncomplicated happiness.

He walked on, his back aching, footsore in the heavy wool uniform. The day seemed endless, he didn't remember sleeping the last night on the ship. He had lost track of time, but the sun was lower now, coasting behind rows of chimneys fanning out of Southampton across the river and on towards Salisbury. Probably mid-afternoon. It would be nice to lie down on a low wall like the one bordering the churchyard there and sleep the rest of the day away, but he needed to go to the demob station and become a civilian again. Once he had done that, he would catch the train home. Civvy clothes and money awaited him. Michael set his kitbag on his shoulder.

Queuing up in a town hall for the trappings of so-called freedom seemed an irrelevance. How were a few yards of flannel and a meaningless amount of cash meant to prepare anyone for life after a war? Michael scowled at his own shadow, bulky with its backpack, as it moved in front of him up the hill.

Rippling giggles and a frantic bike bell flared up behind him, and he jumped out of the road as the mouth organ girl meandered past, perched as a passenger on the back, her arms round a hatless soldier who pedalled and swerved across the road. The girl's pink cheek rested on his khaki shoulder, and they were both singing as they went:

Daisy Daisy, give me your answer do
I'm half crazy, all for the love of you

Her soldier winked at Michael as they passed him, rolling eyes apologetically because he had no hands free to salute. The girl fished her mouth organ out of her pocket and played the melody. The soldier continued singing:

It won't be a stylish marriage
I can't afford a carriage,
But you'd look sweet
Upon the seat

The mouth organ stopped with a squawk as the girl joined in with the last line:

Of a bicycle made for two.

Michael pushed back his hat and clapped slowly. 'You're good, it's the music hall for you guys,' he shouted.

They spun a circle in the road ahead of him. The bike wobbled but kept going as the girl leaned to call, 'I don't know where you're going, but the station isn't far now. Good luck, and welcome back to England.'

With a jaunty trill on the bell, the couple wove away down the road.

The moment of laughter and ordinary human contact was exhilarating. Michael dropped his bag and stretched. What was the rush? Once he was out of uniform, he would be a non-soldier for the rest of his life. A tobacconist was opening up again after lunchtime, in the next street. An old man sat outside with a dog, cleaning his pipe in the sunshine, knocking it on the arm of his chair. Michael negotiated past him into the shop. The woman behind the counter had a brown overall on, a hankie tied around her head and her gaze was direct.

'Can I help you? We're out of newspapers but then

you're the big news around here, aren't you? You lot still coming back, dribs 'n' drabs 'n' all that.' Her mouth was pursed. Michael looked at her curiously. It hadn't occurred to him that anyone might not be pleased they were home.

He spun a coin. 'Could I have some matches, please?'

The smell of pipe tobacco in this little room was reassuring. Michael glanced around, intrigued by the barber's shop room through a glazed door at the back. He wondered if he had time for a haircut. Really, he had time for whatever he wanted. He realised the woman was still talking. 'And I s'pose if you want cigarettes, you just come back and help yourselves. Cigarettes, girls, beer. I don't know where you think this will all end.'

'No,' said Michael. Then on an impulse added, 'Where do you think it will all end?'

She was arranging a stack of matchboxes next to a photograph mounted on board. She stopped, her arm raised, a red matchbox in her hand. The photograph showed a team of young men in naval uniform. Her crossness drained away under his scrutiny.

'Well, I don't know,' she said, flustered by the attention, 'but I do know you'll miss the train any moment. The two fifteen is due in ten minutes and you'll want to be on it, won't you, lad? Got people to be home for. A life to take up. You don't want to miss it now you haven't been killed, do you?'

He looked at her, then at the photograph by the till. A sports team, the names beneath. Another photograph pinned to the wall behind her of a young sailor holding a small, smiling dog. Michael looked out of the window. The same dog was scratching vigorously, its whole body shaking with the effort of applying claw to ear. The shopkeeper followed his gaze, and bent to open a drawer behind her. She pulled out a ledger.

'Your son?' The question hurt like a new bruise.

She nodded, put a hand to the thin silver chain at her neck, blinked hard. 'Don't miss that train, love,' she said.

Michael felt her courage, warm as the sun when she smiled.

CHAPTER 2

The new triptych clock above the kitchen door displayed the time in Kerala and New York as well as Norfolk. New York time was straightforward, the clock had come with it. Something to do with Wall Street and the stock exchange, no doubt: six forty in the morning. Five hours earlier than Green Farm House and Greenwich. Glancing up at it gave Luisa a sense of industry and virtue. It was easy to warm to this reality, she was the urban superwoman, ahead of the game. As a New Yorker, she would have got up – no, make that *gotten* up – especially early to fit everything into her day, she was a busy working mother with an overflowing life, calls upon her time beaming in from every direction. Listen! That electronic ping was probably a very important email from someone requiring her immediate attention, or was it the oven timer? Domesticity. The enemy of promise to some, but not to Luisa. In her busy life, it was just a quick reminder that Baked Alaska waits for no one, and Version One was ready. Version Two, when she had finished preparing it, would just need a few minutes with a blow torch.

She looked at the dog. 'You'll have to eat some you know, Grayson.' He thumped his tail, opening one eye for a moment. 'It'll melt and no one else is here.' The dog sighed, feigning interest briefly, before tucking his nose back into the sleek coil of his body.

Forgetting the dog for now, and the fact that he was sulking in the hope of reminding her to walk him, Luisa was confidently at the helm with all systems go in the kitchen. She had already created two utterly different Baked Alaska puddings, and conceived a recipe for rosewater and cardamom sorbet that would sit exotically between them. The fact that not a single person was here to eat them was just too bad. Another glance at the New York clock and she was completely in the transatlantic zone. It was still an ungodly hour for most of the world's population. She loved those golden moments before the day had truly begun, and all that ambrosial pleasure in having achieved so much in the small hours. It was actually almost midday in Norfolk, but who would know or care if they saw her? Ambrosia. How could she translate that into an ice cream? Peaches and marsala? Honeycomb hit with a dash of vin Santo? What was the twenty-first-century version of the Nectar of the Gods? It depended on who you asked. Tom, like any bloke, would say Guinness, or a decent claret, while Mae would probably go for something typically teenage like rum and Coke. Ellie? Difficult to say, chai, probably, or lassi. Ellie hadn't called for over a week now.

Luisa had last heard from her through a typed Skype message to Luca, 'Tell Mum I'm fine, and I'll be off air for a while.' True, it probably wasn't cause for concern, but it was odd to think of her daughter experiencing so much that she, Luisa, could never know. Or do.

Everyone else in the family was doing their thing. Ellie meditating away in India, or travelling on a bus or a train, or dyeing her hair or whatever a girl let loose on her gap year might be up to. Luca and Mae were busy with exams at school, and so, of course, was Tom, working harder than ever. Leading the history department no less. It was essential, and expected, that she, Luisa, was busy too. She just had to raise her sights, look at the clock and pretend to be in New York, with bustling people, all, according to her sister-in-law Dora, rising at 5 a.m. to go to the gym and maybe therapy before even thinking about breakfast and work. So inspiring. Why be a rural drop out, a Norfolk housewife with an ice-cream-making habit, when, with New York time on the wall, she could be a Manhattan scenester?

Pulling in her stomach, Luisa corrected her posture, dropping her shoulders, as if she was at Spiritual High, her weekly yoga class. Breathe . . . and breathe . . . It was tricky to keep an eye on the fluffing of the meringue as it rose in the mixer while maintaining her spine in the correct position for Tadasana. Three exhalations felt like a marathon and she gave up. There was a time and a place for yoga, and it wasn't here or now.

Luisa removed the block of Amaretto-laced ice cream from the deep freeze. Wrapped in cling film, it resembled a lung, she thought, or a small bagpipe. It wasn't quite the shape she had hoped, it might have been better to freeze it in a mould, but if she chipped a bit away she could make a rectangle. It was the work of a moment to slice a few slivers off it and encase it in the sponge cake she had already cut to shape. The Baked Alaska was going to resemble a swimming pool. That was the plan. She had found the perfect natural food colour on the Internet and turning the meringue blue had worked a treat – Hockney-esque and beautiful, if a little startling. She'd got carried away with the Amaretto, and the whole thing was rather alcoholic considering it was for a taciturn thirteen-year-old's birthday, but, she reminded herself, this was still the dummy run. Maybe it would turn out to be ambrosial. And actually, young Nick Bryer would probably like a punch-drunk pudding, it was his mother who would worry. Much could be tweaked.

She moved down the table to find her notebook. It lay open among a sea of belongings that came and went from the table as family members collected and discarded items. Ah! There was Mae's hairbrush, an elasticated gingham scrunchy bunched like bloomers around the handle. Shame it hadn't surfaced earlier, when Mae, beset by a squall of bad temper, hurtled like a furious bluebottle around the house, banging doors and snatching open drawers in search of the brush. 'I'm not using yours, Luca brushed Grayson with it,' she wailed, when Luisa offered her own.

Luca, hands in his pockets, was bouncing a ball on his foot as he waited for his sister to get ready.

He shrugged. 'Grayson's as clean as you are. Cleaner probably, so I don't see why you have to get so stressed.'

Mae, infuriated, had flounced out to sit in the car. Luca's ball fell off his foot and tipped over the dog's water bowl just as Tom walked into the kitchen, carrying too many folders. One dropped from the pile. It was at moments like these that Luisa took a deep breath and fixed her attention on an ingredient.

Cherries. She had bought a box of them yesterday. It was easy to make them into a sauce of course, a splash of kirsch and they became a stain like an anemone to pour over vanilla ice cream, but there was always another way to do things, that was what Luisa loved. Making ice cream was alchemy. Luisa had learned early the magic of transformation, as eggs and sugar, cream and chocolate or strawberry syrup or drops of precious fragrant vanilla essence, churned in the kitchen at the back of her grandfather's shop. She loved the process, the smell, the fluctuation in form as the temperature dropped, the powdery sparkle that attached itself to sorbets and ice creams as they froze. She might easily have lost interest, but, one Easter when she was fourteen, a bevy of aunts and relations arrived from Northern Italy and made hot chocolate the way they made it in the mountains. Luisa could not believe the sensation in her mouth when she drank the rich chocolate then ate a spoonful of vanilla ice cream.

That was it, she would make mouth-sized cherry-shaped tiny almond ice-cream bombes, and fill them with cherry sorbet, or could she somehow inject them with hot syrup? Ah, but then they would melt. Her notebook page was dense with a list of ingredients and instructions to herself. This could work. She would call it May Day. Every ice cream she created had a name, it was part of the process. The Baked Alaska was called Skin Deep, which had brought a huge grin to the otherwise surly face of Nick Bryer but not to that of his mother Cathy when she commissioned this pudding.

Hunched over the sponge and meringue concoction as she glued the Alaska together, Luisa's back twinged. Oh to really be in New York, with the day stretching ahead and time to practise perfect deportment with a handsome personal trainer. Would Nick like this ice cream? Or rather, would Cathy? Not that she would taste it, of course, she was one of those dairy-free mothers, but she would have an opinion, and it needed to be a good one. It was through the support of Cathy and friends like her that Luisa had been introduced to the new restaurant in Blythe. The award-winning chef who ran it had taken three of her desserts. Luisa rolled her shoulders. He would like May Day, but she might give it a more Italian name for his menu.

It was a shame, it was just the sort of thing Gina, her mother, would love to do, but she had left last week for the summer. Off to stay with her sister near Turin. Every year she made the trip, but since Luisa's father died, the weeks had started to stretch into months. This year she would be gone for three months. Almost as long as Ellie. Fancy having a mother and a daughter both on versions of a gap year. What did it say about Luisa herself, she wondered? Sad old stay-at-home or keeper of the hearth and pulse of the family heart? She'd like to believe the latter, but it was hard.

Closing the oven door, Luisa surreptitiously crossed herself, then sighed, wishing she hadn't. Too many of her mother's foibles were beginning to appear in her daily actions. Had they always been there, silently filling the pool of her subconscious, the part of her that she believed was hers alone, secretly saturating her until the first drips began to spill out again? Would these droplets form faster and faster until the habits and actions she noticed in her mother engulfed her? Would she become her mother at that point? And when was that moment? Her mother was seventy-five, she was fifty-one. The way things were stacked, it looked like it could be quite soon. Just as well Gina was away for a while.

Much as she loved her family, Luisa felt as if she had become invisible. The change had been subtle, but it was inevitable and irreversible. Every mother reigns supreme at the heart of her family while bringing up children, and every mother has to move over at some point. Luisa accepted the natural order of things, she just hadn't reckoned on it coming so soon. Once Ellie had gone travelling, home life had been subverted. Luca and Mae moved up to fill the space

Ellie had occupied, and suddenly the family dynamic had changed and no one was little any more. They were at school, they had their own lives, their friends, and their own idea of what to eat and when. Her children seemed to take their lead from Tom, who whirled through the house, rushing to work or into his study to mark papers, grabbing a banana from the fruit bowl as he passed, not sure if he would be back for supper, shouting 'Don't wait for me' as he banged out of the door and into his car. And now her children, as she still thought of them, had begun to live as though all of them were housemates.

She asked Gina if she remembered this happening to her when she and Cosmo were teenagers, but her mother was implacable.

'I don't know what you mean talking about housemates. Your father, you and Cosmo, you all came home for dinner every night. Housemates? No, we were always a family. A family.' She dusted her hands together, clapping away the strand of thought she didn't like.

Suddenly Luisa's children didn't ask her for anything. The familiar cries of 'Mum, where's my—' or 'Mum, can you help me—' or 'Mum, what's for supper?' vanished overnight to be replaced by a disconcerting silence. They helped themselves to what they wanted and retreated to their rooms with laptops and phones, music and, sporadically, skulking companions she sometimes didn't recognise. None of them cleared up the yoghurt pots under the sofa, the orange peel on cushions, the glasses, odd trainers and endless socks, mugs or apple cores that appeared around every place they sat down, but none of them expected her to either. She had learned it was best to take the line of least resistance. It worked. After all, who wanted to be a slave to housework? The only thing was that it sometimes left her wondering what she was meant to do? Her purpose as a mother was no longer vital, so who or what was she now? Should she pack her bags like Gina and take off? She and Tom hadn't ever visited her sister-in-law Bella, New Zealand always seemed so far, but now? Luisa's thoughts faltered. She wouldn't want to go all that way on her own and Tom was so busy. Maybe she should. She needed to be more independent. All those years as a wife and mother . . . Now the props had been removed, and she was facing the prospect of being herself. She wondered what she might find out about herself.

One thing was for sure, she wasn't much of a time-keeper. Surely the time in India, on the third clock, was wrong? How could it be ten past anything, anywhere? Surely it was five hours ahead? Weren't minutes the same the world over? Luisa felt a shimmer of panic. Had her clock just given India an extra half hour? Or taken it away? More or less time? Which was it? Anyway, it didn't matter, the important thing was that it was roughly teatime. A cosy thought, teatime in India. Luisa felt silly even thinking about it. It was just she hadn't quite got the hang of Ellie being so far out of reach.

Ellie. Warm and open, sometimes stroppy, but mainly even-tempered and a joy to be around. Her elder daughter, and part of her life for the last nineteen years. Almost twenty when one counted the halcyon long ago days of Luisa's first pregnancy. Ellie had always been communicative, she would often call Luisa in her lunch break, waiting for the bus or a lift home from school, and if ever she stayed away, ended conversations and texts with 'Luv u' and 'I love you' and 'XX 2 U Mumma'. Luisa had been quite unprepared for the shock of all this stopping when Ellie left for India. Scarcely a message a week, and when they did come they were short, and just texts or emails, not a single phone call. Luisa felt bereft. Silly, but bereft. It was all very well for Tom to say that the next generation had to be allowed to separate from their mothers, but Fran White called her mother from Mexico, and she'd been gone two months. Joanna Davies, a school mother Luisa had never much liked because she always had to know more than anyone else about everyone else, had the nerve to say Max had bumped into Ellie on a beach somewhere in Cochin. If you listened to Joanna Davies you'd think Ellie was suddenly best friends with Max, when Luisa could definitely remember her kids announcing he was a loser after he was caught cheating in his A levels. Only by asking Mae and Luca to let her see the Facebook posts Ellie had blocked her from, had she discovered anything at all. Distracted by the tantalising photos she could suddenly see, Luisa forgot to write a message. Then thought better of it. No point in annoying Ellie by letting her know she had seen things she was not meant to.

Mae pointed her towards a picture. 'Look, she's fine, Mum. You can see her here.'

Luisa put on her glasses to look more closely. 'What are they doing? Who's she with? It looks like they're castaways. Ellie's got something on her head. Is it a turban? Oh, don't Mae, I'm looking. I need to see her.'

'You don't *need* to,' Mae told her mother firmly. She's blocked you because she doesn't want you to see them. But never mind that. Look what she posted.'

Luisa began following the words on the screen with her finger, Mae batted her hand away. 'Mum, you don't have to touch it you know! Just relax.'

Luisa leaned closer to the screen. What was that thing on Ellie's head? It wasn't a scarf, or a hood.

'Oh.' Startled, the exclamation punched out of her throat. It was someone's arm. Ellie was lying on a beach tucked close into someone's armpit, her eyes raised to meet the armpit owner's. He or she was not visible, but Luisa was sure it was 'he', as the armpit was clearly hairy. Too hairy for even the most defiantly feminist of Ellie's friends, and way too muscly. Luisa clamped her mouth shut. She didn't ask Mae who she thought the mystery armpit belonged to; she'd be struck off entirely, removed from Ellie's contacts if she did anything that could be construed as interfering. So she read the post: 'Going trekking for a few days off the beaten track to a tea plantation. Please guys, tell Mum to get off my case, she keeps hassling me.' The smart of humiliation was sudden and painful as a nettle rash. Still, it was another lesson learned.

She began to wash up, squirting foaming liquid in a squiggle, pulling on gloves that clamped her hands like wax. Bubbles wafted over the sides of the sink and onto the draining board. The muffled crackling noise of the sink filling with foam was a conduit to long ago. When they were small, the girls loved to shadow her every move in the kitchen, miming domesticity, close to her side as if magnetically connected. Washing up was a protracted affair when a six- and a three-year-old took over, a chair dragged to stand on at the sink, sleeves rolled up as they delved for soapy plates and pans. Everything she did, they wanted to do too, mimicking her words and gestures, small mirrors to her mothering.

'Right everyone, that's enough nonsense. Have a glass of water. Just sips you know.' Ellie would say firmly to her dolls, adding, with kindly wisdom, to her mother, 'They just forget to calm down sometimes, like me and Mae.'

In a parallel, equally absorbing world, Mae diligently trundled a small wheelbarrow across the kitchen, stopping every few paces to add carefully chosen items to her load. A peppermill, a glove from the basket by the door, a turquoise tiara, a snake of apple peel and a pair of sunglasses. A photograph of her with her trophies, the sunglasses lopsided on her tiny nose, was propped on the mantelpiece, the edges curling inward with age. They were like little fairies then, but weren't all small children wrapped in magic?

Luisa looked at the clocks again. The pudding would take another five minutes. There was no question, Ellie had been ready to go. On the day she left she had brought her bags down to the car an hour and a half before she needed to go. She sat on the doorstep in the watery spring sunshine with Luca making playlists, laughing as they added tracks featuring journeys.

'That's way too easy, there're loads,' said Luca. 'Let's make it with the word "road" in it. The more restrictions the better.'

Luisa turned on her iPod. Otis Redding poured into the room, 'These Arms of Mine'. Tom called her taste 'slit your wrists music', but Luisa didn't care. She sang along loudly, she knew all the words to all his songs, had done since her brother Cosmo had introduced her to 'Dock of the Bay' when she was thirteen, and singing stopped her checking her phone.

'Burning to hold you'. It was close to sunset in Southern India now, but if this were New York she'd be off to work. In reality, she was at home in the kitchen with the dog, and two puddings he and she would have to eat.

Making ice cream. It was hardly a serious contribution to life on earth, but it was her skill, and she was in demand for it. Three local shops and one tearoom in Blythe stocked the ice creams she made, and if this thing with the restaurant took off, it could be time for a recipe book next. And definitely the van if it could be fixed. Luisa wasn't sure her husband or children had registered her growing success.

'The trouble with ice cream,' she said to the dog as she manoeuvred the spectacular blue baked Alaska out of the oven, 'is that it melts. Or gets eaten. It's just not very interesting, really.'

Except that it was. Mercurial, ever-changing, as fairylike as any child, yet exacting as algebra or chemistry in its creation, Luisa knew the delight of ice-cream making as her forebears had done. She understood the romance. Catherine de Medici was said to have taken her Italian chefs with her when she went to France to marry the Duc d'Orléans. She was just fifteen and, not surprisingly, she wanted ice cream. Luisa told this to Mae and Ellie, hoping to draw them in, but their interest was lukewarm at best. It was her own love affair. She'd always enjoyed the order and the excitement of her science lessons at school, the test tubes lined up, the enigmatic array of powders and liquids, ethers and explosives. This was the edible version. Some, Tom agreed, were pure poetry. 'This is summer on a plate. Nothing can beat it,' Tom had said, with rare lyricism when Luisa made champagne ice cream with elderflowers to celebrate Mae's birthday.

Tom. She had to remember he did appreciate her in his way. He could be thoughtful. He gave her the time-zone clocks after all. A week after Ellie left he put them up for her in the kitchen and called her in to look, 'Here, Tod,' he said. 'You can keep up with her now,' he ruffled her hair affectionately, tweaking nostalgia with the nickname he'd invented when they met.

Luisa loved the myth that had grown up around their meeting, she didn't even really know if it was true or not any more, but Tom was certain of the facts as he remembered them. It was October, she had been wearing a pink fur coat. That was true enough, she'd got it at a jumble sale and wore it all the time. She was always cold, she had bad circulation like Ellie. On this occasion, the day she met Tom, the coat was a lifesaver, worn for her Saturday shift selling ice creams out of the window of a chilly van parked up by a pond a mile inland from the seashore at Yarmouth the weekend the clocks changed.

It wasn't really her shift, or even her job any more, but Cosmo, her brother, sounded under pressure. 'Lou, help me out here, half term's the last bite of the cherry, the last blast, before winter kills the ice cream trade, y'know.'

Luisa had never liked working the vans, too many teenage summer days stuck in the cramped space with a generator pounding away next to her, when her friends were out on the beach, often tantalisingly within view. 'What would you like? Cone or wafer, Flake or sprinkles? Single or double?' Why did people take so long to choose? It was hardly a life-altering decision. A cold breeze flung a shifting veil of geese across the sky, harbingers of weather that would follow from the Russian Steppes, covering Norfolk in diamante frosts with air that bit your breath away. Cosmo had been let down by his mate Franco, who moonlighted from a scaffolding company, and sometimes simply didn't show. She sighed and checked the time. An hour to go.

Tom hadn't even wanted an ice cream, he had actually stopped to let his puppy out in a gateway he'd

37

noticed on this unfamiliar stretch of road. He'd just bought her, Flicka, a lurcher soft as smoke, from a gypsy set-up near Lowestoft, and was on his way home. He always reckoned that the puppy had brought his guard down, so when he saw Luisa, her face framed in the ice-cream van's window, cloaked in pink fur and caught in a panel of gilded sunset reflected off the pond's glassy surface, love hit him like a boxer's fist. It happened there and then at his first glimpse of her on the roadside in the most ridiculous vehicle he'd seen outside a *Flintstones* cartoon. She looked like an off-duty film star combined with a Renaissance painting. He didn't say any of this to Luisa. No indeed. No way. Not then.

Tom's heart may have been hurtling up and down with the brio of a ragtime piano, but he gave nothing away. He sauntered slowly up to her window, taking in the gaudy pink of her van's cab, the twin cones, like flambeaux on a chariot picked out not in gold, as he, an art historian, might have chosen, but in pistachio green and vivid raspberry. Tom squinted in at this girl, moving a jar of gummy bear chews to lean his elbow on the counter, settling his tall frame into an accustomed slouched stance, relaxed. Smouldering, he hoped, though it never seemed to work that way.

Luisa, in a split second of registering surprise that the guy with a mop of hair and narrow grey eyes was actually peering into her van, took in the long denim-clad legs, and—

'Hey! it was the eighties, denim was the image, nothing wrong with that!' Tom always liked to inter-ject at this point.

Luisa was tongue tied, excitement rising as he opened the conversation. What he said was, 'How many ice creams do I need to buy to get you to shut this shop and come and help me take this bundle of puppy for a walk?'

Luisa knew she was blushing, and pressed the ice-cream scoop to her cheek. 'Ow, it's freezing,' she exclaimed.

He reached in, took it out of her hand and opened the door for her. 'Come on,' he said. 'I like that foxy fur of yours.'

'That's sleazy,' she said, and he nodded, looking at her sideways out of his sleepy eyes, then shut them together with a contented sigh.

'Tod' began as his name for the coat, 'because Tod is an old country name for fox, stoopid,' he'd told her, flicking her cheek gently when she asked. Flicka took to it as her bed. 'It's only fair, seeing as you're in mine,' said Tom, when they found her curled up in it on the floor on the first morning they woke up together.

A warm, wet sensation on her hand brought Luisa back to the present, Grayson, grandson of Flicka, was standing in front of her, eyes shining, tail thumping against the cupboard. Good, he was awake. 'Have a bit of this, Gray, and I'll take you out,' she offered. 'I know it's not really your thing, but just pretend, can't you?'

She cut into the blue pudding. The ice cream was beginning to melt at the edges, soft, yielding, unctuous. Grayson averted his gaze, he looked embarrassed. He wasn't going to eat it.

Luisa looked across at him, 'You're usually the first to raid anything with eggs and cream in it. Is it because it's blue?' she demanded. 'Oh well, s'ppose it's up to me, isn't it?' She licked the spoon. Hot and cold, sweet with a kick, smooth, silky, more-ish. Was it the ice cream or the memory of the first date that suddenly flipped her stomach in a knot of desire for her young self? The tug of lust grabbed her when Tom hooked her out of her carefully guarded small-town life, the life of an émigré family, safe, tight knit, a little cloying, and took her into his world. He had been crazy about her. Luisa licked the meringue coating, her tongue exploring the ridge between brittle, chewy meringue and foam-light ice cream. That girl that she had been, Tod, in a pale blue T-shirt and her pink fox fur, flashed her smile at Tom and knew in a slow motion tungsten-bright moment that she would fall in love with him. She sighed, throwing the spoon in the sink. Memories seemed to exist in a different universe. No time had passed since she had opened the oven, and yet, in her mind she had travelled back two decades to her first meeting with Tom. She glanced again at the three clock faces and was propelled to a month ago, and Tom being kind, thoughtful, busy with his mission.

He wore glasses now, small ovals framed in fine wire that caught the light and reflected it back to the dark centre of his eyes. She still loved his eyes. She had opened her mouth to say so, but Tom cut in, polishing his glasses on his handkerchief, a swell of satisfaction riding on a smile. 'I was on the industrial estate, at the tyre place. Had a quick look in the factory shop while I was waiting for the car. This caught my eye. I'll put it up for you.'

He dragged a chair over to hammer a nail into the wall above the kitchen door.

'It's a clock,' he said finally.

Luisa laughed. 'So it is,' she agreed, deciding not to comment as a patch of plaster the size of a coin crumbled off the wall, falling like a ghostly pinch of salt on to the door mat.

'That's wonderful, thank you.' She was puzzled. 'Do I need three? How does that work? I'll never be late again, will I?'

Tom wiped his hands on his trousers, 'Oh it's nothing really, just thought you could do with a way to stay in the loop with Ellie away and all that. This might do the trick.' He opened the glass face of the third clock. 'It's meant for the stock markets, but I'll alter the Tokyo time to India. That way you'll be up to speed on the daily adventures in Kerala.'

He stepped down off the chair, kissed Luisa's cheek, then stroked it and kissed her again. 'You smell nice, Tod,' he said, and wandered out of the room with the air of a man who had thought of everything and fixed it.

A Handel aria, from the opera *Julius Caesar*, ended, leaving delightful menace hanging in the air. It was followed by the song 'Angel From Montgomery'.

Luisa loved the deadpan gloom of the lyrics, *'How does someone go to work in the morning, come home every night and still have nothing to say?'*

Did she and Tom still have things to say to one another? She thought so, but he was so busy at school. Running a big secondary school's history department, his dedication shown by the fact that he had shoe-horned a qualification in history of art into his schedule because he believed it was civilising to his students. He was spreading himself thin, but he was happy. And he was home in the holidays, which meant they could do things together. The trip to St Ives with the children before Ellie left had been precious. All of them in the car, squabbling about what to listen to, playing the games of their childhood car journeys, remembering, bickering, laughing, sleeping. She had treasured those three cold, grey days in February.

Luisa arranged the meringues on the table. They were impressive, definitely impressive. Baked Alaska wasn't a very good name for them, was it? It sounded cartoonlike, and macho, not sensuous enough for the voluptuous puddings before her. The recipe was perfect. It was exciting to be on the brink of success, she thought, although a shame that no one except the dog would notice. For a moment she wished Gina was not away, she would be proud of her. The Amorazzis, her mother's family, had a series of *gelateria* scattered across the low-lying small towns in the Dolomites region and running down the shin of Italy. Uncles, cousins, grandfathers, a great trail of her mother's forebears had worked in or owned ice-cream shops. As a child in her bedroom facing out on to the grey North Sea, Luisa had slept beneath a battered green metal sign, depicting a smudged blue cow drawn out of the letters of the name 'Amorazzi', the last relic of the family business her grandfather had not been able to sustain in Italy.

He came to Great Britain after the war with a hunch he could bring something to life. Working his trade-mark brightly painted ice-cream vans and carts, the new enterprise brought colour and excitement to the seaside towns in Norfolk and Suffolk. He gained a reputation Luisa cherished. Food was a life force, her life force. Antonio Trevi, Luisa's father, had been a market gardener, a prisoner of war in Norfolk, who stayed on and set down roots, finding work at the canning factory in North Walsham. He met Gina ten years after the war. It was his day off and, as he liked to tell the story, he went to place a bet on the dogs at the Yarmouth greyhound track, and won the jackpot, his lovely wife Gina, who was waiting the tables in the restaurant, and had gone outside to sneak a cigarette when Antonio strolled by, his pockets full of cash and his heart singing.

Tom loved Luisa's exotic origins. 'If you've got to have in-laws, make them the Italian mafia,' he always joked. 'The food's good, and an Italian mother-in-law will love all the men in her family, and that includes me!' His enthusiasm made up for the lack of interest the children showed. All that Mediterranean fire diluted through the generations to just a pair of dark eyes and the curl of a cow's lick in Luca's hair.

43

Luisa could never quite believe their indifference, and hid it from her mother. Their genes were different. Her tall, athletic eighteen-year-old son amazed her, his body shape was so un-Italian, miles of legs that meant when he stood next to his grandmother his elbows were level with her chin.

He reminded her of Tom. His light-hearted slant on life was the antithesis of her family. There were two kinds of Italian men, as she saw it, the Amorazzi, who were short, saturnine and swarthy, skittering and frenetic like little bulls, snorting, intensely engaged with life's struggle. And then there were the Modigliani types, as Tom identified them. The photographs of her father's family showed etiolated Trevis picking their way through the back streets of Turin, slight narrow-shouldered men, nimble, orderly and tidy like Antonio himself. Poverty had frayed their sleeves, drawn nervous lines across their faces and given them straight small mouths. The sweetness of disposition that made her father so dear was palpable through the grainy black and white. A hint of softness in his dark eyes, gentleness in a lowered head, hair flopping, a little too long, that essence was in Luca too.

The phone rang, imperiously, Luisa thought.

'Hello?' Splashing sounds and a gasp, 'Oops, sorry, dropped the phone.'

It wasn't imperious. It was Dora. 'Lulu, it's me, are you in the middle of something?'

'Ice cream, why?' Water gushed in the background. 'It sounds like your phone's leaking, what're you doing?'

'In the shower. I'm a bit late. It's on speaker phone so it's not getting wet.'

The gasps were slightly soft porn, Luisa thought. 'It sounds as though you're auditioning for *Readers' Wives* with the shower head.'

'Luisa! Don't be disgusting! I'm just laying a paper trail. You know, making a call to a friend, making sure someone knows where I am. I'm off on a date.'

'Ah, so it *is* an audition. Thought so. Who is it, anyway?'

'Oh you know, the man from the North I told you about. The one from the Internet.'

'But I thought you told him you wouldn't go anywhere far?'

'I'm not. That's the amazing thing. He's coming here, Lou, to Blythe.'

'He can't be. You said he lives in Newcastle. It's miles away, how's he getting here?'

The shower ceased, Dora's voice loomed. 'He's called Bruce, he's actually from Darlington, not Newcastle. He might be amazing.'

'He might be crazy. Be careful, Dora. Was it his idea to come all the way here?'

Everything about this date was a bad idea in Luisa's eyes, but what did she know?

Dora sighed. 'Exactly!' she said. 'So that's why I'm making the phone call. I chose a pub near here because I thought it was good to be visible. D'you think he's a pervert?'

No point in trying to appeal to Dora's common sense, she was cynical about a perfect partner these days, but that didn't stop her from interviewing them. She loved male company. And men loved her right back. With the exception of Maddie's father. Poor old Benji. He still looked gloomily bemused by Dora when he showed up for Maddie's birthdays, even though their marriage had ended more than six years ago, leaving Dora alone with their one-year-old daughter. Dora was always happy to tell anyone who might enjoy her stories, which included her fascinated nieces, that she then began a more dedicated search for a soulmate. Meeting Aaron, as she had done a year later, was the proof that such a person existed. Aaron's tragic death floored her. She had only recently begun to take an interest in meeting anyone again, but even so, there were more candidates than Luisa could keep up with.

'Well,' she said. 'You can't practise tantric sex with him, there won't be time.'

Dora's laugh was full of mischief, 'Not necessarily, but I was wondering if you could pick up Maddie for me? That way if we go for a walk or something I won't have to rush off. I'll meet you in town. She said you and she had a plan to go out to tea this week anyway.'

Luisa smiled to herself, 'I love Maddie,' she said, 'I told her we had to ask you before we planned it. She wants to go shopping with Mae. She's such a darling, Dora, you're so lucky to have someone small.'

'Share her as much as you want to if you feel broody, Lou, in fact, I don't suppose you'd like to share her today, would you? Keep her for tea?'

Luisa thought about her afternoon. Seven was the most enchanting age. She could never resist Maddie. Time with her trumped most everyday activities and Mae would like it too.

'Okay, I'll collect her and then we'll get Mae and have tea. Tell me, Dora, does she know?'

'Know what? About this guy? 'Course not! I never introduce them to Maddie. Except for Aaron.'

Luisa sighed. Aaron. Never far from her thoughts still five years on. He was kind to Dora, and he could play the spoons on his knee and sing whatever anyone asked him to, while looking like he'd stepped out of a Kodachrome snap of the seventies with his burst of fair hair and his beard.

Luisa heard the tiny wobble in Dora's voice. At the time, Tom had said, 'She will never stop loving him, Aaron was the one for her.' That still held true. Silence crackled between them down the phone line, until Luisa spoke.

'Mae and I would love it, you know we would. Maddie is family. Did you tell her it would be me?'

'I said it might be – help! Look at the time. Thanks so much Lou, I owe you. See you later. God, my hair isn't even dry. Oh well, take me as you find me is my motto, or don't take me at all. Bye!'

Dating vicariously though Dora was hair-raising, thought Luisa, returning the phone to its place on the table among a chaos of her notebook, three pairs of glasses, two of which belonged to Tom, so he didn't have any with him to teach today, and a rubber sunflower that came as a marketing ploy for God

Knows What, when the farm suppliers dropped off a roll of fencing wire. What would it be like to be out there meeting men herself? Thank God for Tom. No matter how staid and invisible-making marriage could be, and sometimes it certainly was, at least it removed the stress of first dates. Anticipation was one thing, but what about not getting on? Being bored by someone. Dora was always bored by the men she met.

The drilling command of the oven timer shrilled at her. Why? Everything was cooked. Oh yes, the violets. She'd noticed them by the beech tree this morning, and an experiment was hatching. She would steep them in scalded milk. She was borrowing ideas from an eighteenth-century text she'd looked at in the anti-quarian bookshop in town. The book was vast, the pages frayed and yellowing, and its price ran into hundreds of pounds. Luisa had seen it in the window display and decided to have a go at the recipes. She began with the page it was open on, and the black-currant leaf sorbet had been so delicately fragrant she now couldn't wait to see what would happen with violet ice cream.

A car dashed into her reverie, screeching to a halt outside the kitchen, gravel flying. Grayson raised his head, sighed, and lay back down. It was Tom. He wasn't meant to be back. For better or worse, but never for lunch, that was the golden rule for marriage. Luisa felt a rush of irritation as her husband opened the door, then found that she was actually quite pleased to see him. Another person who could eat pudding. She decided to kiss him. 'Darling, how come you're back?'

Tom threw a bag of books on to the table with the air of a man who was being pushed to breaking point. 'You know your phone's off? I couldn't get through.' He swung the fridge door open, stared accusingly at the contents and shut it again. 'I'm starving,' he said weakly.

Luisa took no notice, it was the same with every family member who opened the fridge. She fished her phone out of her bag, and turned it on. A cascade of chimes announced many missed calls. 'It's always off,' she said, 'I do it so I can't mind when Ellie doesn't call. You could have tried the land line, you know.'

'I did. Engaged.' Tom circled round the blue Baked Alaska, eyeing it with suspicion: 'What's this? It looks like toothpaste.'

'Oh yes, Dora.' Luisa was distracted, listening to her messages. 'D'you want to taste it? I'd love to know what you think.'

Tom dug a spoon in, and nodded. 'Bloody good. Why's it blue though?'

'I thought it looked like a swimming pool so—'

'A swimming pool? Really?' he scooped another mouthful. 'Mmmm,' grinning at her, 'looks more like a car-cleaning sponge to me.'

The Land Rover outside the window wore a patina of dust, sea salt and flecks of cut grass.

Luisa looked from it to her husband. 'Have you ever seen a car-cleaning sponge?' she asked innocently.

He pointed at the pudding. 'I have now!'

She laughed. 'Go away. Why are you here anyway? You still haven't told me.'

'Those sheep.'

'They're out? Again?' Luisa scanned her memory. She'd been in charge of catching them a couple of days ago. Did she leave the gate open? No, surely not. If she had they'd have been out even sooner. 'They're such a menace, this is the third time.'

He nodded. 'I know. Had a call from the Whites at Mill Farm. Some day-tripper in a rush found a bunch of them heading up Sleet Hill and almost ran one over. Thought they were from their yard so he went and kicked up a stink.'

'Oh God, it's the garage,' muttered Luisa, still half-listening to her phone messages. She put it on to speakerphone. 'Listen, Tom, it's about the ice-cream van.'

Jed the mechanic was intoning, 'Welding on the front axle, some of the receptors and brake pads and could need a new front wheel arch panel, so it's good news and bad,' he announced with relish.

What was the good bit? wondered Luisa.

Tom shook his head, 'Dunno, sounds long term to me. You'll have to share my car, Tod.'

'What are you doing?'

Tom had taken his shirt off, throwing it in the direction of the utility room, but it landed nowhere near the door, let alone the washing machine itself.

'That's why I came home on the way,' Tom reached into the explosion of clean laundry on a chair in the corner and pulled out a green shirt. 'Managed to spill coffee all over my shirt when I got the sheep call. It was right in the middle of a timetabling meeting with the Head. Some angry bloke from Newcastle or somewhere was giving the Whites a load of grief. I could hear him in the background. I'm sure the Head could too.'

Tom pulled the shirt on over his head. Luisa noticed how his back muscles moved, working from his spine. He was tucking the shirt into his belt. He tightened the buckle and looped the leather end back through. Luisa put her finger on the belt. 'You always loop it like this,' she said. Tom patted her hand and moved to the other side of the table. He had moved on in his thoughts and was now talking about the mechanic. He was irritated that the work was going ahead on the ancient, rusting ice-cream van she had bought, against his advice, on eBay. Tom didn't have time right now, to deal with it.

'You can't just write a blank cheque for a pile of rotting junk,' he said. 'It needs a fortune spent on it I should think.'

'It's for my business,' she protested. 'I need your help.' In a way, it was a talisman, a memento of how they met, a link to the time when they were passion- ately in love. 'We can sort it out together,' she suggested.

Tom's mind had returned to the sheep and that phone call. 'The guy was ranting away about whether I had insurance for this sort of incident. I had to hold the phone away from my head, and I reckon the whole meeting could hear him.'

Tom switched on the kettle, and waited, drumming his fingers.

'Yeah,' he said, 'I'll have to come and look at the van. But don't make any decisions until I do. I'll get down there this week.' He sighed. 'Life's too busy,' he muttered under his breath, and began flicking through his phone messages.

He wrote down a number and shoved his phone back in his pocket. 'What's the point of letting the farmland if the people who rent it just bugger off all the time? It's a pain in the neck. Jason's sheep are in the middle of the road, and of course sodding Jason's on holiday in Portugal, isn't he? Why the hell couldn't he take his sheep with him? That's what I want to know.'

'Mmm,' agreed Luisa. Luckily, he seemed to have completely forgotten that she was the one who should have dealt with the sheep emergency call. Tom picked up his keys and his cap. 'Come on, Grayson, time you pulled your weight a bit with some sheep herding. See you later, Tod.' He blew her a kiss.

'Tom?'

He opened the door again and leaned in, 'Ye-es?'

She shot him a devastating smile. He glanced at his watch.

'Nothing, it can wait,' she said.

CHAPTER 3

The lane in front and behind Kit's car was a tunnel of shifting green as he hurtled east. The hedgerows on either side of him tumbled with wild honeysuckle, couch grass in a knot, cow parsley nodding. Plant life rattled against the door panels, stones swooshed luxuriously beneath the wide tyres. Kit narrowed his eyes and lowered the sun visor. He'd begun travelling before dawn, and was almost there. Rolling his shoulders, he yawned. He ached, his eyes were tight with the strain of watching the road and he couldn't think about his legs or his back, they screamed, muscles impatient to get out, to move. He would be glad to stop. The car had been going like a dream, but eight hours was a big ask for a thirty-year-old engine. Come to think of it, it was a big ask for the driver too. And he was on the final leg now, the home straight.

Kit found himself immersed in nature, not something he usually took much notice of. The scent of wild honeysuckle blew in through the window, enveloping him, catching in his throat, insisitent and beguiling as a lover. He snorted. He hadn't considered so much as the possibility of a lover in a while. There had been no room, no time. Grief consumes all, Kit had discovered. It might have been different, he supposed, if he had siblings with whom to share the loss.

He braked abruptly as an unmarked junction appeared ahead of him. Leaning over the steering wheel to see if any traffic was approaching, a flash of yellow in the hedge caught his eye. A sprig of gorse had been dropped into the woven bowl of a bird's nest, and it trembled there as the occupant darted away. The bright cadmium jumped at Kit. Gorse. It felt like a sign. He had never thought himself superstitious, but after his mother died he'd begun to notice things. An old yellow mini van, identical to the one she'd driven him to school in, appeared at the garage where he had his car serviced. Radio 3 ran a series on Thomas Tallis, and for three weeks Kit listened to his mother's favourite music and wished he'd made the effort when she was alive. It was absurd, he knew, but he fancied it was her communicating with him again. Gorse was another connection. It was eighteen months after her death that Kit launched the first new fabric in the Felicity Delaware Archive collection, and the yellow gorse flower was the motif he'd picked from his mother's numerous notebooks. The design was selling well. Indeed, an email he'd scanned quickly when he'd stopped for petrol was full of it.

' "Gorse" is on track for a record first month,' wrote Matthew, head of sales at Lighthouse Fabrics. 'Have asked for a few more archive yellows to scan through. Any favourites?'

A thrush darted past the car and dipped herself into the nest, jabbing her beak at the gorse petals. Kit held his breath and fumbled in the glove box for his binoculars. He'd never been this near to a bird. She eyeballed him. Or maybe she didn't, but through the lens, her eyes shone like jet. She opened her beak and a torrent of sound poured out, ceasing as if a plug had been pulled when, without warning, she flew off again. Kit peered at the nest. At the bottom of the mud-lined cup, two bright blue eggs lay like sugar lumps. 'An heir and a spare,' thought Kit, irrelevantly. The gorse sprig had vanished.

Kit drove on, hoping he was still heading in the right direction. Signposts were not part of the Norfolk experience. Norfolk was confusing enough to Kit without getting lost. For his mother to have owned property here and never told him had been impossible to deal with while Kit came to terms with being alone in the world. Never mind that he was a grown man, and had been for decades, grief took its own time. A lighthouse in Norfolk, tenanted and taken care of by a lawyer in a small East Anglian town was best ignored. The thought of investigating it had overwhelmed Kit. Until now. Now he was coming to take possession of this lighthouse. Perhaps it wasn't that odd anyway, his mother always loved seaside icons. Why shouldn't she have bought one? There was probably a very reasonable explanation. Perhaps he could integrate its image into the

Felicity Delaware Collection. Jesus Christ, what was that?

Something large had plummeted off the grassy slope above him in the direction of the windscreen. Kit ducked instinctively, slamming his foot on the brake so tyres and brake cables screeched in unhappy alliance. The car cavorted to one side of the road, burying its front bumper into the bank with a judder that caused a map, the binoculars and Kit's phone to slither off the front seat. Kit was rammed uncomfortably against the steering wheel as the car attempted to lurch once more and stalled. The ensuing calm was a balmy relief. No one around. Thank God. He wouldn't have wanted to be seen making such a hash of an emergency stop. Alf, his godson, who had only been learning to drive for a month, could have done better. Kit opened the door cautiously. He didn't think he was hurt, but his body was crunched and weary, and moving was an effort. Stretching, he grinned to himself. The first time in his whole life he'd seen the point of wearing a seatbelt.

Well, you live and learn, he thought. He leaned on the car, snatching a breath. A few rain drops fell half-heartedly. Whatever it was had disappeared. He rubbed his eyes. Could he have imagined it? All he'd seen was a blur of rushing legs, a black shape hurtling towards him. Fuzzy, and moving fast. A wig? An optical illusion? No. Unless his ears were misleading him, it was nothing so interesting. His car bumper was embedded in the bank for the sake of a bloody sheep. And here came its friends. Bleating assailed him as a woolly ewe appeared out of the scrub on top of the bank, and stood for a moment, chewing, her yellow eyes darting everywhere like a hooligan intent on trouble. That sheep will not be alone, Kit thought wryly. Sure enough, the gap in the hedge broadened to allow through a gang of about ten of them, some black, some white, if anyone could call the greasy grey of their fleece white, but all sharing the devilish gaze and loud complaints of the first.

'You've got no bloody road sense,' said Kit, infuriated as one thumped past him, standing on his foot. He stretched out his hand, resting his palm on the springy wool. Wait a minute, what was he doing? Stroking the sheep like Little Bloody Bo Peep. He snatched his hand back, the sheep carried on grazing.

'You've no idea what a pain in the arse this is,' he said. 'I've got things to do, places to be. I'm meant to be somewhere this afternoon, you know.'

More bleating ewes descended from the field above him. One nudged his legs as she headed for a succulent plant behind him. Her teeth bit through the dandelion stalk cleanly. He wondered, if he fell over if they would eat him. Shades of *The Birds*. Hadn't there been a story a few years ago about a woman whose husband fed her to his pigs? He remembered it because the report had said, 'It is little known that, to a pig, every part of a human being is edible', and his mother, to whom he had been reading the newspaper as was his habit when he visited her, had smiled and said, 'Well, I suppose it's only fair: we can eat all of them, too.'

The sheep in Norfolk were over-confident. They might easily forget the vegetarian habits of a lifetime. Another trotted up and sprang onto the boot of the car.

'Oi!' yelled Kit, banging his hand on the roof. 'Get off there!'

Offended, the sheep jumped down again.

Apart from their unrelenting racket, the rural silence was intense. How far exactly was he from civilisation? And how would he move his car?

A Land Rover burst out of the bend ahead and rattled to a halt, the trailer attached to it squealing and squeaking from every hinge and joint. A head poked out the window.

'Having trouble?'

'Not too bad. But I don't think I'll be going anywhere without a bit of a push,' said Kit wryly.

The driver got out and ambled over. His sleeves were rolled up, and he wore a cap at an angle on his sandy hair. 'No, looks like you hit the bank pretty hard. What happened?'

Kit sized him up. They were the same sort of height, though he reckoned this guy was probably a good ten years younger than he was. A push would do the trick. His hand was extended in greeting as he approached Kit, but the friendly smile vanished abruptly when he looked past the car.

'Those bloody sheep!' he roared, 'I've had enough of them.'

Kit was in cordial agreement, 'Well, I don't know whose they are, I'm not from around here, but they're a real menace. Shouldn't someone put them in a field?'

'Too bloody right,' the newcomer glowered. 'They should be in my field. I've been chasing them around all over the countryside since lunchtime. Did you hit one?'

Horrified, Kit shook his head. 'No, God, no! It jumped out in front of me, and I floored the brakes and got stuck. It could be that one I think?' he gestured towards a black ewe ambling up the road from behind the Land Rover. 'Are they yours?'

'This is a beauty of a car I must say, you had her long?' The stranger had lost interest in the sheep and was walking around the Mercedes, eyeing it appreciatively. He ran his hand along the blue paintwork, and leaned in to inspect the dashboard. 'She's covered some miles hasn't she?' His thumb and forefinger met around the thin steering wheel.

Kit was amused, a car buff was the last person he had thought he'd run into, and a friendly, farmer car buff at that.

He always found it a bit embarrassing to use the feminine pronoun for cars, but other men often seemed to like it, so what the hell. 'Feels like a few too many years when we break down, but she's an old friend.'

The farmer nodded. 'I was more of a motorbike man myself, packed it in for the family, you know how it is. Tell you what, though, I'd trade a hundred of these idiotic sheep to spend a few days in the Pyrenees on an old Triumph Bonneville.' He kicked the stones in front of him, his hands deep in his pockets, and squinted down the lane.

Kit laughed. 'It always looks like a dream, doesn't it? We conveniently forget the breakdowns and punctures, don't we? I drove the Merc back through the Pyrenees. Bought her in Turin, an act of insanity, it was the first free money I'd ever had.'

The farmer pushed his cap back on his head, 'Free money? Sounds good, we could do with a bit of that around these parts.'

Kit smiled. 'In a sense. It was years ago. I'd say thirty years ago now, I won a prize and saw this car advertised in the *Sunday Times*. I didn't know I was looking and suddenly I was handing over the most money I've ever spent on anything to an Italian Mercedes dealer on the outskirts of Turin. The car was only a year old, and she drove home like she was walking on water.' Both men stood the way men do, hands shoved in pockets, chins down, looking at the car.

'Nice prize,' said the stranger.

A phone rang in the depths of the Land Rover, the farmer leaned in to reach it. Through the door Kit could see a chaos of books sliding out of a worn canvas bag. One fell onto the road. Kit picked it up, it was a catalogue for an exhibition in St Ives.

'St Ives? You been down there?'

'Christ, where is it?' The farmer was still scrabbling under the seat for his phone. 'Ah, bingo!' He grabbed something, it turned out to be a small radio, not the phone, which had stopped ringing. He waved the radio at Kit, with a grin. 'Got one of these? Great for the cricket. I reckon I'm probably needed somewhere, so I'd better get going. Oh, did that fall out? Yes, we went with the kids a few months ago. Filthy weather every moment, but St Ives was a delight. That Hepworth museum even got the teenagers going.'

Kit hadn't ever thought that it mattered to him what other people thought of Cornwall, but he couldn't deny he was enjoying his new friend's enthusiasm. It was surprising too. Were there many Norfolk farmers who went all the way to Cornwall and once there, looked at the art? The guy was talking about his daughter now, and his eyes were soft and smiling.

'It worked out to be a good trip for Mae, she's my youngest, and she got right into reading thanks to Daphne du Maurier. She's come on in her English course work like a rocket since then. Look, even this catalogue is covered in notes. God knows how she reads them.' He opened a page at random, waving it in front of Kit. Inside loopy, fat handwriting in different coloured pens vied with the text. 'Better make sure she gets this tonight, it's stuffed with her revision notes. She'll freak out if she realises it's missing.'

His kindness, Kit thought, was almost palpable. He felt a small bubble of well-being rise though him. Norfolk, which could have come in anywhere on his spectrum, from downright alien to neutral to positive, was looking friendly. He wondered if he would know about the Kings Sloley Lighthouse.

The farmer threw the book back into the car. 'D'you know St Ives then?'

'I come from down there,' said Kit.

The farmer whistled. 'Blimey. You're a helluva way from home.'

'Yup, but then everywhere's far from Cornwall.'

They both laughed. 'Same applies here, it's what makes it special though.' The farmer narrowed his gaze, looked around him, sighed. 'Better get going,' he said, 'Shall we shift this car of yours then?' Walking round to the front, he set his shoulder against the bonnet. 'Is the brake off?'

Kit leaned in to check, then pushed with all his might against the driver's door-frame. Nothing happened.

'Okay. Christ, it's not shifting. You'll have to come and push here as well.' The farmer stood up again, waiting for Kit to come round to the front. 'Right, this should do it. Both of us I mean. One, two, three.' A grunt and the car swung back a few precious inches. Kit and the stranger heaved again, gaining a little more ground. They paused. One of the sheep manoeuvred herself in between them and stood, staring at Kit. He resisted an urge to make a stupid face at her.

Kit's new friend grabbed the sheep. 'Right, you can go in the back of the Land Rover,' he said, and posted her into his vehicle, adding, 'Get back in, Grayson,' as a lurcher the colour of smoke leapt out, stretching benignly before wagging his tail and approaching Kit. Kit wiped his hands on his jeans and reached out to stroke the dog. The afternoon was balmy, leaves whispered above them and clouds puffed lightly across the sky like small skiffs on a pond. A bubble of birdsong dissolved in chirps in the hedge above the cars.

'How far is it to Blythe?' He was suddenly over-whelmed by the seeming endlessness of his journey. He longed to lie down for half an hour or so. He'd booked a bed and breakfast, it would be nice to get there. Have a cup of tea. A piece of cake would be nice too. A meeting with a lawyer was not something to arrive at in a state of exhaustion.

The farmer had opened the trailer and, without incident, persuaded the rest of the sheep up the ramp and shut them in. Gentle bleats indicated that they accepted this state of affairs. Kit was impressed. 'I've never seen anyone sheep wrangle with such success. Looks like you've hypnotised them.' He looked at his watch. 'Got an appointment, how far is—?'

'Blythe? Oh it's about ten minutes from here.' The farmer leaned up against the Mercedes, gesturing down the lane ahead. 'Turn right at the top, then first left and then it's signposted. D'you want to start up the engine and make sure these bloody sheep haven't caused you any damage? I'll have to take them back with me, the fencing isn't holding. That goddamn Jason picked his moment all right,' he jerked his head in the direction of the sea. 'Gone to bloody Portugal, hasn't he? He's got a timeshare there. And he isn't answering his phone.'

Kit turned the key and the engine burst into life, its roar silky and familiar, like the crackle of logs on a fire. 'Jason? Who's he? Aren't they your sheep?'

The farmer, or not as it now turned out, banged his palm on the roof of the car. 'No they are not! I'm a history teacher at the school in Blythe. But the sheep live on my land, so I'm pretty sure I'm legally responsible for them if their owner's not around. I'm going to take it up with Jason as soon as he's back I can tell you.'

Kit grinned, taking off the hand brake. 'Looks like you've got them eating out of your hand, mate. You could take them on tour and get people to pay to watch you load them it's so fast.'

His new friend waved a hand. 'Think I'll stick with the day job for the time being. Don't forget: right at the top, then left and you'll pick up the signposts. I'll get out of your way.'

Manoeuvring the car out and on down the road, Kit saw the trailer bump off in a dust cloud. He smiled to himself. If that guy was the sort of person he was going to meet in Norfolk, he was looking forward to his time here. He realised, with a rush of disappointment, that he hadn't asked his rescuer his name. All he knew was that he was a teacher. Would their paths cross again?

Rolling his shoulders as the familiar actions created by so many hours at the wheel sank through his muscles, Kit blinked. He was driving through a village now. A duck pond, an ice-cream van, a queue of children and mothers, one with a pram, another carrying a toddler in her arms. Reeds climbed out of the pond like a line of Red Indians, golden, their feathered tops flickering in the afternoon light. Round another bend and Kit, as used to the majesty of Cornwall as he was, gasped. The sea leapt from nowhere, and above it a vast skyline, electric blue and startling as a kingfisher. His coast-to-coast journey was over. Taking a deep breath, he tasted the sea, and was aware of a shift taking place. Something opened within him, connecting with this moment, as he experienced a primordial sense of his place in the bigger picture. He was part of the scheme of things. But what was the scheme?

Remembering the instructions he had been given, he turned inland. The small market town of Blythe was charming. Lying beneath a great blue sky were higgledy-piggledy houses in flint, or whitewash, the faded blue of painted doors contrasting with soft red brick across which wisteria tumbled. Kit's heart leapt. A sunny afternoon, people sauntering along the pavement enjoying the spring warmth, a lazy pace and a rhythm that suggested all was well and would continue to be so. He had arrived. What he wanted more than anything at this precise moment was a piece of cake.

'Afternoon, Mr Delaware, glad to meet you.'

Kit had not thought what the Norfolk solicitor might look like, but if he had, he would have imagined him just as he was. Grave, avuncular, Kit's age, with a firm handshake and a signet ring on his left hand.

'Yes. Thank you. Indeed,' Kit heard himself sounding stiff and frosty. He made an effort to unbend. 'Fantastic day, isn't it? Have you been following the cricket? Looks like it'll be a long evening. Hope the weather's like this at The Oval.'

Charles Rivett's smile was brief. 'Not my bag I'm afraid,' he said.

The room was hung with the usual prints and discreet landscapes Kit would have expected in a solicitor's office, but smelled surprisingly fragrant. Rivett noticed him looking around, almost sniffing the air, and nodded towards a table by the window. A bowl of flowers swanned above a fan of magazines and a large crystal ashtray. 'My wife brought that lot in. Stuns me that they can give off such a scent.'

Kit stared at the flowers. 'Incredible,' he agreed. 'Did she grow them?'

'She certainly did.' Charles Rivett suddenly looked boyishly proud. He spun his pen on his middle finger. 'She's always digging something up or planting something else. You know how it is. Tea?'

Kit wondered how it was that he had so utterly failed to have a wife to bring flowers to the office. 'No tea, thanks, I've been sitting in a cafe since I arrived.' He smiled wryly, 'I'm used to Cornish cream tea, but I have to say, Blythe's coffee cake takes some beating.'

'True,' Rivett's smile was perfunctory, there was no escaping the business in hand. Kit's heart began to thump. It wasn't a big deal, but suddenly it felt like one.

'Let's get down to it, Mr Delaware. I have your deeds here, the Kings Sloley Lighthouse is yours now, with vacant possession. Have you seen it yet?' Rivett pushed the paperwork across the desk.

Kit was conscious of a great unwillingness in himself to pick it up.

'No,' he said. 'I'm ambivalent about it, to be perfectly honest. As you know, I'd never heard of it at all before my mother's death, so it's all pretty confusing. She never talked about it.' He pinched the bridge of his nose. Rivett looked at him in silence. 'What can you tell me?' His gaze met the lawyer's straight on.

Rivett stacked the papers in front of him. 'Not much,' he said. 'There has never been much to do on this one. It was a straightforward trust, set up by your mother for you. I didn't meet Mrs Delaware, her dealings were with a previous senior partner.'

Kit stared at the desk between them. 'Do you know the tenants? Are they – were they – lighthouse officers?' A prickle of embarrassment smarted in Kit's chest. 'I suppose what I mean is, is it still in use?' He had no clue about how lighthouses worked, and he was at a distinct disadvantage, unsure how much Rivett knew, and painfully aware how few facts he had himself.

'No, it was decommissioned years ago. The tenant, old Jim Fisher, was a bit of a smallholder, he bred rabbits, made hutches and sold them, that sort of thing. He went into a home so his family have been sorting it out.'

Sunlight shot through the dust motes around Charles Rivett. Kit had a sense of floating above the lawyer's polished desk, as if he were receding backwards in his life. His mother reading him *Peter Pan* in his bedroom the summer he was eight and had measles. He had been terrified by the thought that Peter Pan's shadow was rolled up in a drawer, forgotten. An essential part of him removed. Kit blinked himself back to the present. He couldn't shake off the notion that he was folded up in a drawer somewhere else.

Rivett rolled a pen between his fingers. 'It's entirely up to you what you do next. You could sell, and no one would ever be any the wiser. I don't know what you'd get for something like that, but it could be reasonable. You could let the place again, or you could make something of it. You could even turn it into a boutique hotel, if you wanted. It's quirky and it's yours to do what you want with.' The lawyer shrugged, and Kit glimpsed a shadow of a smile. 'Or you could move in and live there.'

Kit was surprised to find himself saying, 'Yes, I think I'm going to do that. At least for a short while.'

Charles Rivett led the way out into the hall. The cool air quenched Kit's impetuous mood, and the scent of beeswax lingered on the staircase, reminding him of home.

The lawyer searched in the cupboard briefly, then shrugged. 'Now, I thought we had the keys, but there was some mess up with the cleaning team at the Lighthouse, so if you'd like to drop by in the morning, Marion, on reception, will give you them.'

Still adjusting to his own statement, Kit answered, 'Don't worry, tomorrow's fine. I could do with an early night before I tackle the unknown.'

They were by the door now. The street was still dotted with shoppers, though Kit thought it must be after five. As if in response to his thought, Charles

Rivett looked at his watch. 'It will be done by now, but I know the Fishers had to get some sort of specialist team in to sort the electrics. Decent of them, they had a hell of a time getting stuff out, so I think you may find a bit of furniture comes with the property.'

Kit's head swam. He had a strong desire to locate the Lighthouse and then drive as fast as he could in the opposite direction. 'You know my business is called Lighthouse Fabrics, don't you? My mother named it.'

'I did notice that, I must say. What d'you make of it?'

Kit shrugged, 'Nothing. I don't know. Maybe I'll get to grips with it after I've been there.'

The lawyer nodded. 'Hmm. I'd like to take you there myself, but unfortunately I have a meeting in the morning. D'you know the way to Kings Sloley? If you time your visit right, you'll get a decent pint in the pub and not a bad lunch. I won't give you directions to the Lighthouse. I'll just say it's striped. Red and white.' He smiled and was gone.

CHAPTER 4

Luisa was in a rush. She'd left Mae in charge of Maddie, and the mother hen instinct was telling her she needed to get back to the pair of them. She had two vital errands: a recipe to give to the chef at Melodies, the restaurant down the road, and posting a parcel to Ellie. Luisa, queuing in the post office with the package for her daughter, found herself standing in a furtive manner. She didn't really want to be seen. Honestly, she felt as if she was sending drugs. Why should she feel like a criminal for sending her own daughter a small token? What was wrong with giving her a very useful, possibly lifesaving wristband from a very practical, sensible Natural Travel Guide website? Yes, it had been quite expensive, but that was because it actually stopped you being attractive to mosquitoes by releasing B vitamins in through your pulse points. Defiant and braced for disapproval, Luisa looked at the wall. If she wanted to save Ellie from malaria, why shouldn't she? And if she was sending a parcel anyway, she might as well put in some sun lotion and the pretty shawl she found in the market, perfect for Ellie to wrap round her shoulders if the sun got too fierce. She hadn't said she was going to the post office, just vaguely mentioned an errand. Mae didn't need to know she was sending things to Ellie, she would only roll her eyes.

'You've got to let her get on with being away without you,' Mae had commanded, thwarting Luisa's supposedly casual attempts to Skype Ellie last night. 'You know where she is, you know she's having a good time. Leave her alone, Mum.'

'Can I help you?' The post office man coughed at her.

'Yes.' Luisa tilted her chin.

'Well?' he enquired.

She looked round. No one she knew was in the post office, no one would know. 'To send this to India. As fast as possible.' She pushed the package through the window, triumphant. She had managed to administer a small dose of mothering to her eldest child, harming no one and indulging her own desire. Once she had paid for the parcel she rushed out.

Hurrying towards the cafe, Luisa deliberately avoided the looming figure of Cathy Bryer, mother of the Baked Alaska client, beckoning from across the street. There wasn't time to stop, she had to hand in her recipe to the chef at Melodies, and she had hoped to have time to talk to him about violet ice cream, and the blackcurrant leaf sorbet. The antique flavours were shaping up well, they could become a speciality. She dived across the road in the wake of a big car moving like a blue whale down the High Street, and was thus able to avoid Cathy altogether. It was best not to be caught by her, she had left three messages over the last twenty-four hours asking for Luisa's recipe for gazpacho. There wasn't time today, and anyway, she didn't want to hand out her recipes. Just because she was making a pudding for her didn't entitle Cathy Bryer to her whole recipe collection. People must come to her to make food. Or they could go to Melodies, or the cafe where she had ice creams. This was how the professionals worked, and she was a professional, born and bred.

Mae and Maddie had chosen a table on the pavement. Luisa threaded her way towards them, surprised that such a throng of people could be squeezed between the brick walls and the tarmac of the road. Fifteen or so metal tables, painted fondant colours, blue, yellow, lavender and pink, all busy. Tea was good business. She had begun experimenting with her own Lapsang-Souchong-flavoured ice cream, keen to have something in reserve, should she ever manage to start an enterprise like this herself. A couple leaned together, spooning sorbet out of a tall glass. That was what ice cream could do! It could make magic, create a frisson, act as a conduit for love, lust even. It wasn't just cones and 99s to bribe children into silence, it was sexy, grown up, erotic. Luisa flourished her phone and took a picture of the tables around her. She would ask Dora for her thoughts on ice cream's eroticism. This cafe had a reputation for cream teas, but today there was hardly a scone in sight. Even Maddie, usually a pushover for a cup cake, had chosen a colourful ice-cream sundae. Luisa slid onto the bench next to her and kissed her head.

'Hello, Miss Chief,' she said.

Maddie's answering smile was missing a tooth. 'You've had the tooth fairy!' Luisa exclaimed, but Maddie shook her head.

'No. It came out today. I've got it in a apple.'

'*An* apple,' corrected Mae gently, and leaned forward to show her mother. 'Look, Mum. Maddie kept it in the apple she was eating when it came out, don't you think that's clever?'

Luisa scrutinised the half-eaten apple, its bitten flesh tinged brown, a small, bloody tooth lying in a dented pit near the stalk.

'Brilliant,' she said, beaming.

'I thought of it myself,' said Maddie with pride, 'so I don't lose it.'

Luisa loved the familiarity of almost daily life with Dora and Maddie. The visits and sleepovers, the ebb and flow of close family life, was natural to her. Ellie was away, and less than three children in the house meant it felt under-inhabited. Maddie was a last tie to a kitchen full of young children. Maddie's ice cream was almost finished. 'Look, Auntie Lou, I saved the sprinkles on my spoon to show you. They're yellow,' she said, bouncing on her chair with delight.

Luisa caught the spoon and looked. 'Good idea,' she commented, 'I did one with saffron and honeycomb once—'

Mae laughed. 'Mum, stop it. You can't stare at stuff like that, it's embarrassing. You would never let us—'

Luisa dropped the spoon, rubbing a fleck of gloop from her dress. 'Sorry, sorry, I just want to have a look at the recipe.' She reached past her daughter for the menu card, 'I was thinking a bit of white chocolate mousse would fold into that—'

Mae nudged her. 'Mum,' she hissed, 'shhh! The waitress is coming. It's like espionage. We're doing the Cold War in History. If this was East Berlin, you could get into lots of trouble for spying, you know, locked up.'

'That's slightly over the top, darling but—'

'What can I get you?'

A quick skim of the menu had shown nothing that demanded urgent consumption. 'A moment on the lips, a lifetime on the hips', Luisa could hear Dora's mantra. She would have ignored it, for research purposes obviously, but she had already eaten a lot of Baked Alaska.

She ordered a pot of tea then called the waitress back. 'Actually, make that a pot for two,' she said, waving across the cafe as Dora arrived.

'Hi everyone, sorry I'm late, I've been. I've been . . .' Dora shouted, then recollected herself as she caught sight of her daughter. 'I've been . . . I've been here and there and everywhere this afternoon!'

She flumped down onto a chair with a sigh. 'What a treat to sit in the sun,' she said, casting her eyes around the tables.

'So?' Luisa raised an eyebrow in Dora's direction. She was basking in the success of her mission to the post office and this unexpectedly pleasant afternoon in the cafe with the children chatting, Mae not sulking and life being sweet. Sunlight seeped in and out of Dora. Copper hair, freckles and the fine hairs on her her arms were all golden. She was voluptuous, creamy, sensuous. Even if she hadn't been having sex with whom-ever-he-was from where-ever-it-was, she looked as though she had. The man who had been licking sorbet off his spoon with his girlfriend had turned round to look at her. A car tooted, a catcall swooped from the wound-down window as it zoomed by. A shadow crossed the sun and Luisa shivered. Sometimes, without it ever being acknowledged, even by herself, she had the sense that she had passed to the other side, the frumpy, invisible side of life.

Dora twirled Maddie's bunches and kissed her daughter. 'Hello, Miss Chief, how was your day? Your hair looks great like that, Mads. Did Miss Kemp do it for PE? Did you and Mae get the torch batteries?'

Maddie wriggled out of the embrace and stretched out her hand with the apple on it as if she was feeding a pony. 'Look, Mumma, my tooth!'

Dora gazed at the apple approvingly. 'Very inventive,' she said.

'Torch batteries? I knew there was something. Sorry, Dora.' Mae stood, and Dora rose next to her to let Maddie out of her seat. When did she get so tall? She'd shot up past Dora by an inch now. Luisa hadn't noticed it before. Maybe it had just happened, a sudden burst like a spring flower and there she was, no longer a child.

'We forgot. We went to buy sweets instead.' Mae held out a hand to Maddie and she smiled at her little cousin. 'Come on, Mads, we'll go and get a treat for Grayson from the pet shop too, he's been herding sheep all day, hasn't he?'

Luisa and Dora sat among the teacups. Luisa poured. 'When's Benji collecting her? Is Maddie excited about going camping?'

'Tomorrow for two nights, she's so excited. Benji's really got it right at last. We've been packing for weeks,' said Dora.

Luisa laughed, 'She's only seven, it's so little to be off for two nights.'

Dora shook her head. 'Oh no. It's fine, and Benji needs to do this sort of thing with her, otherwise he'll miss out completely. You're just such an Italian, Mumma Lou, you'd have them all at home all their lives if you had your way. Sometimes I really need a night off, you know. How else can I ever meet anyone?'

'Dora! What about today?' Luisa nudged her. 'Come on, let's hear it. Was he nice? At all sexy? You have to tell me, it's all about vicarious experience for me.'

Dora made a face, twisting a curl into her hair. 'Frankly, you're not missing much. He was a disaster. I knew it the second I saw him standing by his car.'

'How?'

Dora pulled out a cigarette.

'Here, have a light.' An arm had shot past Luisa and a man, walking past with his dog, was holding a flame steady for Dora. Dora swooped over the flame, shimmering, almost luminous. It would be worth smoking again to have that effect on people.

Dora fanned the smoke away from Luisa. 'It didn't help that he was cross. And late. He was furious. Said his journey was hell. You know, a real moaner. He stopped and had an argument at a farm, he said. Such awful manners, I said. Anyway, that wouldn't have mattered except he was a giant.'

'A giant?'

Dora nodded, scooping up a drip of Maddie's ice cream. 'Mmm, that's so good. I almost prefer it liquid. You know, not cold. Yes, huge! From Giant Land. Not a normal tall person.'

Luisa was laughing. 'How tall is a giant?'

Dora waved her hands to encompass the sky. 'Nine feet tall – well near enough – and he tucked his shirt into his trousers under his armpits.'

'That's quite weird, I agree, it's funny with first impressions, I—'

'First impressions?' Dora was indignant. 'It was more than an impression. He was definitely huge and definitely in a towering rage. He got even crosser when I said I had to pick up Maddie at three o'clock. He drove off! Left me at the table and went back to Newcastle in a huff. Can you imagine?' She puffed a smoke ring and sat back.

Luisa suddenly felt very old. A stressful date with an extra-tall stranger was so much less interesting than a recipe for white chocolate mousse ice cream, or an evening with Maddie coming to sleep over.

Dora squinted at her. 'Mae's looking cute,' she said. 'Wonder if she's got a boyfriend yet?'

'She's only fifteen,' Luisa protested. 'She's too young.'

Dora snorted. 'God Lou, you're prehistoric, can't you remember being that age? She's a hotbed of hormones, she needs to fall in love, she *must* be in love. I was in love with about five people at once when I was fifteen, and the interest coming back my way was precisely zero, except for some pervert who followed me to the hairdresser's once and accosted me on the doorstep of Hair to Impress in King's Lynn and said he'd been watching me.'

Luisa was indignant. 'Great. Is that what you want Mae to find? A stalker? Why does she have to have a boyfriend anyway?'

Dora patted Luisa's arm, and squeezed her hand. 'Calm down, Lou, I was only teasing, Mae's great, and you know it.'

Mae and Maddie waved from across the street.

'Here they come,' Luisa straightened herself. 'I know you think I'm daft, but wait till Maddie's this age. It goes like a flash and then they're almost adults.'

'Tell me about it,' Dora shrugged. 'You know, I sometimes can't believe Maddie's my child, she's so grown up and I swear I only just had her.'

'Ellie didn't have a proper boyfriend until she was seventeen,' mused Luisa. 'God, if only she'd gone travelling with him instead. He's on a nature reserve in Costa Rica feeding baby turtles.'

Dora looked at her affectionately. 'I'm no psychologist, Lou, but that sounds like what you'd be doing if it was your gap year. Given the choice, I'm with Ellie: I'd be hitching round India, smoking opium in a nice den any day.'

Luisa shot an annoyed look at Dora, who was leaning back with a teasingly smug smile on her face, and was just about to say how she was sure Ellie wouldn't know what an opium den was, let alone hang out in one, when Mae and Maddie were upon them.

'Look, we bought these to take camping. In case I get lost in my sleeping bag.' Maddie waved a green neon stick and a whistle on a string.

'Perfect,' said Dora, 'you're all set now, aren't you? Come and sit down here, we're wondering what Ellie's up to.'

Mae slid back into a seat and began tapping at her phone. She looked up again, directing her question at Dora. 'Can you catch a disease of fancying people? Because my friend Lola's started saying she fancies everyone. Literally everyone. Even really rank people. She doesn't have a filter. It's gross, I think.'

Dora laughed, winked at Luisa. 'God, I've definitely got it! I even quite liked the man who was in here a minute ago.'

'What man?' Mae and Luisa spoke at once and bust out laughing.

Dora bit into a biscuit and leaned forwards, demanding conspiracy. 'Didn't you see him? He was at the till when I came in. They were wrapping up a huge coffee cake for him. Probably his wife's birthday.'

'I reckon his daughter's,' said Luisa. 'I can't imagine a man buying his wife a cake.'

'Probably actually his own birthday,' said Mae, still half-looking at her phone. 'Men are obsessed with coffee cake. When I worked at the tearooms in the Easter Holidays it was always the men who ordered the coffee and walnut and the millionaire's shortbread. Women, 'specially your age, Mum, always say they don't eat wheat, and then have brownies or carrot cake anyway, it's so funny.'

'Really? What about ice cream?' Luisa was diverted. 'Do they choose different flavours?'

Mae rolled her eyes. 'Mum, ice cream is ice cream. You are the *only* person who could *ever* think that there are male and female flavours. If I—'

'No! She could be right, Mae,' Dora butted in. 'And if she is, we can make our fortunes on the back of her.'

'Yeah, I bet you, it'll be coffee ice cream for guys.'

Dora bit her lip. 'I'm going to ask the girl at the counter, that way I can find out about the man I saw as well.'

'What was he like?' It seemed suddenly that Mae was nearer Dora's age than she was. Luisa didn't want to be left out.

'Tallish, dark hair, nice voice. Nice shirt, and it was definitely a coffee cake,' said Dora.

'Yeah? You noticed all that?' Mae teased. 'You're ill, Dora. But in a good way. There aren't many grown-ups like you.'

Luisa sighed, content. The afternoon was warm, there was no urgency, the cafe table was littered with teacups and cake crumbs, Maddie was drawing a picture in a tiny notebook, Dora and Mae laughing over a text. This small absorbing world belonged to the four of them. Mae leaned against her, and she felt complete. Her family made her whole. Not family the Italian way, all singing, all dancing and drama, the pitting of strength a constant force, and Gina's iron-willed dominance. This version with Dora, Mae and Maddie, the idle hour after school, no plans and nothing much to do, was the family life she would never have known had she not met Tom. Less intense, less strident than she had grown up with, but no less potent.

Maddie was patting her hand, 'Auntie Lou did you really have ice cream every day when you were little? Mae says you did.'

Luisa bit her tongue not to laugh. The felt-tip pen dripped a blue pool from Maddie's blue mouth on to the notebook and the table beneath it.

'Oops, a bit of clearing up needed.' She dipped a napkin in a glass of water to wipe Maddie's face. 'It's true. My granddad had an ice-cream van, and I used to go with him sometimes in it.' Amazing how forgotten memories could flood in with a word or sound. Apple cinnamon ice cream with a knot of purple bubble gum concealed in the scoop was the big flavour the summer Luisa was eighteen. Her holiday job on the ice-cream vans had seemed like the ideal way to earn pocket money, until she spent three days of a rare heatwave stuck in the van. The hours crawled, and her best friends cavorted nearby in the sea with Matt, otherwise known as The One. Seeing The One giving piggyback rides to Olivia Riscali and racing through the surf with Debbie Marco were low moments in what she had assumed would be the Summer of Love for her and Matt. On autopilot, Luisa had accidentally double scooped glistening balls of Apple Cinnamon Bubblegum ice cream for the queue of garrulous pensioners outside her van, parched after a day on the Great Yarmouth pier. Her inattention, as her grandfather never failed to remind her, had consequences. Even in the ice-cream queue. A gurgling noise penetrated the chatter on that memorable afternoon.

'What did you put in this? It's not just ice cream, is it?' A flustered man waved a half-melted cone at her then bobbed out of sight. Craning reluctantly, Luisa peered out at him, he was bending over a woman who had clamped a handkerchief across her mouth. Out of the corner of her eyes Luisa saw The One throw a towel around his shoulders and walk away down the beach with Olivia and Debbie. Her future was vanishing like their three sets of footprints in the tide.

The man bobbed up again, Luisa recoiled. His face in the opening of the van was wild, his hair fizzing crossness, spittle bubbling up from the corner of his mouth. 'She's got her teeth stuck in the ice cream,' he wailed. Luisa contemplated vaulting through the window and sprinting to join her friends. She might have done it, or so she thought, but as she mustered her strength to spring, Olivia reached up a hand and The One caught it, and held it. She didn't let go. Luisa turned her back and dug a handful of ice from the fridge. 'Maybe she can get it out if you cool her down a bit?' she suggested to the hot-faced man.

The scene had bleached in her memories, and the departing backs of her friends had assumed a nostalgic glamour worthy of a Californian teen movie.

'We actually had six ice-cream vans,' she told Maddie. 'And they were all different. They even had names. My favourite one was Lucky. I thought it was real.'

'Mum, it *was* real, we've got pictures. It was striped and there were cones for the wing mirrors.' Mae rolled her eyes. 'And you've got a Miss Havisham version of it at home. You know, that old wreck you bought off eBay.'

'It's gone to the garage, actually,' said Luisa. 'I mean real as in alive. I didn't know you knew about Miss Havisham, darling?' Always a thrill when one of the children mentioned anything cultural, and even though Tom had told her not to mention it for fear of spoiling it for them, Luisa couldn't resist.

Mae's grimace was perfectly pitched to show disdain. 'We were doing a thing about unrequited love. I hope I don't get it ever.'

'Lucky, lucky, lucky,' chanted Maddie. 'Mummy, can we have an ice-cream van?'

Dora agreed without listening. 'What? Yes, later, we'll get one on the way home. Come on, time to go everyone.'

Gleeful, Maddie skipped at her side, planning a new life. 'We need to make sure it has the right song playing,' she said. 'Something like Jingle Bells, but for summer.'

'Too right,' agreed Mae, linking arms with her mother. 'None of that cheesy piped music. I think it should be rave music, really, that'd wake everyone up.'

On the way to the car, Dora's phone rang. The shadows were mauve, lingering and soft as a shawl. Luisa remembered she had to pick up Luca on the way home.

Dora waved her arm and rolled her eyes at Luisa as she spoke into the phone. 'What? Did he ask you anything? How old is he? D'you think so?' She laughed. 'Well I'm not convinced. I've just had a very bad experience. That's not the kind of thing I'm interested in.' She laughed. 'It's still bound to be a disaster. I'm not desperate yet, you know!'

Dora ended the call. Luisa raised her eyebrows in a question.

'Oh, it was a friend,' said Dora. 'She's just got a job in town, and she's been going on about this guy there. Anyway, she says she's going to set me up on a date.'

'Another one? You're so brave,' Luisa marvelled.

Dora shrugged. 'All I know is you have to kiss a lot of frogs,' she said.

'Mum!' Mae swung round to face Luisa. 'You sound *ancient*. What's happened to you? It's like you and Dad are from another world. When you went on dates they probably didn't even have mobile phones.'

84

'They didn't,' agreed Luisa, laughing.

'How did you know where to meet? How did you get out of it if you didn't like each other?' Mae shuddered. 'It's a miracle anyone in your day got it together.'

'I think we are a miracle,' Luisa agreed. 'It's been more than twenty years now.'

Shops were closing. From the allotments near the car park, the scent of cut grass wafted towards them, while over a wall, the thwack of a ball sounded the beginning of a game of tennis. Blythe settled with audible contentment after a good day. No passion afoot, no teenage love matches for Mae or dates for Dora tonight. This was the beginning of a family summer. A moment to savour. Luisa wished she could capture the essence of now and paint it or bake it or write it. Just do something with it before it was gone. She reckoned her ice-cream van, if she got it going, might just be the living embodiment of this timeless feeling.

Dora pinched her. 'Hey look, Lou, there's the guy I saw earlier.'

'What? I thought you said he went back to Newcastle?'

'No,' Dora whispered. 'Not him, I mean the cake man. From the cafe. Look!' she nodded towards a doorway just ahead.

'Where? I can't see,' hissed Luisa. 'God, that cake box is vast. He must be having a party.'

Her eyes travelled from the cake box held under one arm to his linen shirt, ink dark and crumpled, its sleeves rolled back. His forearms were tanned, he wore a plain watch and was reading the screen of his phone as he walked. Then he looked up. Luisa met his gaze. She was so close she could smell him, and the tang of lemons and hay was fresh and exciting. She walked on, the thin fabric of her skirt gentle as a breath on her skin.

CHAPTER 5

Accidental or deliberate? Chance or choice? The questions thrummed with the rhythm as the train thundered west on the Southampton to Exeter line. Michael smoked in the corridor with a couple of sergeants from the 14th and a lad not more than seventeen years old with bitten nails and a sharp Adam's apple, who'd fired his first shot from a clean unused gun the day peace was declared.

'Where're you headed?' The taller of the two sergeants tapped a cigarette on the pack, hunched himself around the flame, until the tip glowed and he breathed out a feather of smoke.

His friend returned the lighter to his breast pocket. 'Back home to the folks in Liskeard. Gotta farm to run, the wife's been doing it with a couple of land girls.' The words burst out of him, loud across the roar of the train. His lips were wet and red, excitement shaping this first glimpse of his future. Repeatedly, he lifted his hand to his face and swept his palm from jaw to brow, like a magician wiping away all thought and knowledge.

He flipped the open window closed and the ensuing quiet was tangible, warmer and soft. 'My dad's arthritis took him hard just around when I was called up. Reckon Jenny's well worn out by it now, with the little 'uns as well.' He rubbed his fingers in his eyes. 'Don't suppose I'll have as much as a day off before I'll be back to the milking. But you know, I'm glad of it, glad to have something to come back to.'

The listening men nodded, the other sergeant spoke. 'Yeh, it's like that back home for me, I'll be back on the round as soon as I'm outta this uniform. The missus has done it for me, been postmistress of four villages since I was away. I thought she'd like a rest, but she reckons she's off to work in the draper's shop in town. Wrote her she can have her feet up now I'm home, but she's having none of it. Says she likes to be out of the house, so I'll be cooking our tea most nights now.'

The men smiled and fell silent, aware of unease it would be disloyal to share.

'How about you, sir?' The soldiers turned to Michael, an easy camaraderie was established halfway down a burning cigarette, and they looked at him as if from one pair of eyes.

Michael held his breath for a long moment. 'I don't know yet,' he said finally.

Beyond the carriage the world went by, fields, hedges, a river dotted with geese, a few more on the bank, scattered like white roses. Then the grey

rooftops of a farm framed by pale trees. A cart laden
with sacks moved slowly up a hill as the train flashed
past with the sudden shriek of the whistle. Darkness,
a tunnel. Sooty blackness jolted his nerves. Daylight,
a cottage garden, laundry dancing on the line. None
of it had any relevance to Michael. The momentum
of the train was enough, staying on it was all he had
to do for now. He set his shoulders, braced to fend off
further questions. None came. The conversation
shifted to a rumour that the German population was
not so happy to receive its defeated heroes home again
to the Fatherland.

'So they'll have to join the circus, or something, to
keep themselves on the move,' said the tall sergeant
and spun a coin as if in illustration of a trick they
might try.

'Just let 'em try coming near my house asking for
money,' said the young lad, his swagger implicit in his
tone. In the laughter surrounding his comment,
Michael slipped back to his seat.

A plan, that was what he needed. It wasn't enough
to have got on the westbound train, no matter whether
he had done so deliberately or not. He should have
got off again at the first station. By now he would be
on his way to Norfolk. Going home. It was the reality
that had stopped him. There was too much of it. He
was used to being part of a unit, marching. Marching
into war. A number, a uniformed cog in a giant
machine.

'Onward, Christian soldiers, marching as to war.' It
was the marching out again he couldn't imagine. He

was lucky. He kept being told this, he must be. The ticket collector on the train, a woman wiping the counter at the station cafe, a voice in his head, all shared one message: 'You are alive, the rest are not.'

Being alive didn't make him fit to become a husband. He tried to picture himself married to Janey, living in a little house somewhere, wearing a suit and kissing her on the top of her head as he went off to work each morning, returning in the evening, kissing her again. The thoughts pelted him. He couldn't do it. He couldn't marry her and have lunch on Sundays with her mother and father. He wasn't fit for it. He held up his hands in front of him. There could be no small talk, no fabric of domestic life when his palms and fingers were scarred with wounds caused by weapons, and his nights were drenched with sweat, his sleep interrupted by nightmares.

The woman opposite in his carriage was staring at him, a wobble of unease puckered her chin. He shoved his hands back in his pockets and crossed his legs. She averted her eyes, folding her handkerchief into smaller and smaller squares until it was a tiny cube of pale blue cotton. It looked to Michael like a sugar lump, he wondered if she might pop it in her mouth.

The train began to shunt slowly out of the station and Michael settled against the bristly carpet bag fabric and sighed. The only thing he knew was that he didn't know what he was doing. That had not changed in the hours since. His companion had not eaten her handkerchief, instead she had taken out a ball of wool and some needles and begun to knit. Her wedding band moved along her finger as she drew in the wool, and the shadows under her eyes made Michael feel protective of her. She undid her coat, and only then did Michael notice that she was pregnant. He wondered if her husband was alive. A rush of heat stung the back of his eyes and he pressed his thumbs into the sockets to stop tears springing. Lulled by the rocking motion of the carriage, and the quiet click of knitting needles, he drifted into sleep.

At Liskeard Michael woke. The knitting woman had gone and his carriage was empty. He looked out at the platform, disorientated, and saw the tall sergeant jump off the train, dropping his kitbag next to the stiff bulk of his army greatcoat on the platform as he bent down, then cautiously opened his arms to receive the rapturous greeting of a small girl with pigtails. She had hurtled down the platform towing a reluctant toffee-brown puppy on a lead.

'Daddeeee! You're back! Look at Pinkerton, she's my very own puppy! Mummy let me bring her. Come on, I'll show you how she shakes you by the hand!'

'Let him be, Sally, come on now.' A short, bulky woman bustled up behind the child, restraining her with a hand on her shoulder. A sob burst from the woman as the sergeant stood up. The train shunted off, shooting steam around them, wrapping the three of them in a cloud with the puppy and the future, the past and now all tangled up.

Michael should be teaching children like that now. He would have gone to university if things had been different. He had a place. He would have become a teacher, he had a career and a life planned for himself in Norfolk. It no longer seemed possible for that to happen. He could scarcely remember the person he was before the war, he still hardly knew the person he had become. He would not go to university now. His brother Johnnie had never seen the point of it anyway. 'Too much learning can damage your brain, kid,' he said. Michael squared his jaw. Johnnie only ever read adventure stories at school. He farmed with his father from the age of fifteen and he had a motorbike and fixed it himself. He never spent a moment indoors he didn't have to, and Michael, two years younger, looked up to him.

Their mother heard Johnnie's remark, and didn't let it go. 'You do things differently, you boys,' she said. 'Give Michael his head and he'll find his way.' Johnnie winked at Michael, stage whispering, 'Mum's softness is only skin deep.' It became their shared joke, a fast route into familiar territory. Secure.

Michael pressed his knuckles to his eyes, his cheekbones a ridge beneath the sockets. He didn't want to see home in his mind's eye, or any familiar territory. The crush of his hands against his eyelids seeped purple and red blooms across the image of his mother in his thoughts. At Penzance, he hoisted his bag onto his shoulder and walked out of the station. No decision needed there, it was the end of the line. He was dazed, he'd never been to Cornwall, and that in itself was liberating. Striding across the road with a spring in his step, he caught the familiar tang of ozone cut with seaweed and smiled. He had no army timetable to dictate a structure to his day, but his wristwatch told him it was almost six o'clock. He needed somewhere to spend the night.

Penzance had shut up shop for the evening and although a few windows glowed on to the streets, more had the shuttered look of abandonment. Everywhere displayed some level of dereliction, whether a broken window, a collapsed roof, or a boarded-up doorway. The picture he'd held dear of England as a cosy haven, was a fantasy. The war may have been fought across the sea, but it had come home. Michael hugged his kitbag and hurried on as the light faded. Where could he stay? Rubble spewed out of a doorway and a girl, her head covered with a shawl, threaded her way though and clambered into the house behind. A little boy with fair curls stepped from the shadows and she let her hand rest on the top of his head as she bent to speak. Spinning round to shut the door behind her, she stopped short. There was no door, just a couple of planks propped beneath the lintel. The children moved away into the shadows of the house. Michael dropped his bag and stepped across broken bricks to the shadowy entrance. He found a panel of the old door and propped it in the gap, placing a chair in front of it. At least it gave an impression of a barrier. Whether it would protect the children, and anyone who might be in there with them, was another matter. A glance down the street suggested that this was not the only house without a front door.

Michael stepped off the rubble and back on to the road. His gaze was drawn to the sea. He would walk along the coast, following the sunset, and find somewhere to stay the night. The evening's glow pricked through his uniform, and excitement stirred his tired limbs enough to get going. Cresting the first hill, he saw coves and undulating hills, villages tucked into folds falling to the sea, a few houses scattered further away, while to his left a vast grey battleship loomed drunkenly in the sea, small fishing boats floating like toys around it. Lopsided and redundant, it had gone aground on a bank of rocks some time ago, by the look of decay around the rusty portholes and ragged flag. Its colossal scale couldn't stop it looking foolish and comical, like a set for a Buster Keaton movie.

Cheered, Michael strode along the road out of town. The departing sun spilled across the surface of the sea, and he was happy to be alone, striking the tarmac underfoot. He was uncertain how long it would take him to find a place to stop, and he quickened his pace, removing his jacket and rolling it up in a ball at the top of his bag.

The road twisted like a rope into Newlyn. Voices and the chink of glasses through an open door drew him into a pub, a room with a low ceiling, smoke-tinted walls. From out the back wafted a delicious aroma of fresh fish frying. He realised he had scarcely eaten a thing all day and sat down, glad to have got himself somewhere.

'Why Britannia?'

'What?' Michael twisted his head, unsure if he was being addressed.

'Britannia. She's on your collar.'

A man had approached, sunburned, his speckled guernsey textured like chain mail. He stretched a hand in greeting. 'Forgive me, I was just curious about the badge. It's your regiment, isn't it?'

'Yes, the Norfolk's 1st battalion.' Michael was confused, taking in the gentle voice, grey eyes, and sweep of fair hair. He didn't seem like a fisherman. 'Britannia's our talisman, if you like, though she's landed us in trouble I can tell you.'

'She has? Cigarette?' His companion put down his beer to offer his pack.

Michael nodded, mock solemn. 'We're the only regiment to have a woman in our barracks.' He held the match, laughter breaching the awkward gap. 'Lance Corporal Michael Marker,' he said. 'That's ex-Lance Corporal I suppose now, but I thought I'd keep the badge.'

'Paul Spencer. I was in Italy. You?'

Michael nodded. 'Pretty bad there, but then so was everywhere. France, the Middle East, and most recently a bloody great boat we sat on for months. It's taken a while to get home. What about you?'

'Air Force, but I was lucky, we flew straight back at the end of the war. Out of the planes, back to work.'

They both laughed. Michael noticed Spencer's clothes were spattered with flecks of blue paint. 'What've you been painting?'

'Ha! You may well ask. And today I'm damned if I know.'

Spencer stared abstractedly at the floor. The pipe between his teeth looked as if it belonged to an older man, but everything else about him was packed with energy.

'Not walls then?'

Spencer grinned wryly, 'Not walls, no.'

Looking at Paul, lean but healthy, Michael realised he had forgotten that there was a world still turning, where people laughed without a sense of the gallows attached, they ate meals together, talked and went to work and lived beyond the horror of war.

'Are you an artist?'

The question sounded gauche as it came out. Spencer grimaced. 'Some days I think not,' he said lightly, adding, 'You heading somewhere local?'

'Not sure, I don't know this area, but I thought Mousehole sounded good on the sign post.' Michael grinned as Paul Spencer shouted with laughter. 'Have I got something wrong?'

'Not wrong. We forget here that people don't know, but Mousehole is pronounced *Mowzul*.'

Michael laughed now. 'No! The name was the draw for me, it sounded so snug. Right, *Mowzul* here I come.' He reached for his kitbag.

Spencer's hand was on his arm. 'Stay with us if you'd like to. Sheila's at home, it's simple enough, but there's food and a bed, and it's not far.'

Michael felt the hot sting of emotion between his eyes again, and spun a coin from his pocket, wondering if he would cry about everything now the numbness was beginning to fade. It would be a handicap. 'Thank you, I shouldn't impose, but I will. Can I buy you a drink for the road?'

By the time they rolled in at the gate of Paul's home, they were merry. Paul Spencer was a fine story-teller, he had grown up in Cornwall and, as the war hadn't seen him off, he rather thought he'd die here some day. He also had a kind ear for another man's story. Michael found himself talking, tentatively making sense of his lack of plans, and creating some as he spoke. Meeting Sheila, eating a simple meal of fresh mackerel, bread and some radishes from the garden, and falling into a low narrow bed, was all a blur of new sensation. He'd shared bunks and floors and the cramped berths on the ship for so long, to be in a room alone, in peace, was a sensory experience he scarcely felt able to conceive.

The room was piled with canvasses, there were no curtains, and he stared out of the window at stars dancing between the branches of a budding tree. The cottage floorboards creaked, and he could hear the occasional murmur of Paul and Sheila's voices. It reminded him of his childhood, his parents. He couldn't imagine himself and Janey under the same circumstances. What would a house they lived in look like? A whitewashed cottage by the sea like this? A red-brick house in a terrace? A farm? He tried to put Janey in Sheila's place in the kitchen. Sheila, a wiry girl with an elfin air, added another place at the table with relaxed friendliness. Echoing Paul's welcome, she moved back from the table to the light by the hearth after supper and picked up the patchwork she was sewing, 'For the baby.' She spoke quietly and exchanged a smile with Paul.

Michael's thoughts hit a dead end. Janey wasn't part of him, he didn't know her, nor she him. He'd sat on the low sofa and his left foot jumped and jiggled, a tic he hadn't paid much attention to when he was away, but which suddenly stuck out in the company of his new friends. He didn't know when it had started, but he was pretty sure he hadn't had it last time he went home. He realised with a jolt that he knew more about the men he had shared the last months with than he did about his fiancée.

Later he felt as if a curtain was falling, blackout thick, around him, ending an act in his life. He slept, cocooned in rough linen sheets, sedated by the oily smell of turpentine and lulled by the sound of the waves.

He was surprised by how hungry he was when he woke, the scent of bread fresh from the oven seemed to warm the air. He dressed and went downstairs to find Paul cutting into a loaf, Sheila bringing milk in a small churn from a pantry outside. Michael wondered how long it would take for domesticity to feel real to him.

Armed with an address, and an open invitation to return any time, and clad in some old clothes Paul had given him until they next met, Michael was on his way by mid-morning. He had a plan for the immediate future, the rest would come later. His nostrils tingled with the salty prickle of sea spray, and he squinted, trying to take in the view. Small colourful fishing boats were moving out from Newlyn harbour towards the horizon, threading past tumbled concrete blocks and barbed wire as incongruous and ugly as scars on bare flesh. Michael was grateful to be out of his uniform, though Paul's faded blue drill trousers and scratchy knitted jersey contributed to his heady sense of unreality. He was a new man, a different one.

A van passed him as he rounded the final bend and saw Mousehole before him. Slate roofs riding up the hillside, hedges and oak trees suggesting ballast behind the village, the sharp punctuation of the church spire, and streets tumbling towards the sea. Like arms outstretched to catch them falling off the hillside, the harbour walls curved towards one another from each end of the village, almost touching. In the gap, Michael watched a boat bob out into the glassy sea and the world beyond, insignificant as soon as it passed through the harbour mouth.

A palm tree bristled in the garden of the house in Cherry Garden Street, and light flooded through the open front door and into the narrow hall. Michael knocked and called a greeting. Paintings lined the staircase and hung from the ceiling to the floorboards, leaving not a square foot of wall visible.

A voice floated through from the back of the house. 'Come through, I'm flooded.'

'Verity was my uncle Francis's second wife – they met in Oxford in the twenties. He was translating ancient Nordic texts and, although no one ever said, I think she may have been his student,' Sheila Spencer had explained when talking about the owner of this small house in Mousehole. 'They didn't have children, and although she's half-Norwegian she didn't go back there when he died. I think she missed him so much that she began having lodgers to give her people to talk to in the house.'

'She lives up at the back of the village behind the chapel, she'll be glad to meet you,' added Paul. 'She's a nice woman, as long as you like cats.'

Through the front door and out the back was all of half a dozen strides for Michael, and in the yard he found a tall angular figure in blue overalls, a cigarette in one hand, a mop in the other, prodding gingerly at a flooded drain, and watched, with an air of detached disapproval, by two white cats.

'Bloody drains. I suppose I'll have to bail out the garden, I'm not getting anywhere with my mop,' she said, waving her cigarette to signify greeting.

Michael liked her slash of red lipstick and the narrow green snakeskin belt that secured her overalls. The combination, he thought, pepped up the otherwise slightly daunting scene. He wondered if this happened often. Certainly Verity seemed perfectly relaxed in a yard ankle-deep in drain water. 'D'you have any caustic soda?' he asked. 'It's always worth a try.'

By the time they had bailed out the garden and poured caustic soda down the drain, Michael and

Verity were friends. He swept the yard and stood the broom in the lean-to shed, observing his work with satisfaction. Sunlight hit the far corner and the mauve sheen of wet cobbles faded in front of him, a geranium tumbled from a pot on the wall and stones painted white marked raised steps leading to another terrace. Verity made him a cup of tea and the cats, Ossian and Fingal, moved to the kitchen windowsill to continue their unblinking observation of the stranger.

'They must like you,' Verity observed. 'They usually vanish when visitors appear. Come and look at the room.'

He followed her up the stairs and she opened the door to a small room at the front of the house. A candlewick bedspread, curtains made of plaid blankets and a fireplace filled with pinecones. It reminded Michael of a children's book he'd had, and was cosier than anything he had seen in years. Through the window, the palm tree waved at the sea.

'You can move straight in if you like,' Verity folded the note Sheila had sent, and removed the wire-framed spectacles she had put on to read it, absently tucking them into her hair. Michael noticed the glint of a lens from another pair already installed there along with a wisp of a scarf. 'It's good to have a soldier here. There's been too many of them not coming back in this village.' She was by the mantelpiece where a small watercolour depicted the cottage garden. She picked it up. 'Francis, my husband, painted this before we planted the palm tree.' Her shoulders seemed to drop as she held the little painting.

He didn't know what to say, but something was required. 'It's a view I could imagine painting,' he offered, 'though I don't have experience with art.'

Verity replaced the painting, and wiped a finger along the mantelpiece. 'I know. Francis said the same. He was always lost in his books until we came here. Then the sea cast a spell on him. He didn't go a single day without walking down there, you know.' She sighed, staring out at the view, which Michael couldn't really see thanks to the palm tree. Then she clapped her hands on her thighs, changing her mood. 'Anyway, this place needs a duster. I'll sort that out now, and give it a good air this morning while you're out.'

Michael smiled. She was kind, he thought. 'I'd better go out then,' he said, and they both laughed.

Mousehole's streets meandered between huddled granite and whitewashed cottages, doors and windows painted bright colours that the sea and sun had bleached to gentle shades, yards and gardens muddling into one another, so the effect was of a whole toy village more than a collection of separate dwellings. The taste on his tongue of sea salt, the cry of gulls and the soft, inimitable presence of the sea, sometimes hidden from sight, sometimes suddenly there in a doorway or through a gate, reminded Michael of his childhood in Norfolk.

The Ship Inn bustled in the late morning, and the soft spring air was sharp with the smell of fresh fish. Michael glimpsed a skulking cat in an alley beside the pub, carrying something in its mouth. No rationing for felines, he thought. The publican rolled a barrel out of the door and upended it where Michael stood, pausing to wipe the sweat from his face with a large red handkerchief. 'It's warm,' he said in greeting.

Michael nodded, 'It's a great day.'

'There'll be a big catch coming in for tomorrow.' The publican pushed his cap back and stuffed his hands deep into his pockets for the inevitable pipe. A smoke and a chat, it was part of every man's ritual. 'We don't get so many now as when the pilchards came in. Lost a lot of work when they left our shores. And the war.'

'Must've been difficult for work around here,' said Michael, realising as he said it that he would have to find a job. He'd already discovered from Paul that he could sell his watch in Penzance, which would tide him over for a few days, but work was the next step.

He left the pub and took the steps down to the beach in front of him. The tide was out. He could see, from the wet sand, the starfish and scattered shells, that it would cover the whole beach when it came in. He took in the seaweed on the slipway, a tangle of lobster baskets and the echo of rattling masts, and shut his eyes.

The sounds and smells of a seaside town were evocative. His memories of being a small boy swept in like the tide, covering everything that had happened since. Of course, he never went as far as this from home. No, it was Cromer on the train with Johnnie and his mother. His father would join them for a couple of days, but mainly the holiday would consist of Michael and Johnnie and his cousin Angela, building sandcastles and shrimping on Cromer beach. They never stayed for long. Summer was harvest time and Michael's father needed his wife, his sons and anyone else with a spare pair of hands. Johnnie was in his element on the farm, quickest to find the ripe fruit, an expert eye for the weight of a box of gooseberries, a sharp ear listening to hear the rustle of a hen in a bush where he would dive to find a clutch of eggs. Michael preferred the sea, the lick of salt on his lips, the murmur of waves in his ears when he woke each morning. He lined up his shells on the windowsill of his bedroom at home, and hardly had time to look at them as summer days started early on the farm. He'd picked blackcurrants, lifted flints, hefted bales and herded cows between fields, with Angela bossing him and Johnnie always just ahead, shouting to him to hurry and come join him. Edwin, the family collie a shadow on his heel, waiting for a moment when he might turn round and kick a ball for him. Each week of his childhood had stretched like a lifetime, and Michael savoured it now as memories surfaced once again.

He walked along the beach, stepping over rope and buoys that held the fleet of small boats safe in the harbour. Nets hung out to dry, fishermen sat in groups, mending them, or smoking as they hammered planks back on to their boats, and beyond them the tall grey harbour walls gave protection. He could feel every particle in his body that had strained and tensed for so long begin to settle. He couldn't yet contemplate his return to Norfolk. He'd stay a while. He sat on a bench and stared at the gentle waves and an hour passed.

For a few days, Michael explored. He visited Paul and Sheila again. Paul took him to the studio, showed him the paintings he was working on, introduced him to an artist with a studio next to his and a potter they met in the narrow Newlyn Street. He brought them all back to the house, where Sheila was having tea with another couple, Simone and Ivor, both sculptors, and a much older Russian woman who had been a ballet dancer. They sat at the rickety table, pouring whisky into their tea, smoking non-stop and arguing. Ivor drained his cup. 'Is it possible to paint a conscience in a landscape?'

'Why should you?' demanded the ballet dancer.

'Why shouldn't you? Simone's voice was gravelly. 'How d'you expect anyone to work without the shadow of the war hanging over everything they do? It's in the nervous system of our whole generation.'

'There's a lot else to explore too,' said Sheila, who clearly wanted to mollify the Russian, who had twisted on her stool with her back turned to the group. 'There's a lot of change and hope among the chaos.'

'There's more chaos than anything else,' said Paul. 'Hard to imagine a new world order just yet.'

Michael had never come across anyone like these people, though Paul was adamant they existed in Norfolk too.

'Artists I know here went up to your neck of the

woods there before the war. Art's alive everywhere, you see it once you look,' he said firmly.

Michael was intrigued. Paul seemed able to live outside the restrictions of office work, or classroom, or even a regiment. He liked the idea of belonging to this group of people, they were engaged with the act of being alive, but to an extent, the attraction for him lay in the very fact that he was so removed from the artists. He was an outsider. These personalities were intriguing, alluring even, but he knew he could not become one of them. Before the war he and his friends sat in pubs and talked about politics and beliefs, but not with the fire he saw in Paul, Simone, Ivor and the Russian. Not with the whisky either, he thought wryly. He had been younger, of course, but where he had grown up, society was small, parochial, safe. Here it was different, but maybe that was what the war had done. Not that they talked much about what they had experienced. Even the most loquacious of Paul's group skirted around what had actually happened on the battlefields. Michael thought of his local town, the sleepy market square, the dances in the room behind the Red Lion pub once a month, the local station, the medieval church, built to impress by Norfolk's wealthy landowners and traders hundreds of years ago.

On the other side of England lay this wild Atlantic coastline, where a storm could wipe out a whole community, where the sea was a constant supply of contradictions, and the land was harsh. Paul and Sheila's friends weren't local, they were a community of poets and painters drawn to this extreme place, and working and living extreme lives. The cottages they rented near Land's End on the moor among the tin mines were primitive and hard to reach. The art they made was complicated, inaccessible.

Michael, used to looking at a few landscapes and bird paintings in the Castle Museum in Norwich, was both intrigued and cautious. He was out of his depth. The real question, as he saw it, was whether he, or any of them for that matter, could ever belong to anything or anyone again. Everything he had known had been blown apart, and he couldn't imagine how it could come back together as a whole. He was grateful that he had found lodgings in Mousehole, and not in a cottage six miles from the nearest village with no running water or electricity, out on a weather-lashed peninsula like two newly arrived friends of Paul and Sheila's. A bohemian hovel, said Paul, and although it sounded romantic, Michael had no desire for that version of romance. He would walk up the hill behind the village and on for miles, beyond the small farms and hamlets and into the wild where the sky seemed to tear him open. He lay on the grass with the wind like a lullaby, and larks singing around him and the spring earth warming up beneath him and the peace was intense. Sometimes it rained, and he stayed, lying with his face to the sky, eyes closed, drops splashing on his skin, sliding like tears across his cheeks, cleansing him. He had never noticed so profoundly before that he was alive.

In The Ship, a few days after he moved into Verity's house, the publican's wife Esther stopped him as he was leaving one evening. She had freckles and fly-away hair, and a flustered air, accentuated by her crumpled apron which she smoothed as she talked as if soothing herself.

'Reg thought you might be looking for work?' she said. 'Only my brother grows flowers for Covent Garden Market. The plots are up past your place, going up to Raginnis Hill. He needs a man to cut and carry them to the Penzance train.'

Michael heard himself say, 'Thank you, that sounds just the thing.'

He hadn't expected to work outside, but he was excited. Another new departure. He had the farming skills he'd learned at home. He could apply them to flowers. He noticed Esther's eyes were wet and teary, awkwardly he passed her his handkerchief.

'Thank you, it's just that sad,' Esther sniffed. 'William lost his arm at that Verdun. I know we should be grateful, and we are. He's alive, and that's what matters, but seeing him up with the flowers and not able to do so much any more. Well—' she pressed the handkerchief over her face.

Michael spoke gently. 'I can start as soon as he needs me. Shall I go and find him tomorrow, would that suit him?'

Esther nodded, 'It would suit him. Thank you.'

Delaware's bookshop was tucked on a corner behind the Temperance chapel. Outside, two elderly men were netting, their wooden chairs precarious on the uneven path, the cloud from their pipes forming and dissolving like speech bubbles around their rumbling conversation. A green painted shelf of battered paperbacks priced at tuppence each stood outside the door. Most days, Michael pored over them, mentally earmarking them in different sequences. Sometimes he lined them up chronologically, sometimes alphabetically, sometimes he narrowed his choice to a top three. He had been thrilled to find the bookshop. Sheila had told him about it when he picked up a novel by Aldous Huxley in her kitchen.

'Borrow it. I've just read that one. If you like it, you're in the right place. Go to Delaware's bookshop, they'll have far more books you'll want to read in there than Penzance Library. Whenever I visit Mousehole I go there.'

Michael wrote down the address, but until he started work, he had kept away. Buying a book felt like an admission that he was not returning home, as well as an extravagant use of the tiny amount of money he had left from selling his watch in the jeweller's near Penzance station. Once he had a job, there was no longer a need to pretend he was going anywhere. With his first week's pay Michael headed for Delaware's. Tall and confident with money in his pocket, he jangled his small change as he walked. Today he would buy a book, and tomorrow he would take it up the hill at lunchtime and read. His working day with William began at dawn, and by one o'clock, time was his own. The afternoons stretched like a glorious kingdom ahead of him. He would read, and think, and sometime, someday, he would work out what he was going to do. Books would help.

It was after four o'clock when he reached the shop. Today he worked longer than usual. He had cut a frame of violets and another of anemones and packed them in stiff boxes for the train. He had taken the flowers to the station in Penzance, and then driven William Coyne, his curly-haired boss, to the hospital to sign up for a prosthetic arm. William was stoic, 'I was never very clever with my hands any rate,' he joked. 'I reckon I write my name as good with the left one and I don't know who would see the difference.'

Michael crouched by the bookshelf outside the window, the sound of shutters closing above him forcing his eyes to race along the spines. He had to buy something before the shop shut. Anything would do. There would be other times when he could make his choice in a more leisurely fashion.

Moonfleet leapt out at him, familiar: he'd read it in his early teens, though this was a different edition to the red hardback with Johnnie's bookplate in the front. Michael turned it over. The paperback cover displayed a watercolour of a tall ship, sails set beneath a sky where the moon gleamed as bright as a golden guinea. A children's adventure story, set in Cornwall. He couldn't remember Johnnie actually reading it, but he must have, he would have loved it. Even better down here in the place it was set. Known as the family bookworm, Michael had a ritual for reading. He had a den in the hayloft, lined with an old Turkish carpet his mother had been throwing out due to the moth holes in it, and an Astrakhan coat that had belonged to his grandfather, and which he had taken from the attic. He didn't need a ladder, he could swing up on the beams and posts of the hay barn wall, and he would lie there all afternoon in the summer holidays, reading or listening to the sounds of the day passing, his brother whistling to the dogs or an engine firing. He loved the languor of his body combined with the action of his imagination as he read, and the reality of life going on outside around him.

Turning the paperback over in his hand, Michael dug into his pocket for change and entered the shop. It was quiet, the musty smell of books tinged with an exotic scent he couldn't place, and Michael blinked in the gloaming as he stepped towards the desk to pay.

'I'd like this please.'

'Of course.'

Michael had been preoccupied with the small thick paperback, enjoying the silky texture of the cover, the illustration, the font elaborate, embellished to suggest the swashbuckling nature of the book. Only when the shopkeeper spoke, did he realise it was a woman.

'*Moonfleet*. Have you read it before?' She turned the book over. She had beautiful hands, with a tiger's eye ring on her middle finger. Michael's gaze moved up smooth arms, bare to the elbow, and swept across her shoulders. Her face was framed with dark hair, strands of which fell across the fabric of her yellow dress, and his heart jolted in surprise. Everything about her seemed to gleam, from the mother-of-pearl clasp in her hair to her dark eyes, her gaze meeting his, to her skin, peachy in the unlit shop. She smelled of the musky perfume he'd noticed when he came in, and the raw promise of it jumped down his throat. He swallowed, hesitating.

'No. I mean, yes. Yes. Sorry, yes, I have, but a long time ago, before I'd ever been to Cornwall.'

She had the book on her lap now as she adjusted her hair, twisting it up and sliding a pencil through the knot to keep it out of the way. She repositioned the clasp and looked up. She had fine brows, arched and delicate. 'It was my brother's favourite book.' She held the paperback flat between her palms, weighing it up.

He laughed, 'Mine too, well, he had a copy, and I think he read it. I read it, anyway.'

Felicity looked up from the cover, their eyes met, held a smile. Michael felt the hairs rise on the back of his neck, and his voice was hoarse. 'I think he read it,' he repeated.

Felicity reached for a sheet of brown paper. 'My brother always said it chose him, because he was given three copies on the same birthday.' She fumbled and dropped the book. 'I feel bad about selling it, but—' she broke off to search on the floor. Michael couldn't take his eyes from the curve of her neck. There was a glimpse of pale skin at the top of her spine where her dress opened and she was pink in the cheeks when she straightened up.

'It's going to a good home,' she said.

Michael laughed. 'You don't know that,' he protested.

'I do,' she said simply.

Their eyes met for a moment or an aeon, Michael wasn't sure which.

'Don't worry about wrapping it, I'll take it in my pocket.' He leaned to pick up the book and, unexpectedly, his hand brushed hers. He was close enough to lick the musky rose scent straight from her skin. Embarrassed, he leapt back. Reversing out of the shop, he was on the street before he noticed he was holding his breath.

He went back to the bookshop the next afternoon. It was almost five, and he'd read half the book in the sun on the hill, glad to escape the cloying smell in town of the day's catch. Driving a load of lilac and cherry blossom past the fish hall after lunch today, Michael had almost retched at the sight and smell of blood and scales pouring into the gutters. It was warm, the fishermen swept and hauled buckets and trays, their sleeves pushed back, thick wool solid and un-pliable as armour in the heat. Michael couldn't wait to escape up to the hill.

When he arrived home with his copy of *Moonfleet* the evening before, he'd questioned Verity casually, and sure enough, she knew the bookshop girl.

'Felicity? She's the only Delaware left here. When they were small she and Christopher, her brother, were never apart.' Verity led him into the hall, and stooped, scrutinising a small oil painting of

Mousehole, painted from the hill Michael walked to every day. 'That's by her mother, Aileen. They were wild little things, Aileen never kept house much. Some cousin of Francis's, I can't remember exactly. Losing Christopher killed her, there's no doubt. He died in Normandy, though it wasn't official for some time. She knew, a mother always does, they say. Poor Felicity kept on hoping until the final telegram came.' The painting depicted two small figures, blue coats wide like kites, scampering away, caught between their own energy, the gravity of the hill, and the breeze playing in the long grass. Michael squatted next to Verity, haunted. His mother waiting at home, the simple camaraderie of siblings. Captured then in a sweet, almost throwaway painting of children, lost for ever now one of them had died.

'There.' A soothing hand on Michael's shoulder and Verity straightened the painting and patted his back. Michael rubbed tears from his face and followed her through to the sitting room.

'I knit a lot,' she said, gesturing at a corner where baskets burst with knitting and soft lumps of wool.

'What happened to their father?' Michael asked.

Verity arranged herself in a chair, and picked up a pair of stout wooden needles from which a square of grey wool dangled.

'Tristram? Very handsome. He took on that shop and made it into something. His own father had run into the ground what with the drink and the Great War. Tristram brought it back to life.' The click of her wooden needles was regular as a heartbeat. Michael

saw her gaze move from the wool to the chair opposite hers, on the other side of the fireplace.

'Francis played chess with him every week. They
kept it up, even through the blackout, you know. The
only blessing is that he didn't live to know what
happened to Christopher. Went up to London to
show some books to an American businessman and
the bombs at night took him. 1941 it was.'

'And Felicity lived with her mother then?'

'Yes, Aileen was never much around the house,
not a homemaker really, but it's a lovely spot, their
place. You'll know it. The last house after the
violets. The one with the orange door.' She chuck-
led. 'Felicity painted it, she reckoned it suited the
flowers. No one else around here would have chosen
that colour.'

'I'll look out for it,' Michael stood up, restless, for
what he didn't know. He was meeting Paul and Sheila
in Newlyn for a drink. Verity's final words stopped
him in the doorway. 'It's a shame for her, it really is.
Tomorrow we'll be in church for Christopher.
Would've been his birthday, and it's not even a real
funeral, there's been no body brought back. There
won't be, will there?'

Michael shook his head, 'No, there won't.'

He didn't stay long in Newlyn that evening, and
although he longed to ask more about Felicity, he
didn't say a word. Walking home in the moonlight, he
pondered his next move. He could bring flowers, he
could ask her out, he could leave a note at her house.
It seemed terribly important not to do it wrong,

though he couldn't for the life of him think what 'wrong' might be. He wanted to impress her. Perhaps by mending her car, if she had one, or rescuing her from danger. Ridiculous. Chastising himself, he fell asleep. In the morning the only idea he'd hit on was to buy another book.

He was in good spirits as he strolled towards Delaware's. He and Will had planted out three terraces with sweet pea seedlings and tiny snapdragons. The work was satisfying. Sunlight formed a silver skin on the horizon and he'd managed to see Felicity's house. Cornflowers in the garden, a sculpture of a girl sitting coiled like a cat, and the orange door, exotic and eye-catching like Felicity. He reached the bookshop in a heightened state of apprehension. The shutters were up, a handwritten sign tucked into the frame announced: 'Delaware's is closed until further notice.'

Michael's disappointment rocked him, and his stupidity. He knew she had gone to her brother's memorial today. Of course she wouldn't be in the shop. He stared at the door, ashamed that he had forgotten this occasion that meant the world to her. He snorted a sigh, looked up at the shattered facade. Then the door opened. On to the step came Felicity, her arms wrapped around herself, narrow as a shadow in her black dress. Her head rested on the doorframe, her eyes were lowered. Michael thought she looked like a medieval painting. Untouchable.

He was about to wave and walk away when she sniffed. He was close enough to see that her eyes were red, she pressed her fingers into them, dropping a limp yellow flower.

'You've had a big day,' he said. It didn't seem right to pretend he didn't know.

She shuddered. 'It was awful.' She turned back into the shop, speaking over her shoulder. 'Would you have a drink with me?'

From beside the desk she brought out two small glasses and a whisky bottle. Michael didn't move a muscle. This was dangerous. The air between them shrank to one pulse. He ought to leave, but he couldn't. She was sad, and his heart went out to her. He suddenly understood this phrase. His heart strained in his chest to comfort her. She was sniffing and wiping her eyes on the back of her hands.

He had no choice. 'Here, use this.' He gave her his handkerchief, and was lost.

She smiled gratefully and blew her nose.

'That's better,' he said bracingly and picked up the flower she had laid on the desk. A Welsh poppy, bright as sunshine.

'I was picking these today. They're so delicate, it's slow work,' he said. 'We have to wrap them twice before we can send them.'

She passed him a glass and raised her own. 'Let's drink a toast. To Christopher, my brother. And to all his brave companions.'

Michael swallowed. His throat ignited, he choked. 'Christ, this isn't whisky. What's in it?'

Felicity's eyes blurred with tears, but she giggled. 'Of course, you're not from around here, are you?

This is Cornwall. You're drinking our own moonshine. Get the recipe right and it can light up the Lizard Peninsula and all the way to Lamorna. Christopher made it the Christmas before he left. I've got six bottles at home.'

'It's like paint stripper,' Michael spluttered. 'You're obviously immune. Christ, is there a tap here? I think some water might help.' He already loved how her eyes danced when she laughed. 'I've got to tell you, most girls I know would be out for the count on a teaspoon of that stuff.'

She raised her glass again, mischief in her eyes, 'I know it's strong, but we're all brought up on it around here, you know.'

Michael wondered if she was going to knock back another glass. If she did, there was no way he would be matching her, but to his relief, she stopped.

'I thought it was clotted cream and tin and pixies that raised you all in Cornwall?' he said.

'Oh, all that and a bit of magic,' she countered. 'By the way, we haven't been introduced. I'm Felicity. Felicity Delaware. I'm so glad you came by again, thank you.' She began putting the glasses in a bowl to wash them, stowing the bottle on a shelf. 'I should get home now. I just came to drop some books off.'

'Did you read at the church?' he asked.

She nodded, rubbed her hands across her face. 'Yes, I read Milton. A bit of "Lycidas" because it would have been what Mum would have chosen.'

' "*We were nursed upon the self-same hill*". I love that poem,' said Michael. 'What else?'

'You know it?' Felicity's eyebrow's arched in surprise. 'Do you know this one?' She gave him a book, folded open on a page.

'I read a lot of poetry during the war. My mother used to send me pages out of books, I kept them on me all the time. It was—' Michael stopped, and began to read the page Felicity had given him.

'What's this?' He read for a moment then shook his head. 'No, I don't know this, what is it?'

'It's Wystan Auden. You know, W. H. Auden? He's American, I think, I don't know.' She looked at the poem again and sighed. 'It was hard to choose anything. Something that could sum up Christopher. I don't know if I did him justice.' Her voice tailed off, she took the glasses into the little room at the back and turned on the tap.

Michael finished reading the poem, his throat ached with sadness for her, for everyone fractured by the war.

'*The stars are not wanted now.*' He followed her to the sink and filled his glass with water. The tiny space between them was electric. He would have done anything, even drink another glass of the paint stripper to spend more time with her, but he had a better idea.

'Don't go yet. Let's walk up the hill and watch the sun go down,' he said.

She looked at him, doubt clouding her gaze. 'I don't know, I shouldn't. I—'

Maybe the moonshine was powering him, but Michael found he was acting out of character. He took the key from the hook on the wall and held it up, turning it between his fingers. 'Come on, it'll do you good. Lock the shop and we'll go.'

Outside they walked side by side up the narrow path that would take them to the hill. Michael had the sense that he was watching himself from far away as he held out his hand. She took it. Her skin was cool, her hand light in his, skin calloused on her knuckles, and two rings slid on her middle finger. Her fingertips were stained purple and green. Presumably there was a good reason for this.

'I love it up here.' She kicked off her shoes as soon as they were on the grass. 'We came here every day after school when we were little. Christopher used to fly his kite, and we would light fires for the pilchards. I remember watching the boats circling and the water alive with fish. I thought a pilchard was one single huge fish for years.'

They climbed until they were at the highest point.

'What a place to grow up,' said Michael. 'Your childhood memories must be happy.'

The rooftops of Mousehole fell away below them like the little carved wooden toy town Michael was given for Christmas when he was six. It had come in a fine nylon net, slipped out on to the bed when he opened his stocking and the net had glittered, like the sea did now as it shifted with afternoon light. Felicity stared at the horizon, her face lit by the pink haze.

'In Norfolk, where I come from, the sun hits the sea at a completely different angle, so the light doesn't do this,' said Michael.

'Norfolk?' said Felicity. 'That's so far away, the other side of England. Why are you here?'

They were side by side on a stone wall. A petal winked in her hair. Without thinking, he reached up and removed it. Her scalp was warm under his fingers.

'Cherry blossom,' he said.

'What?'

He held it out on his palm but it fluttered to the ground. 'I was packing them for the train to Covent Garden. You should smell the van, it's like a wedding. Or a powder puff.'

She laughed. 'Oh I'd forgotten about powder puffs. They're lovely, I'd love one. My mother had a pale blue one. I wonder what happened to it?'

Her shoulder rested against him, she fiddled with a scarf she'd pulled from a pocket.

He caught her hand. 'Why are your fingers purple and green?'

She curled them, flicking the scarf over both their hands. 'We've got a lot of questions and not so many answers, haven't we?' The tawny stripe in her ring matched her eyes. Somewhere out at sea a ship's horn blared. A breath of wind played with the scarf in her hands. Michael felt he was stepping off the edge of the hill. He leaned towards her. He could protect her, he wanted to embrace her courage, to kiss her, to let her love him. Nothing had ever seemed so right.

CHAPTER 6

'Are you sure that's my key?' Kit stared in astonishment at a highly elaborate wrought-iron piece on the
table between him and Charles Rivett's receptionist.
'It looks like it was last used to lock up Mary Queen
of Scots or someone in the Middle Ages.' He picked
it up gingerly, as if it might bite.

The receptionist looked doubtful. 'It must be. They
brought it in this morning, and there is only the one.'

Kit picked it up, turned it over, his fingers running
over the elaborate ironwork. He placed it on his palm
and noticed that it fitted perfectly between his wrist
and his fingertips. Probably that length was some
ancient measurement. He remembered that horses
were always measured in hands, perhaps it was the
same for keys back in the Dark Ages. The cool weight
of it was impressive.

'It must be some lighthouse,' he muttered to himself.

The receptionist glanced at him again and gave a
small sigh she turned into a laugh. He ought to go.

The key wouldn't fit in the pocket of his jeans, so he rolled it up in his newspaper and turned to leave.

'Ah, the lighthouse keeper,' Charles Rivett appeared at Kit's shoulder. Above Kit's shoulder, in fact, Kit hadn't noticed how tall he was the day before. 'Morning, Marion. Do I have messages?' Rivett asked the receptionist, who handed him a bundle of letters.

'I've put them all through to Jenny, she was in early,' said Marion.

He vanished down the corridor, and Kit picked up his key and prepared to leave again.

Marion passed him a piece of paper. 'Here, Mr Rivett asked me to print out some directions for you, and the postcode. The Lighthouse is at the end of the village, you can't miss it.' She paused, catching Kit's eye and, realising what she'd said, a giggle broke her guard.

'Rather the point of it,' Kit grinned. 'I'd better get used to this, there's a pun everywhere you look around a lighthouse.'

It wasn't until he was in Blythe churchyard that Kit became aware he was wandering aimlessly, like a tourist. The church loomed, its flint facade acquiring a velvety blur in the soft drizzle that had begun to fall. The grass was newly mown, and beyond it cow parsley billowed under the row of beech trees at the edge of the churchyard. Accustomed to small, intimate churches in Cornwall, where the spire often seemed to rise from sand drifts and tiny earth mounds, the height of the tower was a surprise. Gazing upwards, Kit squinted to prevent his eyes filling with the drizzle, and tried to imagine building something like this. It was time for him to take an interest in towers, he thought. Probably time for him to take an interest in a lot of things he'd never made much time for, but the working day of a lighthouse keeper appealed less than a study of how to build a tower. He wondered if there was a second-hand bookshop in town where he could find a useful guidebook to Norfolk's towers, both sacred and profane. Wandering between the graves, he had a sudden sense of Felicity enjoying his quest. 'Lighthouse Fabrics' now had a bricks-and-mortar emblem. There was no question in his mind that his mother had planned this bequest, and even somehow orchestrated its timing, to give him a kick, get him out of the rut of living to work that had become his safety net as he grieved for her.

'Get out and live' was a line of hers, liberally scattered among employees, friends and the young interns who came to work for Lighthouse Fabrics.

A woman entered the churchyard and walked slowly up the gravel path to a seat close to the smaller west door. She sat down and opened a book, which she used as a plate for her sandwich as she unwrapped it. Her bare legs were pale, open-toed sandals suggesting she'd got dressed expecting sunshine. Kit wondered what she did, where she lived, who her family were. Crooked gravestones marked the path, becoming bigger the nearer they were to the church. Outside the door, tombs like moored boats floated in the grass. Was that woman related to someone buried here? Was it a kinship that brought her in the rain for her lunch hour? She had an umbrella up now, and had spread a navy blue nylon jacket across her bare legs. He tripped over the edge of the path, dropping the Lighthouse key, 'Oh bollocks.' The expletive shot out of him. Guiltily he glanced at her. She had folded her crisp packet, and now left, without looking at Kit again.

He moved to the porch and sat down against the cool plaster wall. The air was laced with a mushroomy aroma Kit liked. It smelled of the studio, the distempered walls. He'd grown up as much in his mother's studio as at home. He stared at the vaulted ceiling. A carved angel hung at its apex, painted bright gold like a cornfield, button bright eyes suggesting a recent restoration job. Probably, given the red circles on the cheeks and the rosebud mouth, it had been carried out by a small child with a few felt-tip pens. Kit was curiously peaceful. He hadn't realised he was going to have to find room in his life for anything extra, but on balance, it still felt like an adventure. His life, though he was reluctant to admit it, was small. He had his work, he had his house and he had his friends, but he didn't have any surprises back in Cornwall. The Lighthouse had come along and flashed its beam on his future prospects. Just in time. It hadn't seemed real to him, but now, here it was, and he was holding the key. Time to go and claim the Lighthouse. That was what he was here for.

Kings Sloley stood on a cliff edge at the most northern point of the rim of Norfolk. It hadn't always been on the edge, of course, but nature had decided to focus a destructive force on this particular curve of coastline. Threatened by coastal erosion, Kit had read in a guidebook in his bed and breakfast, a village committee funded by the National Lottery worked tirelessly, Canute-like, against the encroaching sea. Quite what they did was unclear from the literature and, as Kit drove, he found himself abandoning his pre-formed plan to keep himself to himself and even before he had arrived was imagining how he could help. He had experience of this battle between man and the ragged defences he erected against the sea. At home in Cornwall, the widows of the village near where he lived knitted and baked for the benefit of the harbour walls, while the sea crashed against them with the lunatic abandon of a violent drunk.

Aware that knowledge is power, but also somewhat self-conscious, as his landlady danced attentively around him with eggs, bacon, toast and darting comments that suggested she had wildly mistaken views about him and thought he was a famous film star looking for a bolthole, Kit had read a lot of local information over breakfast this morning in between fielding a wide-ranging array of questions.

Mrs Black tweaked the curtain in the small dining room a fraction wider, and Kit's car parked in the driveway loomed. 'That's a big car,' she observed. 'Do you usually have a driver?'

'Not often.' Receiving his plate of eggs, bacon, sausage, tomato and fried bread, Kit marvelled as he always did in this situation, at the lavish spread offered. On holiday anywhere in Britain you really didn't need to bother about lunch.

'You'll notice a lot of people with fancy cameras, big lenses, you know the sort of thing,' Mrs Black poured tea into Kit's cup with a flourish.

'Really?'

'Yes, but don't worry, they're birdwatchers, twitchers mostly, and they don't do any harm.'

'I won't worry,' Kit agreed. 'Do you know Kings Sloley at all, Mrs Black?'

She leaned over him to look at the pamphlet he had been reading, and parked herself for contemplation, her chest level with his eyes. 'In Your Face' was a phrase that sprang to mind.

'Nice those cliffs, aren't they?' The heat of her body emanated through her spotty apron and warmed his cheek. Kit fought rising, slightly panicky laughter, and turned it into a cough and a chance to move away.

Mrs Black picked up the teapot and poured another cup for him. 'The poppies are a real landmark. I should think you could set one of those big weepie films here, couldn't you?' Her eyebrows arched in anticipation. 'I saw a film being made up there a while back, but it turned out to be just a promotion for the railway line.'

She began to clear plates. Kit was not about to get any practical instruction from her, he would have to see for himself.

The road snaked east along the coast from Blythe, through the gorse-ridden heathland, and on to cliffs, crumbling and pale as shortbread above the glittering

North Sea. The rain had stopped and through the open car window Kit caught the gorse's spring aroma of coconut, a scent he still associated with the cheap suntan oil of his youth. Sunshine, the sea, and the faint whiff of sex, all here in front of him. His spirit broke through the layer of mild anxiety he had been aware of since arriving, and soared. This was going to be fun. He hadn't exactly been looking for new challenges, but he had never been one to let them pass him by. He felt renewed. And excited.

In Kings Sloley, he now knew, was a primary school, a pub, a shop and post office. How did the Lighthouse fit in the hierarchy of all this chocolate-box stuff? A quiet village would be a good background to this chapter of his life. It might be quite a short chapter. He wasn't sure of the market value of such things, but the notion of selling the Lighthouse and buying a little house in Greece had crossed his mind more than once. Swimming in the Aegean was a compelling alternative if this lighthouse business was all hard work. After all, he didn't have to keep it. One thing was certain: in a lighthouse, he was going to be visible. He wasn't quite sure how things worked, but it seemed that if he so much as switched on a light to go to the lavatory, the whole coastline would know about it.

He passed a cluster of cottages, a row of terraced houses and then a farmhouse, thatched, the walls lime-washed soft grey, an apple tree blushing with pink blossom as its boughs curtseyed to the ground. Two stone sheep looked foolish on the gateposts.

'The sunny side of the street.' Billie Holiday singing the blues, accompanied by Lester Young's liquid saxophone poured out of the speakers, and spilled into Kit's excitement, trumpeting his adventure. It was like something out of a novel. He remembered the paperback he had picked up from the house before he left Cornwall, Virginia Woolf's *To the Lighthouse*. The book's title was familiar to him, he'd always assumed it was the reason his mother had named her company 'Lighthouse Fabrics', feminist solidarity, the Bloomsbury group and all that. It made sense but he'd never read it. He probably wouldn't now, he'd never been keen on those novels about nothing much, and they didn't even ever get to the lighthouse, or so someone had told him. The book had presented itself to him, in that he saw it on the bookshelf the night before he left home, so he had brought it with him. He hadn't notice that it was inscribed until he'd dropped it when unpacking at his B&B.

The words, in black ink on the flyleaf read: *'I still dream of you, M. 1956'*

His phone rang. He pressed the button to put it on speakerphone.

'Hello?'

'Hello, is that Kit Delaware?'

'Yes, speaking.' His phone showed almost no signal, he moved it to try and hear better.

'I'm Luisa—' her voice cut out.

Kit interrupted the silence. 'Sorry, it's a bad line, I can hardly hear you.'

'Oh. Okay. I'll shout. I'm LUISA. We're neighbours of yours. Sort of. I was given your number by Charles Rivett's secretary. She's a dog-walking friend of mine. Well, she's not a dog-walker, I mean she's a friend of mine and we walk our dogs together. Sometimes.'

She broke off, sighing, and muttered something else Kit couldn't hear.

'I'm sorry, I don't follow?' Kit wondered what the point of this call was. Did this woman think he had a dog? 'I haven't got a dog,' he said.

'Really, what a shame. There are some puppies almost ready to go, they're about five miles away. That reminds me, I promised I'd go and look at them this week.'

Luisa sounded vibrant and attractive. Kit was curious, but he didn't need a dog. 'That's very kind, but I think I'll leave it for now,' he said.

Luisa laughed. 'I'm so sorry, I got carried away. I would love everyone I know to have one, so I thought . . . Oh dear, where did we get to?'

Kit tried to imagine what she looked like. Lots of hair, laughing eyes, attractive. Cheerful and not all droopy and depressed like Virginia Woolf. Was she married? Probably. She said 'we'.

'You were talking about walking your dog,' he said.

'Oh. Sorry, I was sidetracked. So sorry. What I meant to say was that I understand the Lighthouse is your property now and I have to apologise. Some of Jason Tye's Houdini sheep have escaped into your field. Honestly, they never stop escaping. Anyway,

I've only just been told and I'm not sure how much damage they've done, and I'm on my way but my car's blocked in by those people who are digging a tunnel all the way through Norfolk and – Oh! Here comes someone, and they're moving all the traffic. I'm on my way. Are you still there?'

Kit had let the car drift to a halt in the middle of the road so engrossed had he been by Luisa. Sheep, more bloody sheep. What was it with Norfolk and the sheep? Though if they weren't hers, why did she care? Perhaps she was a professional shepherdess? It was more than he had hoped for, but she seemed to be planning an imminent arrival at the Lighthouse. His Lighthouse.

He tried to sound nonchalant. 'Yes, I'm here, well, almost. But please don't worry, there's no need to come all the way here—' He stopped himself from turning her away. What was he thinking of? He didn't want to put her off. Here was a chance to start meeting people, to make some friends. 'Yes, perhaps you should come, could you? I'm not sure.'

Luckily she hadn't noticed his feeble wavering, she was bubbling with excitement and apology, and from the sound of crashing gears, she was under way and driving badly. 'No, no, of course I'll come, and actually, we are really quite close neighbours, just a few miles. They aren't my sheep but I feel responsible and embarrassed. We've all been so excited to hear that the Lighthouse has a new owner at last, and now we've already behaved badly. I'll be there in ten minutes. Are you in?'

Amazing. Who said life was slow in the country-side? Luckily this woman was talkative, as Kit was almost speechless.

'In? No. I mean yes. Almost. I've actually never been there and I'm just arriving with the key now.'

His new confidante was delighted. 'Oh that's thrilling. You've never been there? You must be so excited. I'll first foot you or whatever it's called. You know the old custom? I think I need some coal. Or sugar. I'll stop at the Spar shop. I can't remember which it is, so I'll get both. See you in a minute.'

'Isn't first footing something you do at Hogmanay? In Scotland?' Kit was speaking into a silent phone, she had gone. He laughed. Whistling cheerily, Kit pressed the accelerator swerving through the narrow lanes and round a final hairpin bend. 'Christ!' he hissed, and almost crashed the car. There was the Lighthouse, towering in front of him, larger than life, stripier than he'd imagined, and utterly unreal. It had shot out of a hazy blue field, and the red stripes were hot and bold. There was nothing close by to give it any perspective, the Lighthouse dominated the flat fields that rolled away to a group of cottages and houses. The bizarre contrasts of scale reminded Kit of Venice, and the sudden presence of cruise ships, colossal like painted backdrops behind the ancient buildings. Even for someone used to the biscuit-tin beauty of the Cornish coast, Kings Sloley was lovely. The cliffs stippled with poppies tumbled to a sliver of beach, the edge serrated by the bite of the incoming tide.

Walking up to the front door, Kit felt as though he was in a film, or a children's story. Maybe he should have read that Virginia Woolf book after all, it might have given him a clue on what to expect. Pitted and gnarled with the sheen of age to the touch, the oak door had patterns carved into it, and looked as if it belonged in a church. The key made sense now. Kit held his breath as he inserted it. The door swung open and, as if on cue, four sheep charged up from the garden beyond, bleating hysterically.

Kit groaned, half laughing. 'Sheep? Again? Christ, what do you want? Why are there sheep everywhere I go?' It was like being in some warped nursery rhyme. All he needed now, he reflected, was Miss Muffet in the kitchen eating curds and whey. Whatever they might be. He supposed there must be a kitchen. One of the sheep skipped on to the threshold and trotted into the hallway. 'Come on then, show me round,' said Kit, and stepped inside. As he did so, he felt a pang of loss that could be fathomless if he gave it the chance. 'It's a bit bloody late now,' he said to himself. One of the sheep was chewing a mouthful of something bushy and gazing up at him. Really he could do without them.

'Shoo?' he suggested. Another one jostled forward, something in her tone suggesting dissatisfaction. Kit decided her name was Virginia. Perhaps he was the Woolf?

'What?' he raised his eyebrows at her. 'You don't like it here? The trouble with you is you're never satisfied. You refused to stay in nursery rhymes and insisted on getting into droopy novels didn't you?' Virginia bleated again.

Kit couldn't really take anything in. Everything was wildly removed from his usual experience, and the sheep were, quite simply, surreal. The best approach was surely to tolerate them, or better still to embrace them. But not literally. They didn't exactly represent the approved new-home dream, where a handsome hero carried his bride over the threshold, but Kit found he was enjoying their company, especially now he could be the Woolf. He would show them round, there was nothing else that could be done.

Kit opened a door. The kitchen. Pretty basic. An old yellow fifties dresser, a stone sink propped on wooden shafts and an enamelled stove stood at intervals around the edge of the room. One of the sheep walked over to a bucket on the floor and sank her nose into it. Kit wasn't sure if it was Virginia or not. He patted her anyway, and noticed that her coat was springy and dense. She knocked the bucket over and skittered away. As he walked around, he found himself becoming nostalgic for the old boy who had moved out. The bucket was painted red. A neat red brush and dustpan stood by the door, and a boot scraper painted to match. He wondered if the old man had known his landlord. Had Felicity ever visited? What a gift.

He'd taken a quick look at the interior and now he wanted to see the outside again properly. Craning his neck up, the limitless blue sky framed the light bulb – was it called the light bulb? – in different crazy angles. Spinning clouds, a spiral of red and white like a gondola pole, everything heightened. Kit pursed his lips and whistled to himself. It was hard to believe it had a practical function; it looked like the most wonderful folly. Wrapped in stripes.

He sighed. He'd never classed himself as much of a romantic, but this was mind-expanding stuff. He ought to go back to check on the sheep, though why they all had to be inside rather than out was mystifying. They were still in there of course, though now they had all drifted to the wall, and were standing staring at it. It would be nice to make a cup of tea. As if he expected there to be the essentials, Kit went into the kitchen. The floorboards reminded him of the segments of an orange, curving voluptuously into the walls. Nothing was straight, the effect was giddy-making. The sheep stood staring. They looked like Kit felt. One of them came up to him and leaned against his leg. The insistent pressure was reassuring. Francis of Assisi had nothing on him for animal skills.

He decided to call them all Virginia, it was easier. 'Do you like it here, Virginia? I know you don't approve of the curved walls, you're right they present real challenges to furnishing the place. Lucky the tenants have left a bit of stuff, isn't it? Don't listen to any—'

'Hello?'

'What?' For a split second Kit thought Virginia had spoken. He leapt back against the table. No. Standing in the doorway, vibrant as a flame with sunglasses in one hand and a brown paper bag in the other, was a woman in a red dress. Red as a movie star's lips. Lighthouse red, he thought. She stepped into the room, bringing a delicious scent of summer, hot leaves, or hothouse flowers, he wasn't sure which. She was introducing herself, but he missed what she said. Luisa something, he remembered from the phone call earlier.

'Hi?' It came out as a question. He recognised her, he thought he knew her for a moment. Where had he seen her? How had he seen her?

'I heard voices so I came in, this is wonderful.' She waved the bag and bits of coal shot across the room.

'Oh God. Sorry,' she crouched to pick them up, scrabbling on the floor. She stood up and she was right in front of him. He smiled. 'You know it's not a housewarming thing? It's Scottish for New Year.'

'What's Scottish?' Her face was close, he caught a trace of exotic perfume and the smell of sunshine on her gleaming skin. She had a fine gold chain around her neck, and a red thread was caught in it above her collarbone. He half lifted his hand to remove it, then remembered himself and snatched it back, pointing his finger instead at the bag of coal. 'The coal you kindly brought. It's for Hogmanay.'

'Oh. I thought it was housewarming.' Her peal of laughter was infectious. A second later she stopped, an arrested expression on her face as she looked at him.

'I know you,' she said, 'I've seen you before.' Her hair had fallen across her face, and when she lifted her hand to brush it away their eyes met. Time expanded, stretching the moment. Heat shimmered and a swallow darted through the open door and out through the window. Luisa jumped, her paper bag split and rained the rest of the coal at their feet.

'At least you can light a fire,' she said. Kit nodded. Her dress clung to the soft contours of her body. He liked it. Absently he reached out, put his finger in the cuff of the sleeve, feeling the weight, the knit.

'Italian, isn't it? Silk jersey?'

She gasped, colour rushing to her cheeks. 'That's clever. Actually, me and the dress are both Italian,' she shot a look at him. 'It's an unlikely thing for a man to notice.'

'It's my business. Textiles. I spent a lot of time in Northern Italy, looking at equipment, factories, technical stuff.' He still had his hand in her sleeve. How? 'God. Sorry, I wasn't thinking.' Reddening, clumsy, he snatched it back.

Then her hand was on his arm, cool.

'Would you like a glass of water?' Kit moved away.

Laughter welled up, 'Have you got glasses? Already?'

Kit opened a cupboard, and another. 'Um. No. It would seem not. Just water. Plenty of that,' he turned on the tap with a flourish.

Luisa leaned over the sink, cupping her hands to drink. 'It's really cold,' she gasped.

'Good,' the cold water on Kit's hands was refreshing. The novelty of the Lighthouse, its kitchen, its curves and Luisa in it bubbled inside Kit and came out in a euphoric clapping of his hands and a beaming smile.

The sheep clattered back in, milling around Luisa, she bent to stroke one of them. 'Do you mind them coming and going like this?'

'They've lived here as long as I have,' Kit laughed. 'Which is all of about half an hour. Shall we have a look at the rest of the place?'

Luisa followed him out of the kitchen. 'It's going to be hard for them to come back to the farm when they've got used to the high life here,' she pointed at the ceiling with a smile. 'You may have to keep them.'

Her exuberance delighted him, she made it easy to talk. It was as if they'd always known each other. What had she said about knowing him? How could she? He had to calm down, he wanted to know all about her and her life here, but he'd only just met her, and they were meant to be talking about sheep.

'Oh look, the stairs are incredible. You can see the whole way to the light, I think. Have you been up?' Luisa opened a narrow door, and a wooden staircase spiralled up the wall.

Kit followed her, looking over her shoulder. He touched the leather strap of the bag on her shoulder. 'No, I got here just before you arrived. The sheep were showing me round, but I don't think they're very interested in the other floors.'

'Well I am, aren't you?' Luisa put a foot on the bottom step. Suddenly, she turned, and tried to come back past him. 'I'm so sorry!' She was close against him in the small space. 'It's your house, you should go first, I've just barged ahead.'

'No,' he had his hand hovering above the small of her back. 'Go up, it's fine.'

'Are you sure?' She was climbing ahead of him, chattering, and her voice echoed up the stairs like a bell. 'We saw you in Blythe, you know. I guessed you were a stranger.' Luisa laughed. 'Well, of course you were a stranger, but I mean I guessed you weren't from around here.'

'You saw me? When?' A kick of excitement flooded his body.

'In town yesterday.'

'In town? Really?' He flipped through his thoughts, wanting to remember exactly where he could have been to be seen by her. 'I bought a cake, and . . . Oh yes. I saw you too, didn't I?' He had forgotten. How had he forgotten? Her eyes in the street, meeting his. One tiny moment in time. That's all.

Luisa was a few steps above him, breathless. 'D'you know, I've never been inside a lighthouse before. Have you?'

Laborious to go on about yesterday. 'No, it's a bit like going up a church tower, except the light at the top is real not spiritual.'

Luisa laughed. 'Some sailors lost at sea in a storm might have thought it was spiritual as well as practical,' she said. 'I've been as far as the front door here. Old Jim Fisher used to get very cross about the sheep, so I'd bring him things as a bribe. He loved Scotch eggs. Goodness, it's been ages since I made Scotch eggs, maybe I'll do some at the weekend.'

'So those sheep of yours are recidivist trespassers?'

A door on the staircase yielded to a whitewashed room.

'Good,' Luisa panted. 'It's so steep, I'm out of breath already.'

Smaller than the ground floor, very round. Like being in a salt cellar, Kit thought.

The soft quack of a duck grew louder in Luisa's handbag. 'Oh, it's Dora,' she said, 'Sorry. My sister-in-law,' as she answered it. 'Dora? Hi.'

Kit took in the room, a panelled ceiling, a sagging green sofa, dusty and clearly not worth taking down the stairs, and diamond-latticed windows. He opened one. Already, just one floor up from the ground, he felt high above humanity, the cliffs swooping down the coast into distant obscurity. Luisa had perched on the arm of the sofa. She had whitewash on her dress. 'I'm not at home, I'm catching the sheep,' she said into her phone, her fingers twisting the gold chain at her throat.

Kit wondered how the sofa got into the room in the first place.

'I know, but I didn't do it yesterday.' She glanced at Kit, with a quick smile. 'I've got to go. I'm at the Lighthouse. Going bowling will be fine, it's not make or break, you know.' He heard a change in tone, she laughed. 'I hope we will. I'll ask him. Bye.'

Switching off the phone she walked to the window where Kit leaned. 'I've been told to make sure we can all meet up, so I hope you'll come over for supper or something. What d'you make of Norfolk anyway? Have you been here before?'

'So friendly I can't quite believe I've never set foot here before this week.' He paused apologetically. 'I live in Cornwall, in Mousehole, so I've always had my own version of all this sea and sky and so forth. But this place is quite something.' He shrugged as he looked around. 'I'm just not sure what the something is.'

Luisa gestured out of the window, and a ring flashed on her hand. 'The big skies are what I love,' she said. 'There's room for all sorts of people here. Every lost soul has a place.'

There was silence for a moment before Luisa spoke again, her gaze sweeping the room. 'I'm amazed it's so stark. I imagined it would be full of old hutches and rolls of chicken wire. Jim, the old chap who lived here, used to keep rabbits. My daughters must have had about five of his lop-eared ones over the years.'

The door slammed as a gust of wind caught it. Luisa's hair blew across her eyes, Kit watched her push it away, and a nagging sense of something slipping out of his grasp seized him. To her husband this gesture was familiar, like her scent and her voice and the way she poured tea. Tea. He must offer her some. She was making signs that she might be leaving.

'I might be able to make some tea?' he said, pretty sure as he suggested it that he couldn't.

She got up, brushing her skirt down. 'That's a kind thought, but I should go. I'm supposed to take those sheep back to a field with a proper fence.'

Kit looked at her red dress. 'Really? You don't look dressed for it to me.'

She brushed away a cobweb on the skirt. 'I'm never dressed for anything properly. My husband says I do it on purpose, destroying my clothes to make way for new ones, but who doesn't?'

'Quite,' he agreed lightly. 'And that's the reason people like me stay in business.'

Luisa pulled on a black lace cardigan and looked suddenly Sicilian, exotic. Kit noticed she had big gypsy hoop earrings. She was extremely stylish for a shepherdess, he thought.

'He's right about one thing though,' she was saying. 'I've never worked out how I can blend in with the surroundings. I still feel I'm outside looking in.'

'Red dress, flashing smile. You're almost camouflaged here you fit in so well,' teased Kit. 'But where are you from originally, did you say you're Italian?'

Her eyes danced. 'I'll show you. Come on. Up to the top.'

The height was giddying, the stairs narrowed to steps the size of shoe boxes. Everything seemed precarious, and Kit could have sworn the top of the Lighthouse was swaying. He felt nauseous. Luisa reached the metal railing around the giant light bulb. Kit couldn't drag his eyes from the spectacle of this vast version of a domestic staple, but Luisa was at the window pointing down the coast to a sprawl of containers and cranes in the distance. 'Look, that's Great Yarmouth. You can just see it. That's where my family are from. I'm not exotic, I may be Italian but I was brought up on a fleet of Gorleston ice-cream vans.'

The proximity of her scent, her mouth was easily more interesting than Yarmouth and, with the light bulb, the talk of an ice-cream van Kit felt he was heading into an Alice in Wonderland experience. 'Bring it on' was, he decided, his new mantra.

'Tell me about the ice-cream vans.'

'Oh, it's a long story,' her eyes were lowered, she buttoned up her cardigan, shivered. 'It's a bit chilly up here,' she rubbed her arms under the fabric of her cardigan, Kit heard the silky hiss of skin and her skirt as she rubbed one calf against the other.

'Come on, tell me a little bit. Seeing as we're here looking over your heritage.'

He liked the way she cocked her head on one side to consider, he liked the warmth in her smile when she agreed.

'My maternal family ran a fleet of ice-cream vans in Lowestoft, and before that they came from Italy. My father's father was a prisoner of war in Norfolk. Do you know, they used to sing opera in the camps and they made spaghetti and hung it up to dry on the fences?' She flicked her hair off her neck and Kit smiled at the unconscious act of preening. 'I'm Italian with all the clichés,' she said. 'My mother's father set up one of the first ice-cream van fleets in Gorleston. He was an entrepreneur, he saw there were beaches and no cones. Madness. Now they've got the coast-line sewn up for fifty miles, and all the arcades as well. My brother runs the business since Dad died. It isn't what it was in its heyday, but people will always want ice cream, won't they?'

They were reversing their climb now, Kit leading the way down, his hands on the rough walls for balance, feeling the way on either side. 'Do you like cooking?'

Luisa blew her hair off her face with a sigh. 'I love it. I'm trying to make a business with ice cream myself, but I never seem to get off the ground.'

'Do you have a van? I should imagine you'd be like the Pied Piper around here?'

He was teasing, but glancing round for her reaction, Kit saw a flash of eagerness, and in it her vulnerability, before she sighed, 'I do, but it's derelict. It's my dream. I want to do my own. Not part of my family thing. My idea of a good ice cream is full of elderflowers, or wild-dog rose syrup from the hedgerows. It's a long way from Amorazzi's Tutti Frutti and 99s.'

They had descended to the hallway, now empty as the sheep had disappeared into the garden.

Kit kept his response light-hearted, he sensed that she felt exposed. 'You'll be a wild success,' he said. 'You can definitely give your brother a run for his money.'

Luisa flicked back her hair again and put on her sunglasses, shutting him out with one deft movement.

'Let's go outside,' said Kit.

'What about you?' Luisa raised the glasses and propped them on her head. 'You're the archetype, you know: stranger in town, no family, no ties. What are you going to do with this place? It's amazing, so much more than I thought it could be.'

A warm glow of pride in his new acquisition welled inside him. Kit felt immense gratitude to his mother for bringing him to this place. He might never know why, but it didn't really matter. 'I was left it when my mother died.' He heard himself adapting the story to protect himself, he wasn't sure from what. 'Funnily enough, my mother was dark like you, she was Cornish. Her family were Saltash gypsies and tin miners in the 1800s, and then both her parents were on the fringes of the art movement down in St Ives between the wars.'

Luisa whistled under her breath, fumbling for her keys. 'Saltash? Sounds more exotic than Gorleston. We all wondered about the owners. Around here it was known it was someone from the West Country, but nobody ever came, and everyone lost interest until Jim's family moved him out, then we all gossiped like mad. So your mother owned it, but you don't have connections here otherwise? Does your wife like it?'

They were at the gate. 'Look, the sheep are already queuing up.' He leaned to lift the latch for her, and glancing up from the gate their eyes met. 'I'm not married,' he said.

'Do you have children?' Somehow, the gentle way Luisa asked this meant Kit didn't find it intrusive. He shook his head. 'I did get married, briefly, when I was young, but it was a mutual mistake and, sadly, I had no kids then or later.'

'That is sad.' Luisa opened her car door and put her bag in.

It was a car, not a truck, Kit noticed. 'How does this work then?' he asked, nodding towards the sheep. 'Do they all sit in a row with safety belts?'

Luisa's eyes danced, 'They have to go in the boot. If anyone saw they'd probably report me, but my husband's trailer had a flat tyre.'

Her phone rang again. 'Hi, darling. What? Oh, is he back? Does he want to speak to me? Shall I leave the sheep then? Thank goodness, I was about to put them in the car. He's landing with a thud, isn't he?' She looked at Kit, raised her eyebrows. 'Okay, yes. I'll ask. Half an hour? Okay, bye darling.'

Shutting the phone she shoved it into her bag. 'I must go. That was Luca, my son. I haven't been much use with the sheep, but luckily their owner's just got back from his holiday and he's coming to pick them up. I'm so sorry to leave them, but he'll put them somewhere safe today. I think I've wasted your time, I really apologise.'

Without thinking Kit leaned to kiss her cheek. She smelled of summer grass and orange blossom, his senses whirled as he recognised it and was back in a rush at their brief encounter on the pavement in town. 'I hope we meet again.' His voice was husky.

Luisa's eyes widened. She clasped his wrist and her pulse beat through her fingertips, warm and insistent. 'A goodbye kiss on a farming mission. That's a first for me.' The smile leapt again in her eyes.

Kit laughed, covering his own embarrassment. 'I'll have to let the farmer know you have no control over his sheep, they're a hazard to the lighthouse man's duties.'

Luisa's brow contracted in an apologetic frown. 'We've been such an invasion. How can we make it up? Will you come to our house and have supper some time soon?' She saw hesitation on his face, and flashed a smile. 'I know you want to refuse, but you can't – you've got no plates or pans to cook for yourself here.'

He laughed. She had a knack for making things easy, he liked her relaxed approach. 'I'd like to meet your family.' Once again, Kit heard himself say what he didn't know he was thinking.

Luisa started her car. 'You will. And everyone else in the area too. You're a big fish in this tiny pond of ours, you know. Bye, Kit. Welcome to the Lighthouse.'

He watched her drive around the bend and away, and then he listened. Only when the sound of her car engine was obliterated by distance and the ceaseless whisper of the waves behind the Lighthouse did he turn and walk away.

CHAPTER 7

Since breakfast time, Luisa had been trying to find respite from chores and family demands to scrutinise her text and ponder its significance. Arriving with a quacking sound set for her by Mae, she had almost dropped the phone into the washing up when she saw it was from Kit.

Morning. Can I lure you back to the Lighthouse again? Come for a sunset drink. 6.30. All of you. xK

His phrasing, his sudden arrival into her morning, and his invitation were engrossing. Why didn't everyone send texts like this? She pinged back her reply within seconds.

Nice lure. YES please!

Over the last couple of days she had exchanged a few texts with him, focusing on practicalities, from where he might buy a kettle to whether anyone except crazed lunatics swam in the sea in Norfolk. This one was longer. Five sentences. Practically a note. The quacking that heralded it exploded into a domestic scene as she prepared breakfast for her beloved family.

'Bugger,' she was busy. No time for texts. When she saw who it was from, she was surprised, and the sound she made should have indicated to her beloved family that there was something to interest them in her phone. Not a bit of it. None of the beloveds, from Tom changing batteries in the torch, to Mae, who had, she said, got out of bed by mistake because she'd misread the time on her phone and it was way too early for a Saturday, to Luca, lost in perusal of a football match report from the European cup qualifiers, was even the smallest bit interested in her, her text, or anyone who might have sent it.

The garden offered sanctuary, but not for long. Just as she had settled in the vegetable patch, a tray of broad bean seedlings beside her as her cover, and was examining the message, reading significance into every letter, Luca appeared.

'Thought I'd give you a hand,' he said, and proceeded not to, instead stretching himself out on the grass.

'Is it wet?' Luisa tucked the phone into her bra, a storage spot she favoured when gardening.

'Not really,' Luca propped his feet on an upside-down pot, and flopped his arms out. 'S'relaxing.' He smiled, and closed his eyes.

Luisa wanted to prod him into action, but it was pointless, he would help in his own time. His capacity for being comfortable was endless.

She stepped over him and started a new row for her seedlings. 'Anyway,' she said breathlessly, digging flint chunks out of the soil before pouring a trickle of water into the holes, 'a funny thing's happened. I didn't get round to telling Dad I'd met the new man the other day, and now he's asked us to go for a drink at the Lighthouse tonight, and I still haven't told him.'

'What's the big deal? Dad won't care.'

She hadn't expected Luca to answer, it was more of a thinking aloud exercise. She placed a couple of small plants tenderly in the holes. 'I don't know. Maybe it isn't.'

Her phone vibrated under her shirt. It was another message from Kit.

Help me . . . do I need a giant plastic swing seat from garage? Credit card poised. K

Luisa blushed, glanced at Luca. His eyes were still shut. She texted back, her fingers moving rapidly,

Is it for the sheep?

She shoved the phone away again, biting her spreading smile, pushing back the rush of exuberance she felt. It was such fun, and she felt like a teenager. She poked Luca gently with her trowel. 'Wake up,

Lux, pass those runner beans, could you? Are these rows straight, d'you think?'

Luca brushed her hand away. 'In a minute, Mum.'

She didn't know she was on tenterhooks for a reply until she jumped as the phone buzzed again.

Do sheep swing? What're you up to?

Amazing that just a few words on a phone could have her dancing about in the vegetable garden. This was fun.

Planting beans then making gazpacho. You?

Luisa began to hum, jumpy with anticipation. She was a little defiant. No one noticed what she did, and they weren't interested anyway. Luca and Mae were always hammering away at their phones, absorbed in whatever appeared on the screens, now she was like them. She was in the dance.

Back came the reply, Luisa jumped up and stepped away from Luca to read it.

Manning the Lighthouse and wondering how you make gazpacho.

Luca, stood up, yawning. He stretched and shrugged, gazing blankly at Luisa's plants. 'They're not straight, Mum,' he said eventually. He picked up the hoe. 'Shall I do it?' he suggested.

'Please.' She squinted through a dazzle of sunlight. The familiar tawny flecks in his eyes swam, he whistled and raised the hoe, balancing it.

'Look, Mum, look!' Up it went, high and straight, and Luca placed the handle carefully on his upturned forehead, bent himself to assure a balance and then stood, arms wide, head back and the hoe balanced straight up on his head.

'Wait, I'll take a picture, I can't believe you can still do that. *Stay!*'

Too fast for her to capture it, Luca lost the balance. Luisa clapped, laughing. 'Brilliant, you have such a good life skill there.'

He bowed with a flourish. 'I can juggle too, d'you remember, Mum?'

Luisa thought back to the summer when he was twelve, the circus school and his stubborn refusal to give up on acts more suited to an older person. Tireless hours waiting because to rush him out and away home would have caused bitter disappointment, and anyway, it had been time that she loved giving him. She remembered sitting on a wooden box in the shadows at the back as Luca walked all the way across the sawdust ring on his hands, legs hanging above him, tummy exposed, a pale slice in the spotlights. His whoop of excitement that he had done it was so darling, his confidence boosted so he walked taller already when he waved at her and moved with his group of fellow students to a different challenge.

'Yes, I remember. You've got rubber in your veins instead of blood, that's what the guy said.'

'Wonder if I still have,' Luca suddenly threw himself into a backwards flip, then a cartwheel. He was like a puppy, flailing across the grass, veering beyond control and back. Breathlessly he came to a halt and bounded back to Luisa.

'I'm out of practice. Mum, I need you to make me practise.'

She laughed. 'Come and bounce these plants into the ground. I need help getting them straight.'

She began digging a new row of holes. Luca beside her, delicately placing plants. Luisa noticed that she made about ten times as many movements as he did. As he gently untangled roots and rested little bean plants in their holes, she shook hers, sloshed water over them and patted earth around them before moving on. She was too impulsive. Hers looked shell-shocked. Perhaps she had been too hasty with the texts. Kit hadn't replied to her last one. Or was it her turn? She didn't dare check, Luca was too close.

He grinned, noticing her eyes on him. 'What, Mum?'

'Nothing,' she grinned back. 'It's nice having you here to help. Don't lie down again, please!'

Luca trickled a stream of water onto the seedlings and it seeped in stains across the warm earth, scenting the air with a delicate peppery aroma that reminded Luisa of her father. She could smell the terracotta pots he'd filled every spring with basil and parsley, radicchio and rocket leaves, planted outside the kitchen door in their house near the greyhound track in Yarmouth for Gina to use as she cooked. She realised she had forgotten about them entirely since he died, even though her own interest in gardening had sprung from the hours she spent with him at his allotment.

Luca had finished his row. He stood up. 'Right, Mum, we have to do "straight" my way, and that means string.' He set off to the shed at the end of the vegetable garden.

Luisa whipped her phone out again. A recipe for gazpacho? Her fingers hovered, then she put the phone back in her pocket. He didn't really want to know how to make it, and if he did, she would show him some time.

Googling Kit with Dora the evening before had led to a lot of giggling and too many glasses of wine, and a discussion about whether he would make a good new date for Dora. They had been at Dora's kitchen table, the laptop between them, screen reflecting light on to their faces. Luisa had found the website and scrolled through it. 'It says he runs his business out of a reconstructed tin mine in Cornwall. It's actually really nice. You know, all the fabric he makes. Look, there's a picture of him. Taken quite a long time ago, I'd say.'

Dora refilled their glasses. 'See where he sells it. I'd like to know what it's like in real life.'

Luisa read from the page. 'Working with a design archive founded by Felicity Delaware who set up Lighthouse Fabrics in 1956, the company has grown to employ over fifty people and is dedicated to the continued production of cottons, linens and velvets in the UK.'

Luisa had been impressed, Kit had won awards for

his working practice and had made a success. Further googling revealed that Felicity Delaware was his mother. Dora saw a black-and-white photograph of her sitting in some sand dunes, her arms around a small boy in swimming trunks.

'Look, must be him, the chairman. How sweet.' Dora poured more wine into their glasses, 'She's glamorous. She must've been part of the art scene in St Ives and all that.'

'St Ives? How funny, we went there in February, remember? Before Ellie left for India. It was lovely. Bleak, though, in winter. Wonder how she could bear it. She looks kind of fragile, don't you think?' Luisa enlarged the image and peered at Felicity in her patterned skirt and white shirt. Her hair was up, a scarf wound through it, and she was smiling at her son sitting on a fold of her skirt, hair wet from a swim, holding a shell and a plastic spade.

Dora peered over her shoulder. 'Fragile? No, I think she looks great fun.'

'He looks like her,' said Luisa. 'I wonder how he manages running something like that? It's quite big. I could ask him for some advice for my ice-cream business.'

'I'm sure I've got stuff made from that fabric,' Dora was on a page full of fabric swatches. 'Lou, pass me those glasses will you, I'm always pretending I can see, but to be honest, I'm half blind. How come you don't need glasses?'

Luisa had shrugged, 'I probably do. I keep getting Mae to make the text on my phone bigger.'

It quacked again, and a large letter text appeared on the screen. From Kit again:

Lunch disaster: Heinz tomato with ice cubes is NOT gazpacho. Do you do recipes?

'Luisa, where are you? I haven't got time to sort that van of yours today, I'm afraid. Too much marking. It'll have to wait.'

Tom's voice over her shoulder made her jump. She wiped the mud off her hands and onto her skirt. Tom had a pair of glasses propped on his forehead, and was holding a sheaf of papers and chewing a pen. She shoved the mobile back into her bra and straightened her clothes.

She tried to keep disappointment out of her voice. 'That's a shame. I was secretly hoping to give it an airing at the cricket match next weekend.'

Tom hadn't heard. 'The good news is I think I've broken the back of this marking,' he said. 'They've done all right this year, must've pitched the questions better. Thank God.'

He rolled the papers up and put them in the pocket of his jacket. 'What are you two up to? Am I needed?' He took the jacket off, tossing it into the garden shed. In some compartment of her head, Luisa stored this information, knowing there would be a panic before school on Monday with Tom searching high and low for his lost marking. Every husband had his foibles, and Tom's was chaos. It could have been so much worse, she thought. He would never have an affair, for example, or if he did, she would know immediately. Not for him a hidden phone, shredded receipts, secret texting. The sun went behind a cloud. Luisa blinked, a cuckoo, the first she'd heard, called from the wood across the road. Reality doused her, and she felt embarrassed by her silly texts. She passed Tom the hoe with a smile. 'Weeding would be good. Luca's supposed to be doing it, but—' she shrugged.

'I am doing it!' protested Luca, stepping into the vegetable bed.

Luisa, feeling three was a crowd, stepped out, turning to Tom: 'You know we've been asked to go for a drink—'

'I should have a good case for some more excursions.' Tom scraped the hoe across a nettle root and the fresh, damp smell pricked Luisa's nostrils.

'Mmm, I love the summer smells, you could eat all of them,' she said. 'I'm experimenting with a nettle and watercress sorbet as an intense version of a gazpacho. What d'you think, Tom?'

He was prodding the ground around the new seedlings, oblivious to the threat the hoe posed to the tiny plants. 'Perhaps we can go to Italy next. It makes sense for the course,' he mused.

Luisa pushed him away from her precious plants towards a flourishing patch of weeds. She hadn't been joking when she'd told Dora no one listened. Literally none of her family ever took any notice of her. She tried again. 'We're going to meet our new neighbour tonight.'

Tom had bent to the hoe, jabbing the ground, slaying ragwort and thistles in a swathe as he outlined his plan. 'We'll investigate the Renaissance and explore your heritage, Tod.' He touched her cheek with the back of his hand.

'That'd be nice.' What was the point in minding? Luisa sighed.

Tom ruffled her hair. 'You'd come, wouldn't you, Tod? We'll do it next Easter.'

Luisa nodded. 'My mother will probably want to come.'

'And me,' said Luca.

Tom shrugged. 'Why not? It might entertain Gina, culture-crossing and so on. Bring the family to work, or work to the family or whatever. Might be good to take her as our own personal guide.' He walked to the end of Luisa's row of seedlings. 'It's not straight you know.'

Luisa shrugged. Tom didn't devote any time to appeasing his mother-in-law, it was a game he loved to play, a caricature situation. A light touch was all that was needed.

'You know Gina,' she said. 'She's easy if you handle her right, you just don't always bother. Your best hope with her is to show how much you love ice cream.' Luisa smiled as she pulled off her gloves. 'So, my darling,' she said with mock severity, 'better than planning a trip to Italy, how about you fix my ice-cream van?' She stepped onto the path, 'Oh, and Tom?'

Both Tom and Luca turned to look at her, a synchronised movement, a turn of the neck in tandem that showed their relationship more vividly than genetics.

'We're going to meet our new neighbour at the Lighthouse tonight. All of us. Don't say I didn't tell you.'

Tom shrugged, laughing with Luca. 'I won't, wouldn't dare cross you. And I will sort that van of yours, I promise you.'

'I'm going to call Dora. She wanted to meet him too.'

In the house, Mae was wandering around in her pyjamas.

'Why aren't you dressed?' Luisa snapped. Mae had opened the fridge and was rooting around in the salad box at the bottom, her face lit an unhealthy green by the interior light.

'You look ill, is that why you're not up yet?' That would be reasonable, Luisa thought.

Mae sighed, it was her usual response to comments from her mother. 'I'm comfy, Mum. What do I need to dress for anyway? We're not going anywhere, are we? Where's your credit card? I need to give the number to Ellie and it's not in your bag?'

'You don't need to give my number to anyone, Mae. Why does Ellie need it? Why doesn't she ask me for it?' Luisa rattled out the questions as she lifted a pile of straw baskets. 'I had it yesterday when I bought the shopping.' Mae was searching in the fridge. Not much chance of her finding it there. 'I'd like to speak to Ellie, is she calling back?'

Mae watched her mother turn the baskets upside down. 'I was trying to retrace your steps. I looked in the washing machine as well.'

She hitched herself up to sit on the counter, swinging her legs. Luisa could smell cigarette smoke in her hair. She decided to ignore it. Exhaustion hit her, she sat down, pressing her forehead with her palms. She couldn't face a battle, and probably all fifteen-year-olds smoked. Not that that made it any better.

'Mum, Ellie says I should go out and meet her in India after my exams and travel with her. She says we could go all around southern India for a couple of months. I could get some ideas for my textiles A level?'

Luisa leapt up as if she had been scalded. 'What? Can we talk about this later? You're fifteen years old, Mae, so it's probably illegal for you to fly on your own that far. Of course you can't go to India with Ellie. Just let me sort this thing out, hang on.' She picked up her handbag and opened her wallet. 'I bet it's in here, it must be.'

Mae rolled her eyes and slid off the counter. 'God, you're so stressy, Mum. Ellie needs to book a flight. She's going somewhere else in India. You can talk to her later.'

Luisa pulled out the card with a flourish. 'Ah, found it!' Why listen to children? Of course the bankcard was in her wallet all along. 'You can tell Ellie that until I can have a chat with her I'm not happy to dish out flights all over the place, or to send you to India. And I miss her.'

Sudden tears flooded her eyes. Luisa turned to the sink and splashed her face with cold water. From behind her, Luisa felt Mae slide an arm around her waist and, without speaking, rest her cheek against her mother's shoulder. Warmth, and Mae's soft presence, permeated her body. Luisa kissed her daughter's hand, it smelled of oranges more than cigarettes. 'Sorry, darling.'

'Don't cry, Mumma.'

Deep breathing. Hard not to feel as strung out as a washing line sometimes, but this was nice. Luisa leaned back against Mae. Her hair brushed Mae's face, and she felt her breath on the back of her scalp. Luisa laughed shakily.

'What's happened to my littlest all of a sudden? You're so grown up and thoughtful.'

Mae broke away. 'Mum! I'm not little any more!' She poured a glass of water and drank it, her eyes fixed on Luisa over the rim. The dip of concentration between her brows hadn't changed. Time vanished. Mae absorbed in her world when she was a baby, a small child, a bigger girl, always with the beam of her gaze fixed, always determined. Luisa was glad it was still focused on her sometimes. Luisa blinked. Mae didn't need to go to India. The fewer family members in India the better. Why couldn't everyone just stay at home?

She mulled over her thoughts. A bit of guile never hurt any parenting situation. 'Let's think about it later,' she said with deliberate vagueness. 'Darling, will you help me make a cake quickly?' It was usually best to appear to go along with all teenage plans, safe in the knowledge that for them to actually accomplish anything more arduous than getting out of bed and eating a bowl of cereal was almost impossible. True, Ellie had made it to India, but that was on a wave of action implemented by her whole academic year.

'A cake? Hardly quick,' Mae pouted, tossed her head, swinging her ponytail like a slingshot. She was only fifteen, she'd got lost cycling to Blythe last week because she'd been day-dreaming and turned the wrong way out of the gate at home, she was about to start a summer job making sandwiches in Nellie's Bread Basket on Saturdays. All things considered, she was an unlikely prospect for travel to the Indian sub-continent at the moment.

'It could be quick, we'll do a broken biscuit with a few cherries. We're going to see the man who's moved into the Lighthouse, I thought it'd be friendly to take—'

Mae groaned. 'Will there be anyone there my age?'

Luisa looked doubtful. 'I don't think so.'

Mae groaned again. 'Do I have to come?'

Luisa put a wooden spoon on the table in front of Mae, and a bowl.

'Luca's coming. And we'll go and see Grayson's puppies on the way.'

Mae gave her mother a light shove as they both reached for the fridge door and the ingredients. 'You may think you're bribing me, but actually I'm making my own mind up,' she said loftily.

'Of course,' agreed Luisa. 'Pass me that jar will you?'

*   *   *

There was a festive slant to the evening as they drove along the coast to Kings Sloley. The puppies had been adored and even Tom had admitted he wouldn't mind owning one. Cow parsley lining the verges, waving like a Jubilee crowd, and sun and sea met in a spill of halcyon gold to the horizon. 'Mum, we didn't call Ellie back about the ticket. Let's Skype her later. She's getting a tattoo done.'

'A tattoo? You didn't say anything about that.' Luisa swivelled, Mae's hair flowed smooth as a river and make-up sparkled around her eyes. 'She hasn't got one, has she?'

'No. She wants to. She said she needs to ask you.'

'Ask me? Hardly necessary. She knows exactly what I think.'

Mae sighed. 'You're so predictable, Mum! I said she shouldn't bother, you'd just stress, but she went on about your approval mattering.' Mae shrugged. 'I don't understand it.'

Luca's arm was behind his sister across the back of the car seat. 'Getting so grown up, Mae,' he shook his head.

She prodded him. 'You sound like a granddad. I was just thinking about whether I would tell Mum if I was having one done.'

'Depends on the tattoo, I expect,' said Tom, his eyes meeting his children's in the rear-view mirror. 'I'd be interested to see the design any of you'd like to live with for the next seven or so decades, I must say. Or would you go for "I love Mum"?' He winked across at Luisa next to him.

163

Mae bounced on her seat, indignation squaring her shoulders. 'Dad! What're you talking about? It'd be really lame to have a tattoo that your parents actually *liked*.'

'I'd have a lighthouse,' said Luisa dreamily, as the road swooped over a hill and Kings Sloley appeared ahead of them.

'Wouldn't you have an ice cream, Mum?' asked Luca.

Luisa shrugged. 'You would think so, wouldn't you, but look at that Lighthouse, it's incredible.'

They gazed for a moment at Kings Sloley Light-house, a striped candle, the flame of the glass on top caught by the sunlight. 'It's so joyful,' said Luisa.

Mae shot her mother a speculative glance. 'Can I actually get one?'

Luca laughed. 'Great idea, sis. Why don't you have a map, or the home postcode. Or Mum's mobile number? That way you'll be able to get home wher-ever you are.'

Mae dropped the veil of sophistication she'd applied with her make-up, and stuck her tongue out.

Tom fiddled with the radio. 'There's never any bloody reception around here. We should ask this new chap to get a mast up on the Lighthouse.'

'Oh but phones work here,' Luisa waved hers. 'I've still got a signal, and the other day when I came to get the sheep Luca rang me.'

Tom raised his eyebrows. 'You came to get the sheep? Where was Jason?'

Luisa sighed. 'I knew you weren't listening. His

name is Kit Delaware. The sheep were right inside the Lighthouse when I got there.'

'Oh, I knew that,' Mae leaned forward between them, she smelled of mint and peaches, and her bracelets jangled. 'It's the guy we saw in Blythe the other day. Dora said so. Mum, I forgot to say she rang. She's on a date tonight so she couldn't come.'

'Another one?' Tom snorted. 'Why does she have to go on so many dates? I don't know where she finds the men to go with.'

'Dad!' Mae poked his shoulder, 'That's mean! She's your sister. You're as bad as Luca.'

'She doesn't really,' Luisa caught Mae's hand. It was light, the bones delicate as a bird. 'It's just that Maddie's away, so it's easier for her to go out than usual. She's just having fun.'

Mae gasped. 'Mum, you're such a hypocrite, you haven't ever in your life been on as many dates as Dora has in a week! You and Dad are both un*born* as far as all this stuff goes.'

Luisa laughed. 'Don't show me up,' she protested.

'I'm amazed you aren't trying to set her up with this Lighthouse bloke,' Tom parked the car behind Kit's.

'Dora's seen him. She thinks he's hot, but I reckon he's even older than you.' Mae flashed a smile at Luisa that brimmed with mischief.

Tom wasn't listening. He quickly got out. 'Hey, Luca,' he said. 'Check out this car,' and they wandered ahead through the field towards the Lighthouse. Luisa hung back a little, checked her reflection in the wing mirror, balancing the broken biscuit cake as she fiddled with her hair. Her phone shook in her bag, quacking the arrival of a text and she jumped. Kit? Surely not? She felt suddenly foolish. Grown-ups didn't get excited about texts. Tom would be astonished if he knew.

Mae dug her with her elbow. 'Mum! Stop it, you look like you've got nits when you pull your hair about, and the man can see you. Look!'

'I think I have got nits,' Luisa hissed back, and they laughed together.

Kit was shaking hands with Tom. 'Hey, this is a surprise, you're the pitstop man! My good Samaritan!' They clapped each other noisily on the back.

'Yes, and you're the only breakdown I've ever helped with where I've talked about paintings,' said Tom.

'You've met?' Luisa stared. She had to remind herself to shut her gaping mouth. How could Tom know Kit as well?

Tom reached out and hugged her towards him, laughing. 'Yes, I clocked that car right away. Should've known it would be you. Small world and all that.'

Kit ushered them in. 'A cake, wonderful, let me put it here.'

Luisa followed him through to the hall. A tang of woodsmoke and neroli hung around him. In his dark blue shirt, he seemed exotic, his skin appeared to have a lustrous sheen, his gait an easy energy. His watch threw a steel glint into the shadows. Luisa looked around her. Candlelight had transformed the austere, small-windowed rooms, and the crackle of the fire in the grate was a welcome touch of luxury on a summer night. Kit pulled the cork from a bottle and poured Luisa a glass of wine. His fingers touched hers and she jumped, spilling cold liquid across her wrist. A roar of heat flared up her body, and gratefully she pressed the glass to her burning cheek.

The rumble of Tom's laughter recalled her.

'So what on earth brings you to this unlikely spot? You're not the average lighthouse keeper, or not around here at any rate.'

Luisa winced.

Kit didn't answer immediately. 'Someone else's life,' he said finally. 'Or their death, really. And a fair amount of confusion. I was left this place by my mother. Bit of a surprise, she'd never told me anything about it, or even so much as mentioned Norfolk.'

'I'm sorry about your mother,' Tom's head was lowered as he spoke, moving his glass, watching the wine make a whirlpool.

'Could we go up to the top?' Mae and Luca bounded in, Mae waving her phone, 'Look! I got some photos of my shadow on the Lighthouse, Luca took them.' She broke off, finding herself directly in front of Kit. 'Hi. I like your house – Lighthouse. Whatever! It's really cool. I wish we lived here.'

Kit's face lost years as he laughed. Luisa suddenly wanted to hug Mae.

'You like it? I'm glad.' He gestured to the stairs. 'I haven't counted the steps yet, but I think it's over a hundred. Go wherever you like, and if you count them, come back and tell us.'

Mae darted off, followed by Luca, who mouthed, 'Nice to meet you' as he vanished up the stairs. The echoes of their voices fell like soft petals into the evening.

Luisa shrugged and looked at Kit. 'This is us,' she said. 'There's one more in India.'

'Right,' Kit shook his head, laughing, 'I didn't know what to expect. They're like puppies. So energetic.'

'Not always,' said Tom, drily. 'Try our house tomorrow morning if you want to see them in their natural habitats – bed and piles of chaos.'

Kit picked up a case of beer, 'I hope they like lager. I've got—' he pulled himself up. 'Oh Christ. Have I made a ricket of this? Are they old enough for beers?'

'I'll say so,' Tom picked up a corkscrew and a bowl of ice.

'I was waiting for the sheep,' Kit said with a smile. 'I thought you might have a few stray lambs with you tonight.'

He led the way out through the kitchen. Luisa swivelled, trying to take everything in as she and Tom followed. The strange curved spaces had been softened throughout. The candles, a wood fire dancing in the hall, a pile of books, a rug dropped on an armchair, a big oak chest, and a length of embroidered antique fabric tacked on to the wall, silver threads catching the dying light, gave the Lighthouse a sense of belonging to someone.

Luisa trailed a hand on the back of an old carved

chair, the fabric seat battered and frayed. 'Did you have all this furniture?'

Hands in his pockets, Kit looked around. 'Most of it was in the shed. A bit dusty, but fine.'

Luisa moved to the wall, her interest caught by a small painting. 'Was this in the shed? Or did you find it? Clever to pick up a lighthouse picture already.'

'I've got another actually. That one was in the bathroom at my mother's house. I thought I'd bring it when I knew I was coming to meet my Lighthouse.'

Luisa bent close to the picture. 'It's lovely, do you know who painted it?'

Kit shook his head. 'I always assumed my mother collected lighthouse odds and ends because of the name of her company. Never thought more of it until now.'

Kit led her along the wall to show her a night-lit lighthouse, its beam inlaid mother of pearl. 'I found this and a lot of bits and pieces in a nice old junk shop down the coast this morning.'

Luisa laughed. 'You haven't wasted any time settling in, have you?'

He shrugged. 'To be honest, I'm used to a house full of clutter, this seems very pared down. I like it, I'm realising there's no need for so much stuff in life.'

She raised her brows. 'Oh really? Interesting view considering you've just acquired a three- or four-storey heap of bricks and mortar.'

Kit paused, looked quizzically at Luisa, 'Bricks and mortar? I thought it was a pillar of salt.'

'Or a giant stick of striped rock,' she agreed. 'Oh, anyway. It's straight out of a story book.'

Trying not to meet his gaze she bumped her shoulder against his. The sensation of his breath, warm on her neck, silenced her.

They walked back through the kitchen, where dusty double doors opened out to the patch of grass and the sea beyond. Kit had erected a small round table and decorated it with a jam jar of blue flax and poppies and an array of old plates and glasses. Mae, having announced there were one hundred and thirty-seven steps, collapsed into a chair, Luca supine on the grass beside her. They lolled like lion cubs at ease, chatting to Kit, bright with curiosity.

Luisa had a sudden rare moment of seeing her children through someone else's eyes.

'What's it like living in a lighthouse?' asked Luca. 'You'll need a basket on a rope to get stuff up to your bedroom.'

Mae, rather to Luisa's relief, had knocked over her beer and hadn't noticed as it seeped into the grass. She flitted back to the doorway, flashing the camera on her phone up the shadowy walls of the Lighthouse.

'D'you have kids? They're sooooo lucky, I know which room I'd have if I lived here.'

'I already told you, Mae,' Luisa hissed, but Kit was answering smoothly. 'I'm afraid I don't,' he said. 'No family at all now.' He broke a ripple of wax off a candlestick and threw it into the flames of the fire he had made outside. Luisa felt her heart lurch protectively; she fancied she saw sadness in his face. The firelight encircled them as dusk fell. The big flat pebbles glowed around the logs placed like a wigwam, creating a solid tripod of orange light in the gloaming. Kit had done it just the way Tom always made a fire. In her childhood, if there was an outdoor fire, it was always in something – a metal bucket or a wheel-barrow. Contained. Cosmo would have put it in a brazier.

'I wonder if cavemen lit fires like you do?' she mused.

Kit didn't blink. 'Of course. How else?' He crouched to place another log.

'Unless they were roasting a mammoth on a spit. Or building a pyre,' said Luca.

'I think cavemen are overrated,' Mae flopped onto the seat next to Luisa. 'Cave girls would've invented wheels and ovens so much more quickly if they'd been allowed to.'

'Or Italians,' Luisa interjected, 'we like braziers and barbecues. None of this primitive stuff.'

'The Italians came later,' said Kit, only a slight flicker in his cheek suggesting amusement. 'They were too sophisticated for Neolithic pursuits.'

'Have you noticed how much of the horizon we can see from here?' Tom had been standing apart, clearly lost in this own thoughts, looking out to sea. 'I can see Lowestoft lit up like a battery hen farm.'

'Dad! That's a bit harsh. What d'you reckon about cavemen? Were any of them Italian?'

Luca sprang up and pulled Mae to her feet. Tom sat down in the seat his son had vacated. 'Doubt it, the Italians had too much sense. They waited to join the evolutionary chain around the time of underfloor heating and hot- and cold-running slaves,' he observed.

Luca jerked his head towards Kit, a grin hidden by the fall of his fringe. 'Exactly what Kit said!' He reached for Mae's arm and propelled her away. 'Come on, sis, let's look over the edge. Could be shark-infested waters, you never know.' They loped off, the flax rolling in a blue haze around them to the cliff edge.

Kit and Tom were talking about Kit's business. Fifty employees on the payroll. An annual turnover, manufacturing, owning a factory. He talked easily, legs stretched in front of him. He had an athletic man's ability to appear at ease in his body, and although the chair legs dug into the ground lopsided, Kit, one hand deep in his pocket, the other cupping his wine glass, was as urbane and relaxed as if he had been lolling on a sunlounger by a swimming pool.

A bubble of laughter burst from Luisa and she blushed. 'Sorry, just thinking,' she said guiltily.

'Thinking what?' Tom asked. She shook her head.

'What about your business?' Kit looked between the two of them, 'It's ice cream, isn't it?'

Tom shrugged. 'Oh, that's Luisa's thing. Give her a whisk and a few ingredients and she's off. I'm better on paper than trying to create something.'

'What about my van?' she hadn't meant to sound nagging, but Tom gave her a sharp look.

'It's in hand,' he said shortly.

'Your van? The ice-cream van?' Kit leaned forwards to poke the fire, sending a coil of orange cinders up into the darkening sky.

'I wish I could paint it these colours,' said Luisa, 'like a sunset. Not sure it works for ice cream though.'

Tom snorted, 'It'd look like something off a Meat Loaf album if you did.' He turned to Kit. 'Didn't you say your mother was the reason you ended up here? Did she have a Norfolk connection then?'

'If she did, I never knew it.' A frown drew Kit's brows together. He had nice eyes, Luisa thought, kind. He was telling Tom about his mother's life.

'My stepfather, Joseph, was a BBC photographer in the war, he was partially blind after that, so she was the driving force always. Lighthouse Fabrics was her baby.'

'Your stepfather? What happened to—'

'Mum!' The children had wandered back, and stood beyond the glow of the fire. Mae caught Luisa's eye and jerked her head in the direction of the car. 'It's really late,' she hissed.

Luisa looked at her watch and jumped up, 'We must go.'

Tom's phone bleeped and he walked away from the group to take the call.

'It's early, you don't have to leave.' Kit put his drink down and leaned forward, elbows on knees, and smiled. Luisa immediately blushed, heat stealing up her body, across her chest, over her décolletage, around her neck and, she was sure, flaring crimson on her face. A blatant, literal indication of how uncool she was.

Luca walked up to bid Kit farewell. 'You've gotta have a party here, it's so cool. There's nowhere like it.'

Kit shrugged, but looked more pleased than nonchalant. 'You think so? That sounds good. Who will I ask?'

Luca rolled a cigarette. 'We'll help you ask people, it'll be an introducing yourself to the neighbourhood thing. Everyone'd come, wouldn't they, Mum?'

'Definitely,' she nodded.

'Don't even think about it,' interrupted Tom. He had finished his call. 'Parties are trouble, start to finish.'

'Dad, you're such a killjoy,' Luca offered the roll up to Kit, who shook his head.

'Thanks, but I stopped years ago. Had a brush with long-distance running, and couldn't stand the spluttering. Now I think the only bonus of getting old is that the day is fast approaching when it won't matter if I smoke, or take opium or spend every last penny I have on the dogs.'

'What dogs? You don't have one do you?' Mae moved closer to her mother in order to pinch her arm lightly. 'We went to see such sweet puppies on our way here, they're Grayson's.'

'Grayson?' Kit was confused, 'I was talking about greyhounds.'

'Oh, you mean dog racing. I love that.' Mae flashed a melting smile in Kit's direction, then murmured to Luisa, 'Come on, you said we'd be home by nine.'

Luca had another beer in his hand, Luisa hoped Mae wouldn't do the same as an act of defiance. 'We used to go with Cosmo, didn't we, Mum?' Now Luisa had a child on each side, and was more or less being propelled away from the evening.

'Gambling in the blood then?' Kit winked. 'I'd like to go with you some time. You bring the tips, I'll stand you the Surf and Turf.'

'What's that?' Mae demanded, breaking off to hold out the skirt of an apron hanging on a hook in the kitchen. 'Hey! Look Mum, this has got windmills on it like that dress of Dora's. It's vintage. It's even got the same red frill.'

'It's my mother's design.' Kit lifted the apron off the hook and held it out to Luisa and Mae. 'This is something we reworked from a pattern she was using in the forties, and it's been incredibly popular. We must've printed miles of it over the years. Saved our bacon financially on more than one occasion.'

Mae jumped up. 'She designed this? That's what I want to do. The only reason I'm not running away to India with my sister is that I want to be a fabric designer and I need to get into art school.'

'You do?'

Luisa's astonishment at Mae's sudden change of plan was interrupted by Luca. 'First I've heard of it,' he said laconically.

'Why not?' Tom drained his glass. 'She's good at it. Never knock a dream, eh Mae?'

Kit nodded. 'Young talent is something we've focused a lot of attention on. We want to create opportunities in the whole industry.'

Luisa wondered why hearing of other people's generous behaviour often made her feel stunted and inadequate rather than inspired. Why was she not helping to mastermind an ice-cream makers' foundation for the under-privileged, rather than selfishly concentrating on her own success?

Kit folded the apron and placed it on the back of a chair. 'Perhaps it's sprung from having no kids of my own, but I've ended up on a bit of a soapbox about the importance of creating proper jobs, you know, like the apprenticeships in our day.'

Mae spun away from her mother. 'I could do one!' she pleaded. 'Could I?' Her gaze darted between her mother and Kit. Luisa, trying to read Kit's expression, thought she detected reserve.

'Something to talk about at home, darling,' she fixed Mae with a fierce gaze.

'Why are you glaring at me, Mum? I'm allowed to ask, aren't I?' She appealed to Kit.

He shrugged. 'You can apply when you're eighteen,' he said. 'We've got a strong programme for apprentices, my mother was a great champion of young design.'

Mae clapped her hands. 'Yes, yes please! I'd love that.'

They drove home with all the windows open, the moon a tracing paper disc above the knife-edged silhouette of shifting reeds along the roadside.

Kit had got Tom thinking. 'Inheritance is an odd business. What's a man like that going to do with a bloody lighthouse? He isn't exactly Mr B&B, is he?'

'It's not as weird as him having a business called Lighthouse Fabrics,' Mae interrupted. 'I saw the logo on the apron, it looks just like his Lighthouse, even the little outhouse on the side. Was there a standard look for lighthouses ever? A manual or something? I mean you couldn't look it up on the Internet could you?'

Luisa dragged her thoughts back to the present. 'I suppose they do,' she said.

'You suppose who do what?' Tom yawned. 'I'm exhausted. Nice man, though. I think Mae's right.'

'Right about what? The Lighthouse?' Luisa watched her husband's profile. He was scowling, concentrating.

'Mmm,' he nodded. 'His mother must have come here. It wouldn't surprise me, there's always a link between these artists' colonies. I'm not saying there was one fully established here in Norfolk, but she might have known a few people here. Maybe even come for a holiday some time.'

'D'you think he'll stay here long enough to have a party?' asked Luca.

'I thought he was nice,' said Mae. 'I hope he stays.' She rested her cheek on her mother's seat, her face lit by the dashboard. 'We should get Dora to go out with him.'

The scent of the night air was sweet when they stopped. Luisa stood for a moment after the others had gone inside. Everything about her home was familiar. The sounds and smells of a summer evening, the shadows in the garden, the mown grass damply cool after a hot day. Grayson was in the yard, silently sniffing flowerbeds. She could have drawn the curl of his tail, the gleam of his eye and written a poem on the familiarity of his nose, cool and damp when he pushed it into her hand for his customary welcome. Luisa drank in the sensations. Her nerve-endings hummed with the electric excitement of being alive. She wanted to dance and sing, she wanted to spread her feeling of delight. This was what it was like to be at home with her family. There was a blast of sound from the living room where Luca had turned on the television. Tom whistled and banged the gate as he came in from putting the car away.

Luisa knew every inch of her life, every familiar sound, and yet, she thought, she didn't really know it at all. She only knew it through her eyes. She could see her version, but she couldn't see Tom's, or Mae's or Luca's. Most of life was obscured for most of the time, emerging briefly, like the beam of the Lighthouse.

The kitchen door opened, Tom appeared, taking out the rubbish, and the dazzle from behind him fell across the lawn. He looked at Luisa, hesitated as if he were about to come across to her, then turned and went back inside. After a few minutes she followed him in.

CHAPTER 8

From the window in Felicity's kitchen, Michael could see half the Mousehole harbour, and a sliver of the front of the pub if he craned his head to the left. Mainly, though, his view was out to sea. The nets and boats drying on the quay, and the usual village cats prowling for leftover fish on the slipway were a frame for the expanse of horizon that held him like a spell. He didn't know how many hours he had spent over the last few months just staring at the sea. No matter what the time of day, and no matter what he had set himself to do, he could be stopped in his tracks to gaze at the limitless ocean. He drank in the power of it, and the paradoxes: the silence and the roar, the stillness and the ceaseless exuberance, the swell and the falling away of the tide. He was humbled by the might of the waves, and slowly he filled himself up with its strength until he felt he had his own vitality again. It was only now when he felt he was beginning to be put back together again, that he understood how fragmented he had been. He could think a thought through to the end now, and that was something that he hadn't realised he had lost until he had rediscovered it.

It was low tide, and a small girl played on an exposed crest of sand in the little harbour. The sky was heavy today, clouds moving lumpen and slow, waddling off the hill and scudding out to sea, where they massed and darkened. A summer day with lethargy in the air. A tamarisk shook yellow petals on the slate path to the gate and on to the dry grass of the lawn where they lay scattered like raindrops reflecting the sun. There had been little enough rain in the past weeks, but the cloud today released occasional fat drops which spattered against the window panes. It was August. Frequent summer storms cracked and rumbled out at sea, but few broke over Mousehole. Felicity was at the bookshop, Michael would meet her at lunchtime. A half day. He would help her pull down the blinds and lock up, then, hand in hand, they would walk up Raginnis Hill, not pausing until they reached the top and had a view right across Mount's Bay to Lizard Point and far away beyond. He would bring bread and cheese, apples and ginger beer, and their lunch would be a picnic.

He was back from working on the cutting beds early. He had started at five, dawn rising behind him, rinsing the sky in pink and mauve as Michael weeded and dug to plant a bed of violets to grow on for spring. Michael liked Felicity's half day, it meant he would see her sooner. He was impatient of lost hours, it was as if he had replaced his inbuilt wartime anxiety that something unspeakable was about to happen with a fear of missing something vital.

For the past three weeks Felicity had been working on a painting. A view from the hill, painted while Michael lay and read to her and today she planned to finish it. He wanted to talk to her today, about his family, his brother. He loved her, he would always love her, but he had to go back home. One day he would leave. The weeks had spooled into months in Cornwall, and he'd made friends and a life here. He wrote to his mother, a letter he asked a transient artist to post from London. He didn't want her to know where he was, he owed it to Felicity to protect their world. Writing to his mother, tears smudged the ink so often he ended up writing the letter in pencil instead. He said he was sorry, he couldn't come to terms with all that had happened. He promised her one thing, he pledged on his life that one day he would come home. He needed to tell Felicity about this letter. He didn't want secrets from her. She was his soulmate, and he wanted her to know him. To know his story and his family.

Then there was Janey. Michael found that his mind became a blank fog when he tried to remember her, or think about her. He couldn't see her in his mind's eye any more. He had tucked her photograph into the back of his wallet, and he didn't take it out. Without anyone to talk to about her, he found he could push all his guilt about her, all his snatches of memory, down into the fog. Out of the way. It wasn't good, he knew that, but it was out of the way, and that was all he could bear just now.

Michael opened a pad of paper on the kitchen table. The clock ticked and Rations, Felicity's cat, jumped up on to his lap and began to purr, kneading the twill of Michael's trousers. Pushing him down, Michael stuck one pencil behind his ear, twirled another like a small baton and, whistling, began to draw.

Arthur Castleton would be here in half an hour to make a start in the old sail-drying shed in the garden of the cottage. Felicity needed a studio with a table, a place to make her paintings into silk screens, and Michael wanted to make it perfect for her. He had a hunch his own carpentry skills would not be enough and had enlisted Arthur's help. Arthur was introduced to him by Paul Spencer. Arthur made frames and supplied materials for a number of the artists in this part of Cornwall. There were a lot of them, there always had been. Many had dispersed for the war's duration and, like animals emerging from hibernation, they were re-forming their communities, shaking and stretching themselves as they began to find a way to live in the new post-war world.

Last week, on Felicity's day off, she and Michael had caught the train to St Ives and walked up through the zig-zag streets where the houses were stacked like a staircase to the wide expanse of view at the top. Over the brow of the hill the town tumbled to the brink of the sea, old stone buildings standing squat but solid with their windows blank, waiting to return to peacetime use. The whitewashed, crumbling space of the Porthmeor Studios stood above a sandy beach. Along the shore, the sand was latticed with criss-crossing chains mooring fishing boats, interspersed with canvasses pegged out to dry like sails.

Felicity was excited, dragging Michael by the hand when he paused to look at the building. 'Come on, let's see who's around. I used to come to drawing classes here,' she giggled and put her hand over her mouth. 'God, the first time I came, I'll never forget it, I was so embarrassed. We drew a *naked* man.'

Michael raised an eyebrow. 'Did you indeed? What sort of naked man? Old? Fat? Strong? Handsome?' He loved seeing Felicity laugh. If love was wanting the very best out of life for someone, and being prepared to help them have that, then he loved her with his whole heart.

She leaned forward and placed her forefinger on his chest, tracing his collarbone under his shirt, laughing into his eyes so he couldn't help kissing her. 'Old of course. We never had young models, and the week I was going to do it was the beginning of the war so it didn't happen.'

'Just as well,' said Michael. 'I wouldn't like to think of a whole class staring at you with nothing on.'

'Don't be such a prude,' she laughed, opening a side door to the studios. 'Come and see what they've got on the walls today. You know, during the war these studios almost closed down, but now it looks as though they're thriving again.'

Michael thought the building looked about to fall down, with its rusting tin roof and lichen growing up the walls, but inside the smell of turps and linseed and the white light as crisp and clear as folded linen created an atmosphere so rarefied Michael felt it could almost be sanctified. In its stillness and simplicity it reminded him of visits he had made to rural churches through the long months in Sicily at the end of the war. Until now, he had thought that a place had to be ecclesiastical to create the particular atmosphere summoned by a dazzle of whitewash and warped old glass in windows the size of walls. To Michael, the studios were utterly fascinating. Light poured in on all sides, filling the plain wood-lined spaces above disused pilchard salting cellars, and net-makers' sheds. Some of the doors were open, and varying degrees of chaos were visible within. Stacked canvasses, brushes stuffed into jars, sprays of paint like blood, caught and dried on the walls.

An exhibition in a nearby crypt was hung with a selection of paintings by local artists including Paul and others in his circle of friends. Michael felt quite out of his depth. He had never seen anything like it. The idea of an artist going somewhere to work and doing it as a job hadn't ever crossed his mind before he came to Cornwall. Now he came to think of it, he supposed they didn't all sit around with easels in the middle of the countryside, but the idea of them forming a community and setting up work alongside one another to kick ideas around, was a novel one to him. He found almost everything associated with Felicity was like this, a new thought, a way of looking at things that had not occurred to him before. Sometimes he felt that he was no more than a sponge. Sometimes he wondered if he believed in fate. One thing he was sure of was that he was meant to be here, for now.

Felicity stopped outside one of the studios, the door was open. 'You know, my mother worked here before she had me and Christopher. This studio was hers, look, I've got a picture.' She fumbled in the basket she had brought to carry their lunch, and held out a photograph for him to look at. Felicity's eyes were intent on the picture, though Michael was sure she could feel his gaze on her face. 'She was good, but she didn't really know it, that's what people who knew her always said. I tried to get her to paint more. She always said she would when she had more time, but I think my father dying stopped her in her tracks.'

'Let me see.' He was behind her, Felicity leaned into him. He loved that about her, the way she would stand, as if shielded by him, and when her body was near his, the warmth between them felt like the biggest connection it was possible to have with another person. The photograph was bordered with a lacy frame, small and crumpled. A young woman in man's trousers and a white shirt, slight, with dark hair piled up, face solemn, looked out at him from a clapboard room, an easel beside her, paintings leaning against the wall.

'She looks like you.' He scrutinised the photograph. 'What happened to that picture? It's a lot bigger than the one of you Verity had, or any I've seen in your house. Come to think of it, there aren't many are there?'

Felicity sighed. 'My mother was quite successful when she was young. There's a big mural she did with some other artists in the library in Penzance. I think she sold some over the years, and had work in a couple of shows. That's how Dad met her, he came over from St Austell to look at the famous St Ives school of art.'

Felicity took the photograph back and put it in her bag again. She peered through the door. 'I think she wished she had done more work. That was her only real regret. Apart from Christopher, of course. She died of a broken heart, it was as simple, and sad as that.' She walked down the corridor in front of Michael, her footsteps echoing on the boards, then paused at a door, knocking gently. 'I did some drawing in here with another painter for a while. It was very cheap because it's got no window, but then Ben Nicolson took it on, he actually wanted a studio with no daylight, can you imagine?' Michael did not speak. He realised he was holding his breath and let go a huge sigh full of sorrow for Felicity's mother, and her broken heart. Felicity opened the door and Michael looked past her into the room. It was simple and sparse, an enamel stove, a long table, jars full of brushes again and a chair covered in a crocheted blanket. One painting hung on the end wall, white shapes piled in front of one another, soothing, mysterious. Michael stared at it, the clean lines, the compelling shapes. He thought of the paintings in his parents' house. An oil landscape of the Norfolk Broads, a painting of three spaniels following a rider through woodland. He'd never taken much notice of art before he met Felicity, but suddenly he found his curiosity roused. There might be painters like this in Norfolk. Was there an art movement there? Were there people like Felicity where he came from? He couldn't imagine that there were. He couldn't imagine that anyone else could ever be like her.

On the beach when they had left, Michael put his arm around her. 'You need somewhere of your own to work,' he said. 'You need a studio. Let me build you one.'

The wind blew up, and as they walked a sudden rain shower splashed big drops on to their faces. Felicity paused and tied a scarf over her head, then ran to catch up. 'Oh I wish it were possible. I've got so many things to make and paint and do. I want to design fabric. The bookshop takes all my time and it was never my dream, it was Christopher's. I had to do it for him and for Dad, but I want to create things that come to life around me, that are used for something. Not just buy and sell books to gather dust in people's houses.' The rain stopped, pulled out to sea on a gust of wind. Felicity unwound her scarf, and it fluttered, a white and yellow banner. 'Like this,' she waved it. 'Look at the pattern! Someone made this. Why not me?'

Her spirit touched Michael. She was unlike any woman he had met. Not that he'd met many. What he meant was that she wasn't like Janey, she was so independent, and yet she needed him. He could build her studio. He could help her make her place in the world she longed to go to in her work.

She stuffed the scarf in her pocket, walking backwards in front of him down the beach. 'I've been thinking and thinking, sitting in that shop all day every day. I feel as if I'm closing myself down when I'm there. I'm in a trance, not really living at all.' She laughed and twirled around in front of him, arms stretched. 'Come on, catch me!' Pulling off her shoes she began to run down the beach away from him.

Michael watched her. His mother called his father 'dear'. She kept the house and cooked and sat by the radio, silently sewing. Michael had never seen her display an emotion or utter a wish in her life. He couldn't remember ever seeing her run or jump, and the only time she had ever danced in front of him was at a Christmas party given by some neighbours when he was thirteen and he had been so embarrassed he hid in the cloakroom, inhaling essence of mothball and fur until his father fetched him to go home. This was uncharted territory, and Michael felt a barrier collapse within him. Stopping to kick off his own shoes, he chased her, laughing as he felt the cool damp of sand underfoot and the exhilaration of the wind in his face. He caught up with her by the water and grabbed her.

'Come here,' his voice was husky and he pulled her close. He wanted to shelter her inside his coat with him, and when he kissed her, his blood thrilled through him, waking every nerve, every bone so he pulsed with the excitement of life. In that moment, he knew with a clarity that he would never forget, that he loved her. They left the beach and walked back through narrow streets, past low eaves and windows closed to the summer storm.

Michael drew her hand up to his lips and kissed it, 'I'm going to help you like you've helped me, I promise you.'

He drew swiftly, turning the page to look back, reaching for cigarette after cigarette, smoking them without looking up from his work. He wanted the conversion of the sail shed to be perfect. The Porthmeor studios had beamed roof space and skylights and chimneys for their wood stoves. The old sail-drying shed had the light and height Felicity needed, all Michael had to do was make sure it could accommodate screen-printing tables. The kitchen clock whirred and chimed before he put down his pencil. Arthur would be here any minute. He stretched in a shaft of sunlight in the hall. The sensual pleasure of the sun on his skin catapulted his thoughts to the night before. The bed a tangle of sheets, Felicity's slip silk soft on her thigh, shadows touching her breasts when he woke before dawn. The curtains were open, the moon rode high and fast above the sea, and the night sky was crafted for excitement. Michael looked at her a long time then, her hair curling like a mermaid's on the pillow, her face so peaceful in sleep. He kissed her, breathed her sweet breath, heard her gasp as he shifted his weight on top of her. Her arms opened, her back arched and she moved her hips towards him, skin soft like a peach, like sunshine, like a languorous river, like everything he'd ever loved or yearned for. Her hands were cool on his neck, in his hair, their faces were close together, eyes locked in the moonlight.

Michael heard a step, and with an effort brought his thoughts back to now, this morning and the studio. He strode to the open door.

'Morning Michael.' The gate swung shut behind the slight figure of Arthur Castleton. Michael jumped, reddening as if he had been caught in the act. Come to think of it, he had been, but only the act of thinking. To gain time, he ducked out into the little patch of front garden, looking over the road and down to the sea and walked a couple of steps away before turning to Arthur, patting his shirt pocket.

'Smoke?' he offered.

Arthur shook his head. He was breathing heavily. He mopped his face with a large handkerchief. 'I don't think I will. I've used myself up hill-climbing. It's a hot business coming up here on a warm day.' He limped over to Michael, his crippled leg stiff, his walk a swagger to compensate.

Michael nodded, lighting his own cigarette. 'Looks like rain at last,' he said. Both men surveyed the view towards Lizard Point.

Arthur squinted then clapped his hands together. 'Nothing we can ever do about the weather, is there? Better we try and do the things we can. So what's up here, Michael?'

'Come and take a look. We've got our work cut out, I reckon.'

Since forming the intention to make Felicity's studio, Michael had found a new sense of purpose to his days. He knew it wasn't permanent, he didn't belong here, he wasn't an artist and never would be, but nonetheless, he had changed. The Michael Marker who had left Norfolk for the war was idealistic and cerebral, with little experience of the world. Where was he now? Shed, like a snake's skin, somewhere far away and forgotten. Since his pre-war life within the cocoon of his family, he had seen much that he wanted to forget, and experienced enough to change him for ever. He was still changing. Life could turn, or end, on a sixpence, that much he knew, and little more. Right now, he was an important part of Felicity's world. He wasn't going home yet. Far from it, he was building his sweetheart this studio so that she could make the silk screens she needed for her fabric. His role was taking shape. A plan had been formulating as he and Arthur worked. He could build the structures, create the space that Felicity and her friends needed. He wasn't a bad carpenter, Arthur was good too. Michael liked his methodical approach and his unruffled demeanour. He opened the rotting door to the sail room. A pane of glass fell out of it, Arthur caught it before it shattered on the ground.

'This'll need taking off to fix up.' He placed the glass gently against the wall. He tapped at the door frame, frowned and moved inside to look at the whole room.

Michael followed him. 'We cleared it out the other day, the damp's drying out now we've lit that stove. Felicity's at work, but I hoped we could make some progress so that when she comes home she could use it?'

Arthur crouched to look at a hinge. He squinted up at Michael, 'You mean you've promised her?' He nodded into Michael's silence. 'We'll sort something out, and she'll be happy enough.' He passed a frame covered in cobwebs to Michael. 'Makes sense she'd want a studio for her work,' he said thoughtfully. 'Her mother was some kind of artist. Done a big painting in the library in Penzance of the *White Star* wreck. Way back in 1907 I think it was. They saved almost five hundred lives that day, and my grandfather was among the lifeboat men. It's a great painting. That Felicity'll be right talented I shouldn't wonder.'

'Yes, she'll make her mark,' said Michael, and pride stuffed his chest. Felicity, his sweetheart. A talented artist. She wasn't just his sweetheart. He lived in her house, they were lovers. No one seemed to bother that they weren't married, he couldn't imagine the same state of affairs in Norfolk. Michael thought of the drawings and small paintings Felicity was working on. She had canvasses propped on chairs and watercolour paper tucked under the corner of looking-glass frames around the house. Delicate illustrations sprung to life with colour and charm.

He was eager to talk about her, 'She's talented, all right. She wants to make a business out of her designs, and we've got a couple of hours today to get started on making some benches and shelves for her.'

'It's not a lot of time, but we can make a start.'

By lunchtime Arthur had patched up the crumbling roof beam, made good the door and had gone off to fetch a particular saw he needed for the shelving he would work on while Michael went to meet Felicity.

Up on the hill in the late afternoon, Michael lay and dozed, while Felicity, her painting finished, made new sketches, blurring the page with dots of coloured ink. He kept still for a minute or two when he awoke, enjoying the scratch of grasses and the solid earth warm beneath him. It wasn't sunny: hazy August heat beamed on to his skin and somewhere high above, a skylark sang. Beside him, Felicity's pictures filled half her sketchbook, quick flurries of colour, shapes as delicate as a cloud of butterflies. He didn't ask her what she was thinking. He rarely did, in case she asked him the same question. Today he'd intended to talk to her, but the peace of the scene, the fact that he knew the time was coming when he would have to go, the sheer pleasure of being with Felicity and knowing he loved her, all this stopped him. It could wait.

She closed the sketchbook and leaned over him. Freckles dusted the bridge of her nose and the top of her cheeks. Michael could never quite get over how beautiful she was. Whether it was something to do with Cornwall, or being an artist, he wasn't sure, but Felicity seemed to have a connection with the land and the sea and the weather. She thrived on it. Looking down at him now, her eyes were flecked amber and green like the dappled shade of beech trees. She had her bare legs crossed under her, but she shifted, shaking her skirt, rolling forward to lean on her elbows. Her limbs were tanned reddish gold, her legs were always bare, and the cool touch of her forearm, or a glimpse of the heart-shaped mole on her thigh could make his heart leap. He brushed a crumpled leaf off her shoulder and wound a lock of her hair around his thumb. It was glossy, dark as black treacle. Michael wondered if he was experiencing the beginning of an artistic sensibility within himself.

'I could paint you, I reckon. I've got an idea how I'd do it. I might draw you first.' As soon as the words were out, he wanted to unsay them, they were so foolish. Him! A painter. Absurd.

Felicity rolled over and lay next to him. 'Maybe you will,' she said. 'Anything can happen.'

Michael propped himself up to look at her. He kissed her nose, touched that she hadn't laughed away his thought. He knew he wouldn't really paint her, but he would always dream about it. The truth was, he didn't want to make art, he wanted to enjoy beauty. Felicity's beauty. This sense was new to him, but nothing he experienced with Felicity was like anything he had ever known.

'Come on, it's getting late. We should go home now. This sketchbook is finished, and I've got something I started drawing in the shop this morning I want to look at when we get home. What about you?'

Michael opened an eye, squinting through his lashes at her. She had a splash of ink shaped like a tiny butterfly on her forearm and another on her knee. Her thin dress, sprinkled with yellow flowers looked like part of the hillside.

'You belong here, don't you?' He sat up, blinking. He wasn't sure how long they'd been up here, but it had been a while.

Felicity jumped up from the grass, shaking herself. 'There are elf kings in Cornwall, you know,' she said, reaching to pull him up too. 'They live in the tin mines and have castles and kingdoms but humans can't see them. I belong with them. I'm going to put a spell on you one day, you wait and see, so you'll never want to leave.'

Michael laughed, 'You've already done that.'

Felicity didn't hear, she was running down the hill towards town.

In the weeks that followed, Michael found that he was happier than he had ever imagined he could be. He and Arthur finished building the screen-printing table and whitewashed the studio over three intense days where electric storms alternated with sultry sunshine. The air smelled of sawdust and wet paint when it didn't smell of damp, and any silence in that time rang with the thwack of hammers or the drum of raindrops on the roof.

When Michael swept the last of the wood shavings out of the studio, Felicity announced she was closing the bookshop for good. 'If I don't do it properly, I'll never know if it could have worked. What d'you think?' She was sitting on the new padded screen-printing table, swinging her bare legs and eating an apple. Pots of mixed dye stood in a row by the open door, and the studio danced with sunbeams and an air of anticipation.

'It's what I hoped.' Michael pulled a fleck of wood shaving from her hair, and she caught his hand between hers. Her skin was warm, she vibrated with life and energy. 'You can't be shut up in a bookshop all your life.'

She jumped down, pulling sketches off a shelf. 'I know what I'm going to do. It's this.' She waved a piece of board at him. 'Starting with three designs in four colourways. Look, here they are, Michael, I've got no excuse.'

He knew he was avoiding his own life again, for another slice of time, when he answered, 'I love them. I've got an idea. Let me sort out the bookshop for you while you keep this work up. I'll get them all catalogued for you to sell.'

Felicity threw the apple core into the flowerbed outside and began to select brushes from the earthenware pots on the windowsill.

'Maybe,' she said dreamily, but she wasn't really listening. Humming, she bent to sift through a wooden box full of paint tubes on the floor.

Everything was in its place. The paintbrushes were next to a pot of paint-covered palette knives, and Felicity had picked a scratchy bunch of sea lavender sprigs and plonked them in a third. She moved across the studio, picking things up, arranging them, making the space her own. She reminded him of a swallow, swooping back and forth to the eaves of the house so as to build a nest. Finally she piled a collection of white stones and a sea-bleached seal skull she and Michael had found on the beach. It had smelled of fish. Michael tried to discourage her from picking it up, but Felicity pretended not to notice. It was her favourite technique, he had begun to realise, for getting her own way. Now the ivory gleam of bone in the sunlight and the blue-grey shadow of sockets and hollows sat on the shelf, scrubbed clean by a summer outside, smelling of nothing.

He liked things that didn't smell of anything, they had no memories attached to them. The war had smelled of mud and rubble and death. Michael sometimes evoked a fragment of it in his thoughts or his nightmares, where it emerged cloying and chilly like a damp corner, generally hidden but not forgotten. Mousehole, by contrast, was breezy, and the air smelled of fish and sea and flowers, zest and hope. It smelled of safety. He loved the aroma of newly cooked bread in the mornings when, just after dawn, he passed the bakery on his way to work, his senses still suffused with the lingering intimacy of Felicity's scent when he had kissed her goodbye in their bedroom. The pub smell in the evenings when he and Felicity bicycled to Newlyn to meet some friends was exciting, run through with sawdust and yeasty hops, the lush whiff of a woman's perfume, a snatch of tobacco smoke in the air as a cigarette flared against the sulphurous spark of a match.

It was an easy habit, formed through the summer, and Michael liked the fact that he and Felicity fitted without effort into the group that met up in the Sword-fish. A few pints of beer, a game of darts or backgammon and people to talk to. In the pub, everyone had a story. For some, it was of a past they couldn't yet lay to rest. Paul Spencer had flown Hawker Hurricanes in the Western Desert during the war. His passion for flying blazed as strong as his art through his talk. Another painter, Kit Barker, leaned at the bar, a black eyepatch giving the air of a pirate to a man who, as a conscientious objector, had driven ambulances through Belgium during the war. Listening, discussing and tentatively putting forward his own thoughts, Michael found himself more in harmony with these people he was meeting and befriending than he had ever expected to feel again. Across the room, Felicity was at a table with Paul's wife Sheila. Their heads together, laughing. He loved Felicity to be happy, and he smiled and raised a silent toast to her before turning to take his turn at the dartboard.

Sometimes, in a quiet moment, he wondered how long he could continue living in this way. In his heart he knew that no matter how much he talked and laughed and bear-hugged his new friends, he was not one of them, he did not belong here, and his usefulness was limited. People came and went, it was the nature of the artists' colony, but Michael could see how they worked together, potters and sculptors exchanging equipment, collaborating with one another, writers, printmakers, painters, falling in love, setting up house, making art, creating exhibitions and bringing up children. No one had much money but, to Michael's mind, they all had a future he didn't share. How many studios and picture frames could he build? He was neither an artist, nor a skilled craftsman like Arthur. He was enjoying it, but it couldn't last indefinitely. He thought of home with a jolt one evening, when a chance remark revealed that some of the St Ives artists had spent time in Norfolk one summer before the war. A connection he hadn't anticipated, breaching the distance from home to here in an instant. He swallowed a whisky chaser after his beer, swilling the liquor to try and lose the metallic taste of guilt.

It was a Thursday evening in September. Michael had harvested a crop of asters, and decided he didn't much care for them. The pink and purple petals seemed lurid to him, the centre of each flower an offensive egg-yolk yellow. He laughed at himself. Here he was, a soldier back from war, the epitome of stalwart masculinity, fussing around with bunches of flowers. He took the asters to Penzance station, boxed and piled for the London train. Having passed them over to the stationmaster, he walked into the pub across the road from the station in search of Arthur, who had said he would like a lift home. He found him, sleeves rolled up, a pint of Guinness in front of him, with the newspaper. Arthur had been making wooden plinths for sculptors in St Ives, and he drank his beer with the air of someone who had earned every drop of it.

'Blast me!' he said when he saw Michael, his top lip decorated with creamy foam. 'Some of those women artists are hard work.' He rolled a cigarette and lit it, drawing deeply. 'Had to make a sodding great stage for their bronzes, and then they were all shouting about how wrong it was that there had to be steps. But if they want to get up to them, they had to have steps. One of them walks with a stick, for God's sake, she can't just spring up on to a stage.' He ground his cigarette under his boot. 'I left them arguing about it. Reckon it'll all be forgotten next time I go back over there. S'always the same with those sculptresses.'

Michael nodded, 'Seems that making art is a lot more complicated than I thought. Felicity doesn't get angry, but it's as though a curtain falls and she disappears. She forgets everything when she's working.'

Arthur nudged him. 'Neglected are you? Let's head for the pub back in Mousehole and we'll catch up with some of my buddies. We're finalising the team for the cricket match against St Erth, d'you reckon you'd be up for playing?'

'For sure, you can count on me,' said Michael, flushing, happy to be included. This was what he was missing. Friendships, cricket, a life in common. It would be there at home in Norfolk, it was everywhere that families lived, children grew up and people went out into the world. And came back.

The thing about Felicity was that she didn't talk about practicalities or plans, she wasn't interested. She just wanted to mix dye and make patterns. She was absorbed, and he knew her well enough now to understand that she was happy whether he was there or not. Her work was what drove her. She was working until dark every night, and the designs were becoming more intricate and beautiful. Themed around the sea, she had made flowing patterns of seahorses and cockle shells, birds and fish, sometimes closely detailed, some more abstract, all dancing on paper and fabric that she hung around the studio. Michael was sure she would sell them if she wanted to. She sidestepped any conversation about the future, or even the present, if it was about their relationship. He liked it like that. She didn't scrutinise his motives, she didn't cross-examine him. She was, as she teased him, from another world and the lack of demands from her were helping him heal his confused and anguished memories.

The working day in Mousehole was over, shop windows were being shuttered as side doors opened and families spilled on to the street. Here a woman sweeping a step, there a child pulling a wooden dog ran across the cobbled street. Michael breathed a deep sigh. The salty seaweed air in his nostrils tingled with exhilaration. Arthur was sunburned, his sleeves rolled up above arms that showed the strength his legs might have had. He rolled a cigarette and passed his tin to Michael. 'You'll be taking Felicity to the summer barn dance on Saturday?'

Michael looked up quickly. 'Yes, of course. Yes, we're going to the dance. Are you?'

Arthur sighed. 'Hmph. That's something. Me? Got no one to take. Got no missus, have I?' He stood up and crossed the road to the quay. The fishermen had lifted everything that was coming off their boat into a small tender and were landing alongside the harbour wall. Arthur called to the younger one of them, and reached a hand for the rope.

'Hey, Diccon, you got much of a catch today?'

'Nothing to make a song and dance of, that's for sure.' Diccon had curly black hair and a red face, even redder than usual now after a day at sea. 'What's the plan for Saturday? You umpiring?'

Arthur grunted affirmation, the fisherman nodded back. 'Tide's in the morning, so I should be back for the second half if you need me?'

'Come on, Diccon, we'll never be home for tea if you keep us talking,' the older man threw rope in a coil into the hull of the boat.

Michael shivered. The sea was swallowing the orange orb of the sun, and long shadows hung like cloaks on the hills above the village. He stood up stiffly, and took the empty glasses into the bar. Arthur had gone with the fishermen, hadn't said goodbye, just wandered down the village street. He could see him now at the far end of the harbour, talking to Diccon and his brother outside a white painted cottage where they were spreading their net across the garden wall. He waved. Arthur waved back. It was time for him to go and talk to Felicity.

She wasn't in the house or the studio. Michael stood in the room he'd made and looked around, his hands in his pockets, relishing the white light bouncing around him, the cat curled tight like an anemone on a cushion by the stove, and a spray of buddleia arching a silver green leaf towards the mauve spearhead in a jam jar on the windowsill. There was a smell of paint, and an acrid aroma of rubber, and on the table, daubed painted marks were building up a patina of colour on the worktop so the studio already had an atmosphere of industry. From where he stood he could see Felicity in the garden, hanging flapping bits of fabric on the washing line. Strung between the walnut tree and a post Michael had slammed into the ground with a mallet, the washing was not domestic. The swooping clothes line resembled a canopy from a medieval painting, hung with celebratory flags becoming bolder and more beautiful the more Felicity pegged out the fluttering squares of madder rose and indigo cotton she had made.

She secured the last one and turned to Michael. 'Look, these are almost finished I think. I tried a new technique today and it worked!' She came towards him for a kiss. He noticed her hair was held up by a small spear-like paintbrush.

'Looks ready for a couple of knights to do some jousting,' he joked.

'Jousting?' Confused, Felicity spun round. Michael pulled the brush out and her hair tumbled down her back with a swish that sent a shiver through him.

He waved the brush. 'Yeah, you know, banners, this little miniature lance, colour, music, pageantry. It's exciting.'

'I'm your lady fair,' Felicity danced a few steps and curtseyed to him, then rose and snaked her arm around his neck, 'and you're my valiant knight,' she whispered.

Music curled out of the studio behind him, the click of the gramophone needle like a beat in time with the floating jazz hanging in the air. Michael wanted the moment printed on to his memory like one of Felicity's linocuts. He needed it etched and pressed and stamped safe in his mind, where it would never fade, but would shape itself to fit him wherever he was and who ever he became, close to his heart, for ever. His pulse flew. He should have told her before. The beat of adrenalin opened a throttle, the muscles in his neck knotted, and he swallowed, pressing his lips to the top of Felicity's head, touching the soft fragrant mass of her hair.

This was nothing like the bombast of war, nothing here to haunt him, and yet this anxiety was grimly familiar, tightening inside him, stringing his nerves like banjo wires, and unleashing his blood so it fizzed and pounded through his veins. He hadn't realised how far he had moved from this old lurching pattern of fear and anticipation. Felicity had saved him, he could never forget that, and he was about to hurt her. His throat was dry, he wished he'd drunk more in the pub with Arthur. Brandy would have done the trick.

'What's the matter?' Her face was lustrous, happiness chased in the delicate lines of her smile. 'You look like you've seen a ghost.' Her hands were covered in ink. As usual. She leaned on him lightly, her chin on his shoulder, and rubbed her finger along the buckle of his belt. 'Verity came up today with a pie she baked, so lucky, as I don't know what we would have eaten otherwise, I've been lost in this all day.'

Michael pulled her against him, pressing his face in her neck, shuffling to be closer, her hip hard against him, her body fitting his like a glove. It was time. It wasn't the right time, but it was time. 'There's something I should have told you, Felicity.'

She pulled away, arching her back to see his face, keeping close.

She smiled. 'You look so anxious, darling, please don't worry,' she cupped his face in her blue-stained hands. 'It's funny you should say that, you know,' she was whispering, her lips close to his ear, 'because there's something I should have told you too.'

CHAPTER 9

'What the hell?' Kit braked hard. He didn't need roadkill on his conscience. A moorhen and her three chicks, black like ink blots, legs a red blur, dashed along the white line in the middle of the road before swerving into the undergrowth. He watched the leaves quiver and close behind her then a movement shimmered between the trees and he noticed cricketers spread in front of a rickety pavilion, and a mown pitch. He'd always liked the thought of village cricket, but he'd never got round to joining a team. Travel, work, running in circles just to keep up with life. It didn't matter what the excuses were, he'd always been too busy, too keen on going it alone. Ironic, considering how much of his business was about building the team spirit. Hannah, his PA, never stopped arranging trips and bonding experiences for the employees of Lighthouse Fabrics. And here he was, by chance, at a Norfolk cricket match. Was this another epiphany? Why not? He'd stop and watch the game for a bit. Where was the harm?

Parking in a hedge opening, he wandered through to the cricket ground in time to see a wicket fall. The stumps flew and a beefy batsman trundled back to the pavilion, red-faced, hair flattened to his forehead under his helmet, the fractured smile of defeat shiny beneath a film of sweat. The next man walked out on to the pitch, clapping a friendly hand on the shoulder of his teammate. They nodded as they passed one another.

Kit had always subscribed to the belief that self-sufficiency was the ideal, but life had become solitary. He pulled a toothpick from a row of them clamped like a pointed fence in a cardboard packet and bit down. The cinnamon taste spread reassuringly, and he sauntered towards a cluster of people standing near the old shed. Sorry, make that the pavilion. Until coming to Norfolk to get to grips with his Lighthouse, he'd been subconsciously shedding stuff. Possessions, even people. No girlfriend. Sure, there had been the odd date, an occasional weekend, but no one serious enough to introduce to his friends. He'd thought he didn't want that intimacy. Couldn't be bothered with it. He had felt comfortably selfish, securing himself, after Felicity had died, in a world where he called the shots and he knew the way.

His phone pinged with a text. Pulling it out of his pocket he squinted at the screen.

How old is your car?

It was from Luisa.

He typed Very, then added a kiss. Then deleted it again and sent the message. Another chimed back, straight away, What do you know about rust?

'Get off the pitch!' A man in a white coat and brimmed hat gestured with his thumb, his facial muscles a shrug of astonished righteousness. Kit, legging it, almost ran straight into the next batsman walking in. It was Luca.

'Hey,' he put on his helmet, brushing Kit's shoulder with a clumsy gloved hand.

'Good luck,' Kit turned on his heel to watch Luca take his place at the wicket.

Thank God he'd deleted the kiss from his message to Luisa, he thought, and sent another one:

At cricket with Luca. Why r u not here?

No going back from a sent text. The cinnamon taste in his mouth reminded him that there might be coffee here somewhere. His toothpick was chewed to a splinter, he spat it onto the ground, encountering a severe look from an elderly lady perching, parrot-like, on a red plastic chair. He nodded a greeting and hurried past her. At the pavilion, a line of chairs and a picnic rug were occupied by cricket bags, cool boxes and a few spectators. Luca faced his first ball and the crack of the bat rang out.

'Don't you think it's a bit like duelling?'

'Duelling?' Kit repeated blankly. A woman in a yellow dress had got up from a rug to clap.

'You know, two men face one another over a short distance and fire. I just thought the bat sounded like a shot. Of a gun.' She swooped to pick up a daisy chain she'd dropped to clap. 'Well done, Lux,' she called as another shot cracked into the sky.

'It's a four.' Kit clapped too. 'I see what you mean,' he agreed. 'The clearing, the wooded surroundings. Should be pistols at dawn, but bats at midday is in the same spirit, I guess.'

A small girl cartwheeled on the rug beside Kit and pulled at the woman's sleeve. 'Mummy what did he do? Why didn't he run?'

'Oh, they're always running or not running,' murmured the mother. Kit stared at her dress. He blinked. Yellow crêpe de Chine, bright silk-covered buttons and tiny orange feathers tumbling across the fabric. Unmistakable. And rare. It was a Lighthouse design from the 1970s. The woman caught him staring and held out her hand in greeting.

Kit shook it, her skin was cool. 'Hi,' she smiled. 'I think you must be Kit? You're Lou and Tom's new friend.'

Kit must have looked surprised, she dropped her hand on to his arm, 'Don't worry, it's just village life, we don't have enough to talk about. I'm Dora, by the way, Tom's sister.'

'Tom? Oh yes. Luisa told me about you. Well they both did.'

In his pocket, his phone buzzed, he didn't dare get it out, too embarrassing if it was a text from Luisa.

'This might sound odd,' he said, 'but I'm curious about the dress you're wearing. Where did you get it?'

Dora giggled. 'That's a new opening line,' she said, and lowered her voice. 'The old biddies are peering at us, I'm always in trouble for making too much noise, bet they think something worth watching is about to happen. Why d'you ask, by the way?'

Kit laughed. 'It's Seventies. My mother designed that fabric in collaboration with Biba. Not many were made. I gave one to the Costume Museum in Bath about three years ago. It was so tiny they had to use a child's mannequin to show it. Silk crêpe, bias cut and far too many buttons for nowadays. Where did you get it?'

Dora looked down at herself. 'I'm a props buyer, so I go to a lot of vintage fairs. Funnily enough, this came from one down in Bristol.' She smoothed the dress over her hips and sucked her stomach in. 'I love it,' she said, then blinked at him. 'You're from that neck of the woods, Lou said?'

'Yes, Penzance, bit further than Bristol,' Kit said. 'Makes more sense for one of these to appear in the west country than at a Norfolk cricket match.' His mind raced through an imagined conversation between Dora and Luisa where he featured in an excellent light. Was she coming here?

'Really? I love Bristol, don't get anywhere like that much now.' Dora raked a hand through her hair and sighed. Kit hoped she was not about to unburden herself, although there was the hope that she might talk about Luisa.

'So you're old friends with Tom and Luisa?' he sat down on the rug beside Dora.

She raised her sunglasses and narrowed her eyes. 'Old friends is one way of putting it. Or you could say, as I just did, that I'm Tom's sister.' The sunglasses clamped down again and she raised her chin. Clearly a girl who was used to having a man hang on her words.

Kit laughed, 'Sorry, yes, of course, you did. I was side-tracked by the dress. So do you live nearby?'

Dora's nostrils flared. He watched uneasily. She could go either way. Cross, or not. After a moment she sighed, and although she ignored his question, she didn't appear actively cross. 'Your mother was the designer? That's fascinating. I've come across Lighthouse Fabrics a lot over the years. Tell me, though, how do you catalogue your archive? Luisa and I googled the company, but it was difficult to see it all.'

'Luisa? Did she? I mean, did you?' The nostrils flared again. Dora chewed her lip.

Kit realised he was sounding over-eager. 'Yes, our archive. It's a headache, frankly, but of course we do it. Next month, when I get back to Cornwall, we'll be putting the whole thing in order. In a new order.' A shout from the pitch flew high as a fielder lunged to catch a shot and landed heavily. Kit winced. 'Ouch, seems a pretty hard-hitting match. Which team are you on?'

Dora smiled. 'Luca's team, of course! But I'm not really into cricket. I'm meeting Luisa here. Maddie

211

loves coming to watch, although it's the picnic and the play area rather than the performances.'

Luca hit another shot low towards the boundary, a fielder raced in pursuit. 'Luisa's coming is she?' Kit simply couldn't resist repeating her name. The sibilant syllables thrummed in the air above the picnic rug. He sneaked a glance at his phone. He had to roll off the rug, crushing some of Maddie's daisies, so Dora didn't see the message.

On way, how great you are there.

Luckily Dora wasn't looking. She was fishing about in a wicker basket from which she pulled a bag of carrot sticks and a pot of green paste. 'Have some,' she urged. 'Luisa's bringing cucumber sorbet, she's obsessed with making ice cream, you know.' Dora bit into a carrot stick, putting more on a plate for Maddie with cheese and a packet of crisps. 'I've got a few other vintage dresses, you know, I mean ones with the Lighthouse label in them.' She broke off. 'Maddie, come and eat this. Where was I? Oh, it doesn't matter. Oh yes, it's just that I always thought they must have been made by an artist, they have such unusual detail. I've got one with butterfly nets and shrimps. It's one of the nicest dresses I own.'

'We do the fabrics really, not the clothes,' he said. 'That's what we sell, and that's what Mum sold. I've worked in the business all my life, travelled with it, and lived and breathed it. When my mother died I took it over.'

'Look, Mummy!' Maddie jumped up from her picnic. Luca's batting triumph had ended on a catch. He walked in dragging his bat.

'Luca Ducca! You . . . Are . . . Out!' she shouted. 'Come on and let's play over here!'

Luca flicked her cheek. 'Shh! Don't tell everyone,' he whispered.

'You can't hide it,' she said severely. 'But you can play with me now.'

'I will if you get me a drink. There's some Coke in there, Mads,' Luca folded himself into a chair and squinted at Kit. 'How's the Lighthouse?'

'Pretty good, thanks.' Kit offered a carrot stick, Luca shook his head. 'I'm still besieged by farm animals. Those sheep your parents took away seem to have been replaced by a herd of piglets. Apparently they've come to do some digging in a kind of compound just outside my gate.'

Luca rolled a cigarette and lit it. 'Yeah, it's like that around here. There are way more animals than people, you know, and if you think about it, where you live in the Lighthouse, most of your neighbours are fish.'

Kit's laughter made Dora turn her head. 'Luisa's here. Hope everyone's hot. She was telling me earlier that she's bringing her gooseberry and ginger ice cream. I hope she has – it's incredible. It's in a weird metal hand cart thing she says she bought on eBay. I wonder if it'll keep it cold or just give everyone Legionnaires' Disease?'

Luca rolled his eyes, and sighed. 'Oh no. Mum

said she'd got some sort of mobile stall she was threatening to bring. I hoped it wouldn't happen.'

Kit looked round and saw her. Luisa had positioned herself in the shade by the pavilion. She had rolled up the sleeves of her purple shirt and kicked off her shoes. A queue had already formed around her, and she looked in her element as she scooped pale green ice cream into bright pink wafers.

'I'm just going to say hello to your mother,' he told Luca.

'Good idea, I'll come too.'

They got up and made their way towards Luisa.

'I know it's not a proper cone, but it tastes like one,' she was saying to a suspicious pair of boys. 'You can just taste the cucumber sorbet if you like?'

'It looks a bit weird,' muttered one.

'Yeah, I'd prefer a Magnum,' said the other.

Kit had a powerful desire to bang their heads together. He made do with scowling. He was almost breathless with anticipation as he approached Luisa. His gaze flickered from her face to the crumpled shirt, the worn belt defining her waist. Her arms. She had piled her hair up and held it in place with a pencil. His mother had always used a paintbrush in her hair. How funny, he'd never noticed anyone else do that. He shoved his hands in his pockets and twisted around in a circle. As he turned back, Luisa shrieked, dropped the scoop and stepped back.

'Bugger, I'll do you another,' she said to the small girl who was looking doubtfully at her ice cream, upside down on the grass.

'Mum quite often seems to spill it when we're around,' Luca commented.

'Does she always make such an effort?' Kit was mesmerised. Luisa popped a raspberry on to a mound of ice cream and gave the cone to the child.

'Yeah, you can't stop Mum. Ice cream's her thing. She can do anything with it. She used to make it in castle shapes with dragons and stuff for our birthdays when we were kids. Her hands would go blue.' Luca stretched his fingers in front of him as if to check the colour of his own extremities. Kit did the same. Blue fingers, quite some dedication, he thought.

'Once she fainted and we had to put a hot-water bottle on her head, but nothing stops her. I felt a bit sorry for her that we got too old for pirate parties and stuff. Her talent needs more scope.'

'Or scoop?' suggested Kit.

Luca laughed. 'Scoop or scope. Whatever, she's obsessed. Maybe you should get her to cook for your party? Are you really having one? The Lighthouse is the coolest venue ever.'

Luca's sweet-natured enthusiasm charmed him. 'I'm going to make it a painting party,' he announced, surprising himself as much as those around him. 'I've got to get the place decorated for the new tenants, and so far all the local decorators I've contacted are booked up or they say they can't do curved rooms.' Kit nodded to himself. The plan was falling into place. It hadn't been a plan at all, but it was now. 'So I was thinking,' he said, thinking it there and then, 'that if I ask people to come and help me paint, we could have a big feast with music and plenty of drink afterwards. It'd be the Lighthouse whitewash party, I suppose.'

'Cool,' said Luca. The monosyllable was the seal of approval Kit needed. 'I'll come.'

Dora had wandered over to them. 'I'm dying to see it, and I like the idea of painting a round room.'

'Just about anything you do is fun if you do it in a round room,' agreed Luisa, who had made a beeline for Luca with an overflowing cone. She licked her fingers. The ice cream and Luisa's lips were deep pink. 'Quick, you've got to try this. Dive in before it melts.' Luca took the ice cream.

Maddie had been surreptitiously sipping Coke from a plastic cup. She waved it at Luca. 'Here you are. Sorry. Most of the Coke fell out.' She looked at Kit, weighing him up. 'Can I come to the Lighthouse party? I've always wanted to go to one of those.'

He rested a hand on her head, then snatched it away again. Who was he to go around patting children's heads? 'Everyone can come,' he said.

'Mum, you can make the dinner,' Luca suggested. He nudged Kit towards the pavilion, 'Come on, mate, I'll introduce you to some more of the team, they'll come and paint.'

By the time Kit left the cricket ground, his party was shaping up, and a summer storm had turned the sky a hectic purple. The Lighthouse was a magnet, everyone knew it, and everyone wanted to see inside it. Next Saturday was mooted, and free beer mentioned, and suddenly the whole cricket team wanted to meet Kit. He had more friends in an hour in Norfolk than he'd made back home in years. Watching Luisa negotiate her car out of the gateway, scraping her bumper, the orange parasol fluttering out of the car window, speckled by rain, Kit was bemused. Where was Tom? The ice-cream stand had taken three of them to load, and it still looked as though it might fall off at any moment. What sort of man leaves his wife to heave great metal contraptions around on her own? Reversing on to the road he looked out of his back window and flinched with embarrassment. Luisa's grass-stained plimsolls were on the back seat. He'd picked them up, and without thinking he must have put them in his car in the rush to be done before the rain came. Driving with one hand on the wheel, he got his phone out and wrote her a text.

Kidnapped your shoes. Will return.

He put his phone away, turning the windscreen wipers to their fastest setting. Lightning flashed, and he imagined Luisa running barefoot across storm-drenched grass from the car to her house. She would be soaked.

Sunday dawned bright after a night of storms, Kit rolled over and squinted at the face of his watch. 'Christ!' He leapt up. Almost ten o'clock, he hadn't slept this late for years. Downstairs he made coffee, padding around the ground floor. 'You could call it the round floor,' he mused. The curved walls, the red stripes and the limitless views of his dwelling had lost none of their charm or surprise. It was like living in a cartoon. He flung open the double doors, blinking, juggling his sunglasses and the coffee while he switched on his mobile phone. Would there be a message?

'Morning.'

'Shit! Ow!' Hot coffee splashed Kit's wrist as he leapt back. He didn't know whether to focus on the torrent of buzzing from his phone or the two people in his garden. The individuals fiddling with a fence post just metres from the door watched calmly as Kit dropped his phone and stepped back into the hall. He was only wearing his jeans, and they were covered in coffee. His phone vibrated helplessly from the stone doorstep. The younger of the two men stepped forward to pick it up, wiping it on the sleeve of his T-shirt, and offered it through the open door to Kit.

It chimed again. 'You're popular,' he said. 'We've mended the gaps in your boundary this morning.' He proffered a muddy hand, 'Jay Hopkins. That's my dad, Bruce.' Bruce wiped his forehead on a big handkerchief. Behind him, two pigs sniffed at the wheels of the pick-up truck the Hopkinses had parked.

'Pigs. Yes, of course, the pigs,' said Kit. 'I'm never far from a farm animal at the Lighthouse,' he raised his coffee cup to Bruce. 'I'll get dressed and be right with you.'

Jay remained on the doorstep. 'We would've asked you where you'd like the opening, but you didn't stir out of the house and we didn't want to wake you.'

Kit coughed. Nowhere to go with this one. He'd been asleep. Not that they seemed bothered. His phone vibrated again. Amazing how a supposedly inanimate object could be so imperious.

You solved my shoe mystery . . . How much is ransom? x L

His thumb hovered to respond straight away, but he stopped. Better get dressed. Bruce and Jay, having peered past him through the open doors, had seen enough.

'You're all right,' said Bruce kindly. 'No rush. We'll be off now anyway. You know where we are if you need anything?'

'Now you mention it,' said Kit, his hand on the open window of the truck, 'I don't suppose you know where I can get hold of a few trestle tables for Saturday?'

'We'll sort you out there, no worries,' said Bruce.

Alone again, Kit texted Luisa.

Shoe ransom urgent! Food for 20 including ice cream of your choice. Deliver Saturday in person. X

No sooner sent than regretted. The last part came under the heading 'Going too Far'. 'Self-control is all,' he remembered, too late. 'Think before you act.' As if this gave him licence, he then sent another text to Luisa.

Seriously though, feast required. How much do you charge?

An answer pinged back.

Lighthouse Ices under starter's orders! Do you need a slave girl?

Lighthouse Ices? Good idea. Perhaps it could become a subsidiary of Lighthouse Fabrics. It could be the moment to have a business conversation with Luisa. The prospect was a lot more appealing than talking to his accountants. He tapped in his reply and sent it.

Kit didn't have any expectations of his party. Secretly, he hadn't believed anyone would come, but escorted by Luca and Mae, at Luisa's suggestion, he had gone to Steddings, the Blythe hardware store, and bought quantities of sandpaper, filler, paintbrushes, rollers, tins of paint, masking tape and dust sheets. Just in case. Early on the appointed morning, he looked at the pile of decorating materials and laughed. Who was he kidding?

How could he have been idiot enough to think that he, Kit, a newcomer, could ask a community to give up their time for little more than a square meal? And where was that, come to think of it? He'd left three messages for Luisa, and heard nothing. His back ached from lugging furniture around. He had a banked-up series of emails from Cornwall, politely asking what decisions he would like taken in his absence, and whether the meetings that loomed with the accountants should be rescheduled to allow him time to recover from his 'sabbatical'. The disdain was palpable. Kit ignored it, but he couldn't ignore the question that beat in his own mind. What on earth was he doing here?

It was a sunny morning, and he thought he could hear a skylark. Kit shoved the decorating materials outside, left the front door unlocked, just in case, and took himself off for a walk. He needed to think.

He returned just before ten o'clock to find people in his garden, the trestle tables promised by Jay and Bruce set up in a horseshoe, and Luisa picking corn-flowers and arranging them in jam jars.

'I didn't think you were coming,' he found himself flinging his arms wide and then hugging her in greeting.

Luisa's eyes widened, but she kissed him on the cheek, smiled, and stepped back. 'Hi, there. We didn't think you were here.'

Kit rubbed his hands through his hair, hiding confusion by keeping his eyes on the ground. 'Sorry. Sorry, I don't know what—'

Luisa touched his arm. 'Don't worry, we weren't going to leave you in the lurch, you know.'

Kit looked up at the Lighthouse. All the windows were open, he could hear voices from each floor. 'I really didn't expect this—'

Luisa handed him a bacon sandwich. 'Here, I saved you one.'

He bit into it and groaned, the bread soft and light around salty, crumbly bacon and a sliver of butter. 'Bloody delicious,' he said.

'We didn't know if you were here this morning, so we started anyway. I hope you don't mind.'

'No. Please. Amazing.' He spoke through a mouthful, and was about to offer her a cup of tea when she turned on her heel, calling over her shoulder, 'I've got a lot to finish off, I'll be back later.'

By lunchtime, the top room was painted. Kit found Luisa, barefoot again, fanning herself and sitting on a straw bale, eating an apple.

'Ah. No shoes.' He sat down next to her. 'I'd better return them.'

She wriggled her toes in the grass. 'I've got to try to be less of a gypsy,' she turned towards him, flipping up her sunglasses. A fleck of paint on her cheek ran into her hair. He was reaching out to wipe it before he realised what he was doing.

'Paint. You've got paint on your face.' Just in time he'd managed to divert his thoughts, and point instead of touch her.

'Have I? Where?' Luisa grimaced, held her sunglasses in front of her and rubbed at her skin. The half moons at the base of her nails were pale. Her teeth were white and even, she smelled of sunshine and fresh paint.

She was speaking, he realised, and he wasn't listening, 'What? Yes. Yes. Whatever you like. I'm with you entirely.'

Luisa giggled. 'I was asking if you've got a favourite bedroom lined up.' She didn't wait for his answer. 'I really love this place, you've made it yours so quickly.

I hardly know why we're painting it, to be honest. It's so pretty already. Where did you get all the furniture?'

'That's a compliment.' Kit shifted as he peered into the basket she had at her side. 'I can't take a lot of credit though, the stuff was mostly here, I just hauled it out of the shed, and then made a return visit to that junk shop I told you about, and another about three miles further on. They're good here, really good.'

Luisa drummed her fists on her knees. 'Oh, I wish I'd known!' she cried. 'I'd have come with you. I *love* that kind of shopping, I'm looking for fifties Formica for my van, to put outside and create a kind of cafe atmosphere.'

'Ah, now I may be able to help you,' Kit raised an eyebrow at her and flicked through the photos on his phone. 'I saw this yesterday at another place. The chairs are piled up at the back. I really like the colour, don't you?'

'Oh look!' Luisa had swooped to see the screen. 'That green is great. I'd love to look at them.'

'I'll take you. Just name the day.'

'Name the day for what?' Both Kit and Luisa jumped as Tom appeared in front of them. He dropped a hand on Luisa's shoulder. 'Anything to drink, Tod?'

Luisa returned Kit's phone to him. 'Thank you, I will.' She pressed his forearm briefly and leaned to rummage in a basket at her side. She pulled out a bottle of water with a flourish. 'God, it's hot today isn't it? The paint'll be dry after lunch. Oops, missed!' A splash ran down her hand as she passed Tom the bottle. She licked the water off the back of her hand. Kit's gaze flicked between her mouth and her eyes, then rested on Tom.

The day softened to dusk as a fluid riff of saxophone notes drifted out of Luca's speakers, and the bats began their habitual swooping dance around the Lighthouse. Kit was exhausted. He had painted two round ceilings single-handed and countless small window frames, never exactly part of any of the teams at work, but joining in everywhere he could find a space and a spare paintbrush. With Mae's help, he'd dragged straw bales into position, and now the table was ready, covered with sheets and decorated with the jars of cornflowers. Sparks shot through pluming smoke as Luisa lit the barbecues. Kit found her wielding a blow torch at a metal brazier. 'That looks serious,' he said.

'It's meant for crème brûlée,' Luisa twisted her hair off her neck with her free hand, and leaned over the fire. 'I don't know why people bother with matches.'

'Let me help you.' Luisa's neck was damp, tendrils of hair catching in her earrings, the light catching her fine gold chain. Gilding the lily, Kit thought. Taking the blow torch from her, he moved to the next brazier. 'I love the smell of woodsmoke, don't you?'

She nodded, gazing into the flames. 'I'd like to find a way to have a fire on board the ice-cream van.'

Kit blinked. 'Really?'

'I was thinking about the elements. You know:

earth, fire, water, air. All that, and I thought I could make something work so I could make bacon sandwiches and marshmallows as well as ice cream.' She balanced a log on the fire he had just lit and they moved to the last brazier.

'Why not?' Kit had been ready to laugh, now, he found, he was ready to help her. 'You could do it. You need a bit of a business plan to get your ideas harnessed, but it sounds good to me. You'll be up and running before you can blink.'

'Really?' There was a note of hope in her voice that he found endearing.

'Really,' he smiled. 'I tell you what, I'll get my company manager to give you a call and talk you through the strategies you need. Don't worry, it's not impossible, you know.'

A smile fluttered briefly across her face. 'I keep getting stuck. Somehow it never gets off the ground,' she said. 'It's really great hearing what you think, after all, you actually run a business, so you know from the heart what it's like.'

'Hey Mum, can you come and see if these are done?' Mae called from where she was turning sausages over the fire.

Luisa sighed. 'I'd love to talk to you about this again?' she said. 'If it isn't too tiresome?'

'It would be a pleasure,' he said. 'I think you've got a great idea.'

The radiance of the smile she gave him left Kit reeling as she walked away.

Snatches of chatter fell from the windows above.

'Wow, have you seen this room. It's a lot better now.'

'Look, you can see right the way down the coast. Yarmouth looks like Las Vegas tonight.'

The voice was Dora's. He liked Dora. Earlier in the evening he'd found her by herself, cross-legged on a patch of grass near the clifftop, facing the sunset. She looked up when she heard him.

'Hi, this is a really peaceful place you know.'

Kit gazed back towards the building, figures grouped, music and laughter drifting around them.

'I know, I can't take any credit,' he said, 'it seems to have its own energy. Life force, even.'

Dora nodded. 'It's true. There are people like that, you know, who just make a difference by showing up. Who change things.'

Kit was curious. 'Change things?'

Dora sat down again, wrapped her arms around her knees. 'I was in love with someone like that,' she said.

'Hey, Mummy!' Maddie appeared out of the dark and pounced down on the grass, breathless. 'You know I'm having a striped house when I grow up, even if it's not as tall as this one. I'm going to be a lighthouse keeper and make sure it stays lit up for ever.' She leapt up and danced away again.

'Maddie's already one of those people,' said Kit.

Dora smiled. 'I met Aaron when Maddie was two. He taught music technology at a university out to the east of London, and used to cycle there.'

Kit stretched out on the grass next to her, her

profile outlined against the sunset. Pretty girl, he thought, and wondered what the magical element was that made him fancy Luisa and see Dora as a nice friend.

She had hunched up her shoulders. 'A lorry hit him on a roundabout in Silvertown. In the inquest the driver said he never saw him, it was as if he was a phantom already.'

Kit winced. 'When was this?'

'Oh five years ago, a bit more.' Dora stood up and shrugged, lightening the mood as she listened to a melody breaking from the speakers by the Lighthouse. She gestured towards the sound. 'I always thought Aaron would have written a song about it if he hadn't been the person who—'

Kit had squeezed her hand. 'He was a keeper of the flame. A good thing to be, unforgettable.'

Nodding, Dora squeezed his hand back.

Kit had, for a while, lost sight of Dora and Maddie in the melee after that, but when he glimpsed her in the throng, he felt both protective and appreciative. He had, he thought, made a friend.

By eleven, the party was in full swing. Luca and another lad his age had climbed out at the top below the Lighthouse glass, and wedged themselves between the rail and the light. They had binoculars, and their commentary floated down to Kit. 'This is like reality TV. Look. Here comes Jay Hopkins, back from a slash behind the tree.'

'Yeah, and he's forgotten his flies.'

'I said it was reality TV.'

Below, Kit laughed to himself. Out in the firelight, Mae turned up the music.

No curtains on any of the windows, but Kit had a strong sense that it was late when he woke on Sunday morning. Groaning, he reached for the glass of water he habitually placed next to his bed. It wasn't there. God, he must have been drunk. He dragged himself to the window and looked out at the remnants of the party. It was messy. Decadent, but also rustic. He'd never seen himself as one to embrace bucolic life, but that, like much else, appeared to have changed. The wheelbarrow which had contained the beer barrel had tipped over, allowing the barrel to roll drunkenly into a table, tipping it up in a trail of chaos. The cloak of unreality brought by a hangover was a blessing, he thought, peering at the ketchup-smeared plates dotted around the grass, and on the wall. He felt no anxiety as he noticed glasses half full of forgotten drinks, smoke blackened storm lanterns or the dish of butter wiped to a smear and decorated with cigarette butts. He pulled on a shirt and jeans, adding sunglasses as a precaution before he left the bedroom. He couldn't see a thing to navigate the stairs, but he was damned if he was going to take them off, the light was sure to be bright outside. He staggered down, holding on to the walls. He found he still wanted to dance. He had danced for the first time in God knows how many years, and from the moment Luisa pulled him to his feet and got him moving, he'd loved it. Thank

God the neighbours had been there, or they might have called the police.

Bruce Hopkins had made something of an entrance, walking up through the blue flax field in a yellow suit as the sun set behind him. Maddie thought the yellow suit made him look like the Cowardly Lion in *The Wizard of Oz*, and Kit couldn't get the image out of his head. Whether the image, or the drink had made him more comfortable with Bruce, he'd ended up with his neighbour among a circle sitting around the dying embers of the fire, swapping bike versus vintage car stories. Bruce, he vaguely remembered, had been surprised to hear Kit's mother had no known connection to the area. He was insistent that no one could just randomly own a lighthouse, especially a woman from the other side of the country. Kit couldn't remember how they'd left it, but he had a feeling Bruce would be looking for some answers and, come to think of it, he wouldn't mind some himself. That could all wait. Right now he needed coffee and breakfast a lot more than he needed answers.

He wondered who would be in the house this morning. His money was on Luca and the fairy-like girl who'd arrived late on a bicycle, with a whippet puppy in a straw basket. Tom, who had started the evening by taking on the role of barman, had brought Kit a drink as he was turning steaks on the barbecue and rolled his eyes towards the front door. 'Luca's brought along a new flame,' he said. 'I teach her History of Art, she's called Jemma, but everyone calls her Shrimp. She's full of tricks and he's falling for every one of them.'

Kit and Tom had watched, unnoticed, as the girl gazed at Luca, twirling her hair around a finger, pressing the puppy close to her. Luca remained hypnotised as she filled his arms with first the puppy, then a fluffy dog bed, and then various scarves and trailing bits of fabric. The puppy looked embarrassed, Kit thought, and frankly, it had his sympathy, as did Luca.

The girl tripped towards the bar.

Kit nudged Tom. 'Look, she's leading him up the garden path.'

Tom laughed. 'Christ, you're not wrong. Ah well, we all have to go through that phase, don't we?'

They'd got on well, he and Tom. Kit examined his conscience, and regretfully decided there was nothing he needed to hide from his new friend. He and Luisa had danced, but she'd danced with Bruce Hopkins too, and he'd danced with Mae and with Dora. It had been a great evening. Humming, Kit opened the door to the kitchen. Sure enough, there was the fairy, eating yoghurt straight from the pot and muesli out of the box. Like Kit, she was wearing dark glasses.

'Hi,' she whispered. The little whippet was curled up on a cushion. The fluffy pink dog bed was nowhere to be seen. As well as Luca, who was making coffee, and the girl, there was a huge vase of sunflowers on the table and a pile of Sunday newspapers. The girl occupied the only chair in the room. Kit wondered how long it would be before Luca found her as irritating as he did.

'I'm Shrimp,' she said and stretched a tiny pale hand towards him.

It reminded Kit of a pipe cleaner. She reminded him of a pipe-cleaner doll, he decided. His focus alighted on the puppy. 'Has she spent the night there?' he asked.

'No, Dora brought you that cushion. She's outside, getting chairs.' Luca passed Kit the cup of coffee he had made.

'Dora? What's she doing here?' Kit strode to the door, the sun was suspiciously high. 'Jesus, what time is it?'

'It's almost midday. You've slept all morning,' piped Shrimp. 'I'm about to go, but thank you, it was such a cool party. I love your place here, you're so lucky, you know.'

'So I'm told,' said Kit politely.

Scooping up the puppy, Shrimp beckoned Luca, and they began assembling her scattered bangles and scarves. Kit was delighted she was leaving. Then he felt mean. She wasn't bad, she was polite, and pretty, and neither of those was a thing to hold against a girl. He stepped into the hall, and trod in something soft.

'Urgh! Shit! That sodding puppy! Christ,' he yelled, and hopped outside, cursing Shrimp under his breath. His phone beeped.

A message from Luisa.

Swell party Kit, and BTW thanxxxxx for chat, I am really excited, and you've made such a difference.

The damp grass and lazy pigeons, the hiss of the sea and the light dancing high above him flowed

231

through Kit like oxygen. He sighed, cleaned his foot, and wandered right round the Lighthouse. Pleasure, all a pleasure, he wrote, and pocketed the phone again. He must remember to give her details to Hannah. What were PAs for if not to help his friends?

An unexpected and blissful sight greeted him where the party had been. Dora and Maddie had cleared the tables, and several black dustbin bags bulged in a heap near the Hopkinses red truck, which had the look, impossible to pin down but unmistakable, of a car abandoned the night before. The tables were empty, and Dora had just shaken the last of the dust-sheet tablecloths. Maddie sat nearby, wrapped in a pink fluffy dog bed.

'Dora, what a saint you are.' Kit realised as he stretched his arms to hug her, how truly fond he had become of his new friends. He was blessed. Especially now he didn't have to clear up.

'Oh Kit, we thought we might miss you. We're going in a minute to have lunch with Luisa, but we brought you a present.'

Kit shook his head. 'You don't need to do that,' he said. 'You all made the party a success, I just provided the Lighthouse.'

'But that's the best part!' said Maddie.

Dora nodded, patting his arm. Kit noticed how fragile her wrists, her forearms, her collarbones were. Her touch was feather light. 'You made time for all of us,' she said. 'Thank you, what you said was so thoughtful.'

'What did he say, Mummy?' Maddie tugged at her waist.

Dora hesitated. 'He was kind, that's all,' she said lightly. 'But mainly, Kit, we had so much fun, and Maddie was up early, so we thought we'd come and clear up to say a big thank you.'

She was like a hind, or a doe, he never knew the difference. Maddie, with her big eyes and bouncing personality was a real-life Bambi. He saw Dora, like his mother, bringing her child up alone. Tragic that Aaron had come along and then gone like that. But at least she had loved him. What had Luisa told him? Maddie's father had remarried and lived in the Midlands, he visited occasionally, and had just taken her camping for the first time. Dora had all the responsibility of moulding a child's life without a partner to share the anxieties and the triumphs. He had only been small, probably younger than Maddie, when his mother met his stepfather but, even so, he had always been aware that Joseph, with his pipe, his beard and slow speech, had saved her, and therefore him.

Maddie pulled Kit's arm, excited. 'And I said Mummy could give you the cushion after all.'

Dora raised her eyebrows. 'We agreed it, Maddie. Remember, we've talked about it a few times, and because it belongs to both of us, we had to agree, didn't we?'

Maddie was dancing on tip-toe. 'And we always had to agree if it was washed,' she told Kit, 'because it's an Air Room, isn't it Mummy?'

'Heirloom, Mads,' said Dora. 'But we thought we'd just give it to Kit because it belongs here, in the Lighthouse, doesn't it, darling?'

233

Maddie nodded at her mother. 'Yup. Kit's got a picture too. Let's hang it near the cushion.'

'What picture?' Dora followed Maddie into the hallway.

'Look!'

Dora looked, and laughed. 'Oh that's like those old ones of Dad's. I think his generation were always out in the landscape, it's sweet. See if anyone signed it, Mads darling.'

Kit's voice boomed for a syllable then subsided to a groan. 'Dora, where have you got to? And what cushion are you talking about? Christ, I've got a headache.' He wanted to sit down. His hangover was lurking behind every blink of his eyes, or so it seemed. A proper breakfast in a house with straight walls was what he wanted. A vision of Luisa leaning over a table wreathed in the aroma of coffee and bacon floated before him. He was beginning to miss his solitary life in Cornwall.

Maddie appeared beside him. 'Come and see. It's in the kitchen. I put that puppy on it. She looked so sweet.' She led the way, skipping ahead. The cushion was still in the middle of the kitchen floor. Maddie pounced on it and brought it over.

'It's for you.' She thrust it towards him.

Kit laughed. 'I like your delivery methods,' he said.

'Our housewarming present.' Dora and Maddie exchanged a look brimming with excitement.

'What's this?' Kit got the message that this was a big deal for them, and had removed his sunglasses to examine the embroidered picture. He looked sharply at Dora, then back at the cushion and whistled a long slow note.

'Well,' he said. 'Well I never.' A blue background, a red striped tower, cliffs foaming with the crests of waves. It all belonged to the Kings Sloley Lighthouse. The stitching, the looping signature, the colours and the patterns, however, belonged somewhere quite different.

His mind whirled, he opened his mouth to thank them. 'How thoughtful. It's beautiful, Dora. It's old, I think, where did you find it?'

Maddie brushed her hand over the picture, and a frown puckered on her forehead.

'On the sofa at home. Don't you want it? We thought you would be so pleased.'

Dora was eager to show the detail to him. 'We thought that with your fabric business and everything you'd love it. I know it's a funny present to give to a man, really, but it captures the Lighthouse so brilliantly, don't you think?'

Kit had not moved. He held the cushion on his hands, absorbing everything about it. It was as if a lid had been taken off a box and the memories fluttered around him. The Lighthouse had been embroidered in silk, using tiny stitches, and followed through to the finest details. Nothing had been left to chance, nothing forgotten. There was a red bucket on the doorstep. Kit could make out a scatter of different small flowers by the gate, poppies a tone or two darker than the stripe of the walls, blue cornflower stars, and a pair of seagulls floating in the sky. On the sea, an angular grey ship lay beneath the horizon, turrets and a sliver of mast hinting at its past. The Lighthouse itself commanded centre stage and, even allowing for the fade of colour over time, was still as bold and beautiful as a jewel. Kit was caught by something he saw at a window just below the light. A snippet of curtain had been embroidered. A flash from within, skilfully suggesting depth. A tiny pattern of peacocks exquisitely drawn on the detail of the tapestry.

He sighed, tearing his eyes from the design. 'Of course I want it!' he said. 'And yes! I'm very pleased. It's beautiful, it's beautiful,' he repeated. 'And you're right, this is where it belongs.'

He rubbed his hand across his face. 'Where did you say it came from?'

CHAPTER 10

Luisa was beating batter to make pancakes. Lunch had changed to brunch because no one was up so there hadn't been any breakfast yet, and no one would want orange and watercress salad and frozen pepper gazpacho. Hangovers required bacon and pancakes. Ladling batter from the bowl to the pan, she trailed a puddle across the hotplate and watched it blacken and burn. Her mind was full of snatches of the evening before, and she hummed, dumping a pile of forks on the table beside the stacked plates. She wasn't in the mood to lay the table, she didn't want to create an occasion. Ever since she'd got up she'd been edgy.

'Hungover, are we?' She spun round, startled. Tom's gaze held a challenge. 'Here, you need a bit of zest,' he added, and threw a lemon.

'No! I can't,' she wailed, ducking. 'I can't catch it.' The lemon hit the wall behind her, 'See?'

'You should have more faith,' said Tom. 'Here, have another go.'

'Tom!' she shrieked. 'Don't. You know I'm useless at this.' He lobbed another, Luisa stuck out her hand, more in self-defence than with any hope of catching the lemon mid-air.

'My God!' she laughed. 'I caught it!'

Tom's nod was curt. 'More faith in me,' he muttered, dusting his hands on his trousers and pouring himself coffee.

'It was fun, wasn't it?' Luisa pushed her hair back with her forearm. 'Such a great evening, I thought.'

Tom yawned and stretched. 'Great place. Never thought anything could be done with those old lighthouses, but Kit's really turned it around. Luca'd like to move in there I think. And Mae.'

Luisa returned to the pancakes. 'I know. Even Jay Hopkins was full of compliments. I didn't know he was into interior decor, but he said he thought Kit should be on one of those prime location shows on TV.'

Tom poured more coffee and gave a cup to Luisa. 'You'd be better on a dance show,' he said, his face deadpan. 'You know, *Strictly* whatever. You danced for hours.'

'I love dancing.' Luisa waved her wooden spoon, turning towards the radio which was on in the background. 'I could dance now, I just need a partner. Breakfast's ready, by the way.' She glanced at the triple clocks. 'Or should I say lunch, it's almost one. Where are the kids? And Dora's supposed to be here. Let's ring her.' She looked round, but Tom had gone, his voice floated back from the hall.

'I'll be back, I'll call the kids. Are they even here?'

Luisa smiled to herself and, humming, turned up the volume on the radio.

Last night had been like a wonderful spell. Excitement winged through the air, cinders crackling and leaping, through the music and the alcohol and the uncharacteristic warmth of the night. Kit might have been new, but he had a knack for making people feel welcome, and the Lighthouse was thrown open, every room lit with candles, sparse furniture and the odd dash of colour.

'Where did he get all that stuff? It's great.' Dora, usually quick to see room for improvement, was enchanted. 'This place is heaven,' she said. 'Kit's somehow found his way to that junk shop I love, Luisa, and he's plundered her textiles. Look at this patchwork.'

'Isn't it beautiful.' Luisa opened her mouth to tell Dora she'd sent Kit to the junk shop, then she shut it again. Kit had come over and asked her to dance, and the moment passed.

'Ow,' she was holding her hand under the kitchen tap, waiting to feel hot water, and had forgotten about it, her mind full of the joy of dancing under the stars, dancing anywhere. It was so much fun. Luisa shook the colander of rinsed strawberries and tipped them into a bowl. They shone, water droplets like beads quivering on the red flesh. Last night she had danced until her knees actually shook. Where the energy came from, she didn't know. She bit the end off a strawberry and shut her eyes.

Euphoria, that's what it was. Kit had set her off laughing, and the laughter was like rocket fuel for dancing, especially with all that alcohol. She was euphoric. Though Dora had been cross and said she knew another word for it. They were in the doorway as the party vibrated around them. Beyond them embers flew like dragonflies, and the moon raced creamy and voluptuous above the sea. 'Look at the night, Dora, this is heaven, don't be cross, please.'

'Well, stop behaving like a crazy teenager.'

'I'm not!' Luisa wailed. 'Why can't I have fun?'

'You can,' hissed Dora, 'but just try to tone yourself down a bit. That dress is too tight for a start.'

'Oh shut up,' Luisa had flounced away. She wanted to dance more. Tom had gone off to help someone pull their car out of the field. Secretly, she had to admit, she quite liked the feeling of being a naughty teenager. Suddenly she understood the power of sulking, as displayed so often by Mae. Where was Mae, come to think of it? She would find her and persuade her to dance. She had spun round to find Kit right behind her. Churlish not to dance with him again, especially as he caught her hand, held it high, looked at her and said, 'You look incredible.'

That was probably the moment she'd felt most electric all evening. And she had to make sure her back was very straight and that she stood tall because the dress was tight. So tight she'd had to use the hook of a coat hanger to do up the zip, but who needed to be told that? No one. Mind you, it was pretty obvious, as she noticed when she'd turned sideways in front of her bedroom mirror, and saw a poured-in silhouette, all curves and cleavage that she couldn't possibly pretend was appropriate for a barbecue where she was actually cooking, but never mind.

She remembered once reading in a novel that the hero had 'raked' the heroine with his eyes. It sounded painful, but Kit did it. So did Tom, and he also patted her shoulder and said, 'Good effort, Tod,' as though she was a rugby forward in his team.

'That's some dress,' said Kit as they danced. 'You look—' he pulled his handkerchief from his pocket with a flourish Luisa had noticed was an habitual gesture. 'Well, let's just say I don't think the Light-house had ever seen anything to equal you.'

Today, Luisa found she was suffused with a gnawing regret for the things she had never done. She hadn't ridden a motorbike or slept in a gypsy caravan, she hadn't travelled round the world or lived in another country, and she hadn't kissed the wrong man.

Tom had stood chatting by the fire while she danced with Kit. He drank beer from the bottle, and when she broke away from Kit and walked over to him, he put his arm round her to whisper, 'Please don't make me dance, Tod' and her euphoria evapo-rated, leaving her feeling like a limp balloon. The pounding heart, the static in the air as she danced was easily crushed. The thrill was ultimately just a moment. Luisa had put her apron on, and hidden herself behind her formidable *batterie de cuisine*, a barricade of spatulas, wooden spoons, baking trays and sharp knives. Luisa was aware of Kit as he wove in and out of the crowd, filling glasses. Luisa had arranged sausages in rows, shook out salad, scattered flower heads on top of the leaves and checked the fridge where the pudding waited, formidable and over-ambitious, a floating island ice cream construction cut to look like the cliffs.

'Will it last?' Tom had leaned in as she shut the fridge door.

She shrugged. 'Don't know. It's risky, but we'll see.' She had a small toy lighthouse in her hand. Tom looked at it.

'That's nice. Thoughtful,' he said.

An explanation burst out of her. 'I got it in the newsagent in Blythe. It's nothing really, but I thought it was too good to resist. I'll put it on the pudding when I bring it out.'

The night sky was purple over the sea, the horizon a pale fire flickering in the distance. 'The Northern Lights,' Tom told Mae.

'They look like a lava lamp,' she commented.

Luisa brought out the Cliff Top dessert in flames, Luca at her side with his lighter poised, feeding more brandy onto the surface.

Kit was touched by the trouble Luisa had gone to. 'That's a real show stopper,' he finally said, after the general applause had subsided. 'You are a force of nature, Luisa, there are no other words for it.'

Luisa didn't look up, she was intent on rebalancing the teetering toy lighthouse, which wanted to career over the cliffs, rather like Virginia Woolf, she'd suddenly thought. Oh, but she was mixing everything up. There was a book about a lighthouse. Poor old Virginia had actually thrown herself in a river with stones in her pockets.

Kit tapped a glass with a knife. Luisa wasn't sure if he was drunk, but she knew Tom was. She saw him on the edge of the light thrown by the fire, his head back as he downed a glass. She felt cut loose, reckless. Kit's eyes were on her every time she looked at him.

She tossed her hair off her shoulders. The party fell quiet, someone turned the music down, and the sea breathed a hush over everyone.

'Superb dinner, thanks to Luisa.' His glance took in the range of guests, and Luisa sensed him choosing a line. 'I think most men here will agree that it's way off beam to believe that we blokes only want one thing. We also want food.' A crack of laughter showed he was spot on. Her shoulders, which she hadn't realised were tense with a degree of trepidation for him, relaxed.

'I want to thank you all for welcoming me to Kings Sloley. I didn't know I had a connection here until very recently, and now I have a lighthouse and all of you new friends.'

There was further clapping, and Luca turned the music up again. Luisa stood on the edge of the rug, hugging herself. The air was a delicate veil across her skin. A few people, Dora and Mae and a couple of other girls and some children, were all dancing. Luisa shut her eyes. Flames from the bonfire threw dramatic shadows across the Lighthouse walls, turning the dancers into spirits conjured from the depths of the sea, the earth and the fire.

'What're you looking at?' Kit was beside her.

'They look like nymphs,' she said.

'They do? That's one way of looking at them I guess. I see something more straightforward – the extras from a cult film, for example.' He looked at Luca, and Mae, who, with a couple of others, were collapsing with laughter as they inhaled the helium from Maddie's bunch of balloons, and then spoke in fast, ludicrously squeaky voices. Luisa caught the infectious laughter and began giggling.

Kit's hands were clasped on the top of his head as he turned a full circle, taking in everything. 'I've never given a party where the thing everyone has in common is the only thing I don't share with them,' he said.

'What? Is it a riddle? If it is, the answer's usually an egg.' Luisa dragged her gaze from the heap of teenagers, collapsed with laughter.

'You all belong,' Kit said. 'I'm the outsider.'

Luisa shook her head. She'd drunk enough to be forthright with him, she felt superhuman, wise and utterly happy. 'No! It's the opposite, silly! The thing we all have in common is you.'

'Me? Not sure about that.'

Luisa could feel his body heat at her side. It was getting late, the evening was cooler now. 'Come on, let's dance,' she pulled him towards the music.

She'd thought, as she twirled in the dark, breathless, unable to stop, that she would pay for her fun the next day. But oddly, she wasn't really hungover. All that laughing probably sorted it. Didn't it bring oxygen to the brain? She picked up her phone to send Kit another text. She'd already thanked him in one earlier, and now that didn't seem enough. She would ask him to lunch. Now. Oh dear, she should have thought of it sooner.

She scrolled idly through her phone, deleting old messages, wondering what to write. Suddenly she noticed a text she hadn't opened.

Got you in my mind's eye, dancing. Sweet dreams Kx

It had been sent at 2.41 a.m. Straight after the party. Her throat tightened, and a prickle of embarrassment crawled up her chest to her face. She threw the phone on to the table, then snatched it back, shoving it in her pocket. She must delete the message. The phone vibrated, she didn't look at it. At the same moment, the house phone rang, and a gurgle from the computer in the corner of the kitchen announced a Skype call. Luisa fought an impulse to hide under the table. The smell of burned butter forced her back to the cooker. One blackened pancake glared back at her. She threw the whole frying pan into the sink.

'Oh God,' she muttered, reaching for the computer to answer the Skype call. She wanted to talk to Ellie, no one else. There she was, pixillated but present. Luisa was instantly cheered.

'Ellie! Hi there, sweetheart. I'm just making pancakes. What are you up to?' It would have been impossible just a matter of a week ago, but she hadn't spared a thought for her beloved eldest child for days. 'We've been so busy here, and there's so much to tell you. I can't remember when we last spoke. Weren't you off on some trek? Anyway, since then we've got a new neighbour and—'

'Mum! Keep still, can't you?' Ellie's voice was scarcely audible above the background street sounds. Luisa drank a glass of water. Ellie was surrounded by alien sounds, the spattering of a clapped out engine, a cacophony of car horns and tuk tuks beeping and tooting, and the storm of busy chatter surrounded Ellie.

'Gosh, it's so colourful,' she said. 'Oh Ells, you look lovely,' Luisa couldn't really believe that she was somewhere so vibrant, it was like a filmset. The other Skype conversations they'd had had all been in hostels and hotel rooms.

'Mum! I'm at a cafe in Hyderabad. I've been in the countryside for so long, I can't get my head round the city, it's insane. Last week I was in an Ashram, and I've still got the meditations ringing through my ears. This city is crazy, it's so busy. The view on the screen shifted suddenly, as she lifted her laptop to show Luisa. Grayson started barking and she could hear a car arriving.

'Damn,' said Luisa, 'they're all coming back.' The new pool of pancake batter was smoking in the pan, she had flour on her hands and she didn't want to wreck the computer.

'Darling, I really want to catch up properly, but

there are so many people about to arrive and I've burned the pancakes and—'

Luisa was spared the need to cut her daughter off as the screen froze then blacked out. She'd try later.

'Oh! How did you know to come?' Kit walked into the kitchen, startling Luisa. 'I was going to invite you, but I didn't,' she said baldly.

'Thought I'd bring you these back,' he said pointing to the basket full of roasting tins and plates he was carrying. He leaned to kiss her cheek. 'You were phenomenal. It was sensational, I don't know how you do it, and I'm about to write you a large cheque in thanks.'

'Oh. Yes. Good. I don't know where everyone is but they're on their way. Coffee?' Luisa couldn't meet his eye. Too embarrassing. It was as though they had slept together. She sneaked a look at him, but he was also determinedly looking elsewhere. Was he embarrassed as well? Did that make it better? Or worse?

'Where's everyone?' Kit opened the door and peered into the garden.

'Well they're not out there,' Luisa snapped.

His eyebrows flew together. 'Okay,' he said mildly, and moved the pile of bowls he'd brought off the table, making room for himself to perch there. He rubbed his forehead. Luisa noticed he had circles under his eyes. He was probably hungover. She opened the window. The kitchen had closed in, clogged with steam. There was too much going on, the recklessness she had embraced the night before now felt dangerous. She pressed a

247

glass against her face and took a deep breath. Now was the moment.

'Kit, I—'

'Hey there, something smells good.' Luisa spun around as Tom walked into the room. People flooded in behind him. Luca, Dora and Maddie stepped in from the garden, repeatedly banging the door against the wall until the glass juddered. Luisa wondered if research had found that noise actually *was* louder when made by teenagers. Mae emerged like a dormouse from the hall and snatched the laptop.

'Mae. Don't start on anything,' pleaded Luisa. 'The pancakes are ready. It's time to sit down.' She flipped the final golden disc and slid it onto the stack in the oven. Everyone was at the table, and the party post-mortem was interspersed with requests for butter, milk, sugar and lemon.

Dora poured a glass of water, and drank it in huge gulps. 'Sorry, I didn't think I drank much last night, but I feel like I'm on another planet today.'

Maddie waved her fork, festooning liquid chocolate over the table and her sleeve. 'Watch out for my laptop,' shrieked Luisa.

Kit stood up suddenly, cleared his throat and fumbled at the side of his chair.

Amazing, thought Luisa, he's going to give another speech. Must have got a taste for it last night. She bit her lip, then thought better of her intention to eat nothing, and tucked into a twist of bacon and a mouthful of Luca's pancake.

'Mum,' he muttered. Kit was clearing a space on

the over-cluttered table. He placed a cushion on the cleared table in front of him.

'I need to talk to you all . . . I am . . . Oh, God. Let's just say I didn't see what has now become very clear.' His smile was apologetic. 'Anyway, I'm going to seize the moment. In the midst of the family.' He looked vulnerable, young.

Luisa suddenly wondered how old he was. Funny, she'd never thought about it before. He was looking at Tom. Tom stood up, ran a hand through his hair and said something to Kit, their heads close. Luisa didn't hear his words. She didn't hear anything except blood thumping in her head. In that moment, time shifted its pace, and her world became no bigger than the distance between Tom and Kit as they stood side by side. The sounds in the room, the movements of cups, food, hands and cutlery, the vapour trail from the kettle, the rhythm of voices stopped. Ceased. Vanished. The plumes of steam that had curled up to the ceiling to hang in festoons evaporated, and within Luisa's body and mind, the charge of energy and excitement, the exhaustion and the laughter and the fun, all became still. In the midst of this stillness, her gaze met Kit's. An ache of silence passed between them, subtle and vital as a heartbeat. Tears sprang in Luisa's eyes, and she dropped her fork on the floor. She bent to retrieve it, a coward's impulse pulling her down to hide under the table. She straightened herself again. There was no need. Who was she hiding from? What was she hiding? There was nothing. There never had been, there never would be. In the room, movement had begun again.

'Dad, did you really not know?' Mae was asking, 'I mean we did the Second World War in history. How come you didn't tell us what happened to our grandfather at the end?'

Tom shrugged. 'You know, it did come up, Mae. Your grandmother, whom you won't remember really, used to say that my father,' he paused, looked across at Kit, and their eyes met, '*our* father, lost a whole swathe of time. He came back from the war a couple of years after VE Day, and I don't know where he'd been. No one did. My mother always said she wouldn't ask him, she said if he wanted to tell us, he would. So we never asked.'

He dropped a hand on Kit's shoulder.

Dora, chin propped on her hands, elbows on the table, stared at Kit. 'We never asked,' she repeated slowly, 'but I think Bella knew something.' She turned to her brother, 'D'you think Mum knew, Tom?'

Tom sighed, 'Hard to say. Perhaps she guessed and didn't want to rock the boat.'

'Some things are better left unsaid,' Dora hugged Maddie at her side.

'A brother from another mother,' said Luca, his smile spreading as he dragged himself up from his seat and moved between Kit and his father. 'Uncle Kit. The man from UNCLE. It's a film, isn't it?'

'It was TV first, but it's a film now. This is the man from Cornwall,' said Tom.

'The man with the Lighthouse.' Luca shook his head.

'How long have you known this?' Luisa heard her question hit the room like a felled tree. Or so she thought. No one heard her. She cleared her throat and asked again, 'Did you know when you came to Norfolk?'

Kit didn't meet her gaze. He shoved one hand in his pocket, and looked across the table and out of the window to the lawn where Grayson was lying flat on his side, his tail occasionally swatting an invisible fly.

'I've only just realised,' he said after an endless pause. 'It was the cushion. When Dora said it had belonged to her father, everything fell together in an instant.'

All eyes flew to the embroidered cushion on the table. 'It didn't make any sense to me that my mother had this Lighthouse, but when I saw this, it did.' He ran his fingers over the bright stitches. He shrugged and looked at Dora again.

'And then there was the painting. You saw it, Dora, you even said it was like one your father did. I brought it with me from Cornwall, like a talisman, I suppose. It was in Mum's house, and I never really looked at it, but the initials are MM. Michael Marker.'

'It fits,' said Dora, tipping back on her chair. 'It makes sense.'

'She loved him,' Luisa found tears rushing, and hid them in her cup of coffee.

Kit nodded, 'Yes, I think she did. I suppose she didn't tell me because it wasn't her story. It was his. Norfolk, the Lighthouse, and in the end, all of you, belonged to him.'

Dora leaned over the cushion with Maddie. 'Weren't there any letters?'

'Ask Bella,' said Tom. 'I've never seen a thing, but we can have a dig around.'

'I haven't seen anything in my mother's papers,' Kit said, 'but maybe we'll discover something now that we know what to look for.'

'Do we?' Tom opened the back door.

Luisa sat among the breakfast chaos and picked up a strawberry. Its taste pinged her back to the morning, the post-party happiness. Kit was following Tom outside, tapping something into his phone. She shivered, goosebumps along her arms, as all the things she hadn't done with Kit picked themselves up and stole quietly away, shadows insubstantial as wisps of steam, and vanished into the air.

'Right,' she said briskly, 'basil ice cream it is. Maddie, do you want to help me pick some basil? We're going to make green ice cream.' She stood and held a hand out to her niece. 'I made a mint version the other day,' she explained, to the top of Maddie's head, 'and it gave me the idea. Herb ice cream sounds medieval. It might be medicinal, even.'

'Eugh. I don't want medicine ice cream,' Maddie swung ahead across the lawn, then broke into a run towards the greenhouse. Luisa followed, soothed by the tranquil air. She wasn't sure what basil's healing properties were supposed to be, but if she made an infusion with the leaves, the delicacy of the colour, the taste that would be so subtle it would be as much a scent as a flavour. Could be amazing.

Tom was standing in the vegetable garden, alone, hands in his pockets, looking up at a crack in the wall.

He patted Maddie's head absently. She ducked and opened the greenhouse door. 'I'm looking for a butterfly,' she called.

'This needs mending,' Tom said, his eyes fixed on the wall.

'Are you okay?' Luisa's eyes were on his face, it was inscrutable.

He sighed, but didn't speak. She tried again. 'I wasn't expecting that, were you?'

Tom snorted a laugh. 'Not really. Nothing's exactly dull when Kit's around, is it?' He raised the lid of the water butt by the greenhouse door and peered in, poking with a stick at the flat green surface. The film broke and ripples spread in gentle circles. Tom pulled the stick out and threw it far across the garden. 'You know, Tod, I never really thought about my parents having any emotional life. I can't imagine what my father must have gone through. I was never close to him.' He bent to lift a broken pane of glass from the path.

Luisa nodded. 'Or what it was like for your mother. Or Kit's mother,' she said.

Tom's expression was uncertain. He looked young. Much younger than Kit. She suddenly wanted to protect him, to protect all of them.

'True,' agreed Tom. 'I'm not sure what I make of it. Having a brother I mean. Mae just told me she thinks we should christen Kit,' he laughed, 'so the kids have obviously got no problem with the whole thing.'

Luisa pulled a dandelion with gossamer threads at

knee height from the path. 'That's not a bad idea. We could do it when Ellie gets back. What would Kit wear, I wonder?'

Tom grinned. 'Some fabric made by his company? 'Maybe a robe covered in windmills—'

Luisa touched his shoulder. 'No, it's got to be lighthouses!'

Tom's hand on her back spread warmth, he kissed her and wandered off towards his car.

Maddie emerged from the door to the greenhouse with a jam jar. She slid it under the lid of the water butt to fill it. 'I'm taking some water to the hens. They like it in their dust bath.'

'Okay darling.' Luisa entered the greenhouse, and inhaled deeply. Earthiness hung around the ripening tomatoes, so intense it was almost physical. The aroma mingled with the pungent scent of basil rolling together like some exotic oil poured into warm bathwater. Luisa, picking basil stems, was immersed. She held her bunched basil close to her face and closed her eyes, shutting out everything except the sensuality of a Mediterranean afternoon. A lazy day water ice, basil, tomato and a hint of strawberry. Sultry, sunkissed summer.

Everyone always said the summers in the war had been incredible. Luisa thought about her own family. Her Italian father, toiling in a stony field in Norfolk, far away from home, from any pungent basil crop or ripe crop of tomatoes. Making spaghetti when he was worn out from a day of hard labour, his need for home tastes and sounds so vital. He sang Puccini, *La Bohème* was his favourite, she remembered from her own childhood. She wondered what he yearned most for while he was a prisoner of war. It can't have been home as an actual place, because he stayed on. A toss up then, between love and Italian food, and he had found both with her grandmother. She would make this basil ice cream in his honour. Maybe it would become her signature flavour. She wondered if she would have thought of it under different circumstances, or if she would have missed it. Impossible to know. She placed the basil in a flat wooden box and crouched to select a bunch of tomatoes.

CHAPTER 11

The months before the baby came were happy. Michael found his day-to-day life in Cornwall had purpose and happiness he had not thought possible. As the country began the slow process of putting itself back together, rebuilding and coming to terms with some of what had happened, the local landscape changed. As the outsider, Michael was well placed to observe these changes. They reflected shifts of perspective and new thinking he experienced within himself, as well as heralding a renewal that gleamed through the tattered veil of rationing and endurance that continued into the 1950s. Britain had undergone seismic change. Across the distance of time, life before the war was unreachable, unimaginable, and impossible to recreate. No one even tried. Years had been spent yearning for this time after the war, and now it was here, it was all the country could do to keep moving forward. Rebuilding was slow, painstaking and beset by lack of money and lack of manpower.

In Cornwall, Michael and Arthur worked together, using driftwood and ingenuity to resurrect studios and potteries for the expanding colony of artists who turned up in ones and twos from all over the country. In London and other cities, the constant difficulty of living in bombed streets with the haunting reminders of derelict houses, shops and businesses crumpled into rubble, made it difficult to move on from the war. Painters, writers, artists found the fractured urban environments impossible to work in. The reputation of St Ives, through artists like Naum Gabo, Barbara Hepworth and Ben Nicholson was growing fast. Everyone came. Michael was under no illusions that his part was significant. He was probably more vital to William Coyne, digging over and planting up the flower terraces, but he liked the physical act of making things, building spaces, and he was becoming good at it. So he was quick to accept whatever carpentry and building work came his way, without ever missing his days with William. To be busy and to be useful was his daily aim. Beyond that there was nothing.

An old mill on the hill above Newlyn, derelict since before the war, was stripped out by a group of potters, enamellers and printmakers. Michael and Arthur worked through long winter evenings, partitioning the spaces and making rough doors for each new studio. They planned to finish the work on the shortest day of the year.

Michael walked there through the darkness before dawn, and saw the sun rise in streaks of red and orange, on fire in the windowpanes of houses and shops, shining a path through the sea, and he felt this rich, deep glow might have come from within him. He had a role, he was providing. Felicity needed him, he had friends and work. Soon there would be a baby who would need him too. He liked the routine that his life had taken on.

That morning, as he did every day, he had got up in the dark. He went down to the kitchen to make tea, and the early morning kitchen was like a womb, warmed by the embers still flickering in the stove. The chimney rushing and whispering with the odd gust of wind, the tiled floor was warm underfoot like the earth would be in summer. The sputter of the tap as he filled the kettle, the whine of it on the stove, like a distant engine notching up the gears as the water heated within, even the luxurious sound of Rations purring on the cushion on the chair in the window, were familiar to him now, the fabric of his daily life. He made the tea, tucking the pot under the crocheted tea cosy Verity had made for them. He added mugs, a small jug of milk and a teaspoon to the tray and took it up the narrow staircase to Felicity. With the daily repetition of these simple rituals, Michael's memories and his conscience were ebbing, drawing the vestiges of his old life away, sucking them out of him, out of the house, and away into the depths of the sea to sink and lie dormant for evermore. Michael was planting himself, putting down roots, and the tendrils of love and intimacy clung to the slate and the stony soil of this peninsula.

The bedroom was silent, a sliver of dawn between the curtains bright in the darkness. Michael threw twigs on to the embers from the night before, and the fire crackled, throwing a gleam across the hearth.

Felicity sat up, and smiled sleepily. 'Hey, soldier, have I missed anything?'

'Not much, it's wild and windy, you should go back to sleep for a bit longer.'

'I will if you will,' she teased.

Michael sat on the bed, handed her a cup. 'I would if I could.'

Felicity sipped the tea. 'I've only got a bit of time this morning. I want to finish the peacock print today.'

She smoothed the quilt. Michael caught her hand. He loved the way her fingers were always dyed with at least two of the colours she was working with. Purple had faded beneath deep emerald, and tiny splashes of both freckled her wrist.

'Honey, if I get back into bed with you, there'll be no time for peacocks,' he drawled, faking an American accent. Of course he wanted to climb back under the covers with her, to be with her, to hold her. Felicity was everything to. him, she had made his life different, better than it could ever have otherwise been. Sometimes he succumbed, dived back beneath the heavy blankets and pulled her on top of him, seizing precious moments of skin touching skin, touching the warm curve of her belly growing with their child, their eyes meeting in the silence of the early morning, enthralled by every movement and every moment of stillness between them. Today, though, he resisted.

He dragged on his clothes, tucking layers of vest and shirt into the brown tweed trousers he held up with a pair of red braces. Even his cap was on before he let himself reach for her again. Clad in the armour of the day he wrapped his arms around her and buried his face in her neck. She smelled of wintersweet and something musky, the essence of passion, he thought. Her heartbeat was a magnet, she brought him a sense of peace he'd thought he'd never know again. There were times, such as last night when they had made love and Felicity was curled against him so her breathing felt like his own, that Michael fell asleep wondering what on earth would have happened to him if he hadn't met her.

The clock on the mantelpiece ticked the minutes away. He was expected at work, he had to leave. Felicity came down to wave him off, clattering plates in the sink, flinging open the back door to let the cat out, stoking the kitchen stove, the room warming up as activity rubbed out the chill of night. Michael took the winding road out of Mousehole to Newlyn and the last day on the building work there. He looked back, he could see the lamp in Felicity's studio, high above him on the hillside, its glow flickering like the broken beam of a lighthouse.

Felicity was obsessed with her work. Michael knew that without him returning to her in the evenings, she would never tear herself away, and would forget to eat or sleep. She loved the workshop Michael had built for her at home, and she didn't want to leave it.

Michael saw it as cramped and isolated, and wanted her to show her talent to the world, by joining the other artists who were flooding into the region. After much cajoling on his part, she agreed to take a space at the newly built Newlyn Studios. Today she would make her last work at home. Her fabrics had begun to swamp the old sail shed over the months, and already orders for her printed cottons and silk were steady. Felicity needed printing tables and space.

A letter lay on the desk in their sitting room from Liberty's of London. A journalist from *Vogue* had come to St Ives to interview the sculptor Barbara Hepworth, and had admired the scarf she was wearing. Felicity had screamed with delight when she opened the letter, and twirled with it around the house, with Michael laughing too, though wondering why.

The buyer had seen the scarf in the article, and on the strength of that scrap of fabric, she wanted to come and see Felicity's work. Would the fourth of January be convenient? Felicity was five months pregnant and fired with energy. She'd already sold her first designs to a department store in Bristol, after an old schoolfriend Annie Preen had put two scarves in the window of her family's haberdashery shop in Penzance. The rose madder silk with grey seahorses dancing on sliced, abstract waves, was arresting even behind the yellowing cellophane covering the window display in Preen's. They had been there for a morning when Christina Bishop, wife of the proprietor of the West Country's leading department store, walked past and stopped in her tracks. She was, she later explained, intrigued by the bold colour and abstract shapes in Felicity's work. The fabrics were sophisticated and modern, unlike anything else, and they stood out like priceless gemstones in a toy crown.

Mrs Bishop took both the scarves and left her card for Felicity.

'She hung around me while I took the scarf off the mannequin you know,' Annie had told Felicity. 'It was like she thought I'd hide it or something. She said they'd be ordering more of your designs for their shops, and that we'd done well to get you. She reckons you're commercial and classy.' Annie made a face and giggled, but admitted she was impressed, most clothing sat around in the shop, most customers hummed and hah'ed, and changed their minds, Felicity had done well. Felicity laughed, inclined to brush it off as Mrs Bishop's whim, but Annie was right. Three weeks later, Felicity sold ten scarves in each of her six first designs to Bishop & Steel's in Bristol.

Michael had no experience of anything relating to the process involved in screen-printing, let alone running a fashion fabric business, and he found Felicity's fearlessness exhilarating. Felicity sold the stock from the bookshop as a job lot to a friend of her father's, and used the money to buy printing inks and silk. The newspapers were full of articles about the post-war art movement, and Cornwall, in particular St Ives, was at its heart. The circle of friends that Michael found himself in through Felicity included ceramicists, sculptors, glassblowers, printmakers and textile designers. Unlike many of her contemporaries, Felicity was committed to working as a commercial artist. 'I don't just want to make things, I want people to want them,' she had told the *Lizard Peninsula Herald* when they interviewed her about closing Delaware's bookshop to open Delaware's Textiles.

Michael loved her determination, and her application. With the money she earned, she bought more cloth and hired an assistant, Molly, to work with her. Michael asked the local bank manager for advice. Felicity appeared to ignore him when he told her, but in fact she was shrewd. Delaware's Textiles began to flourish. Sketches of shells, seahorses, fish and gulls, more fish, starfish, boats and nets, feathers and pebbles and the crashing waves against the rocks covered her studio. Felicity blocked colours in ink around the drawings, stuck leaves, scraps of paper or fabric, flowers, chips of pottery, stones, anything she could find to bring the palette she wanted together.

Michael thought he loved her most when he saw her in the studio, moving back and forth, lost in concentration, a pencil twisted to hold up her hair, her head on one side as she worked, turning the tones and shapes of her world into her palette. Stone and lichen, gorse yellow, rose quartz pink, bruised mauve and greys and greens as soft and changeable as the clouds and sea. The colours caught her imagination, and Michael grew used to small piles of stones, squares of fabric and swatch after swatch of vibrant silk marking Felicity's progress around the house.

The next stage though was more practical. Each

colour on the cloth took two days to fix. The garden and the studio became like a medieval apothecary's shop, with cauldrons of dye, tins of pigment and stirring sticks steeped in colour like a rainbow of magic wands. The screen-printing tables filled the room, and Michael felt that he had stepped through time and become a medieval craftsman as he poured dye into frames and raked the colour across the silk before sliding it, like a cake heading for the oven, into a rack in the dark room. The dark room was an old potting shed Michael had adapted in an afternoon.

There was nowhere to put anything, so raw fabric, delivered in bolts, was shunted like a group of formal visitors into the drawing room and left there. Tall cylinders of silk in stands, the exotic visitors stood close together as if in secret conversation. One group, led by a stout bolster of bold cherry red, tipped over one morning, startling the cat so he ran up the curtains and knocked two pictures off the wall. Felicity conceded that it was time to move.

The Newlyn Studios, housed in a largely derelict mill whose last use had been making uniforms in the war, was perfect. Michael even managed to salvage the cloth-cutting tables. There were outbuildings she could expand further into, and there was practical help and chat and advice, both sought and unwanted, from the rest of the artists. As Michael unlocked the space the morning before her move, he knew he had just one final touch to make: his Christmas present for her. He began to draw.

*   *   *

Christmas Day was soft and grey. There had been snow the night before, and it lay in mauve ripples along the hedgerows and as an apron on the lawn. The sky was full, dropping erratic flurries from clouds that bulged like over-stuffed pillows tumbling off a bed. Lighting the fire in the sitting room after a walk to the church, Michael crouched, staring into the flames. It had taken easily, the coals from the evening before still glowed orange beneath a layer of ash. He and Felicity loved fires. Coal was scarce, but Michael always had a sack of wood off-cuts and handfuls of shavings from his work, and they lit a fire any time they sat down in their house. He felt a twinge of disloyalty for his parents' home, the cold black hearth at Green Farm House. In his childhood, Christmas Day was the only time in the whole year that a fire was lit before lunchtime. He wondered what was happening there this Christmas, but the thought was too painful to sustain and he rubbed it away with a hand across his eyes.

He leaned into the crackling heat, pushing a small log into its heart. The roar in the chimney, the faint whiff of sap burning, stirred him. He could taste childhood excitement and smell the sweet exotic scent of the orange he and Johnnie always had in their stockings. An orange, some marbles and a stick of striped candy cane. Memories of childhood. Building a marble run in the seams of the eiderdown on Johnnie's bed, blowing the whistle so it shrieked their parents awake and the heap of laughter that he and Johnnie subsided into. Michael didn't move. The fire held him, he fancied he could see all of time in its heart.

To see a world in a grain of sand
And heaven in a wild flower.
To hold infinity in the palm of your hand
and Eternity in an hour.

How many times had Blake's lines, learned duti-
fully at school, come back to him? How many more
times in his life would they do so? What lay ahead of
him? The revelation he thought he was waiting for
had not come. The answers continued to elude him,
as more questions formed. Was this how it would be
now? Forever?

At the beginning of December, he'd read in the
newspaper that families faced terrible difficulties in
trying to trace relatives missing overseas. Whitehall
was besieged with requests to find sons, sweethearts,
husbands, soldiers who'd vanished. The backlog
had hardly moved, wrote the journalist, since peace
had been declared. Michael burned the paper before
he finished reading it. Guilt rattled through him, left
his throat dry, empty as an old can. Sadness knocked
insistently at his conscience. He mourned his mother.
In his mind's eye he saw her waiting, hoping. His
parents would have another Christmas of sadness
and uncertainty. He was not a father yet, but for his
child to disappear without a word would, he already
knew be an act of unbearable cruelty to Felicity. For
himself, he thought it would be no more than he
deserved.

He wrote again, this time a Christmas card. *'Mum
and Dad, dearest Mum and Dad, I'm getting well. I love*

you, and I'm sorry not to see you for Christmas. I will see you soon again. As soon as I can. Your loving son.'

He was not ready to be traced to Cornwall, but he could no longer hide. Sorrow, suspended, like an instrument of torture, hung around the women queuing at the War Office, years of waiting drawn into set expressions of endurance. He couldn't go back yet. It wasn't time, although every day, in small but palpable ways, he felt the repairs to his shattered self growing, the holes in his second skin shrinking.

He dreamed of violence less frequently now. He no longer saw the broken bodies of his comrades, or heard the deafening sounds of battle in his sleep. On Christmas Eve, he dreamed about Johnnie for the first time. Johnnie had walked towards him from the sea. He wanted Michael to tell their mother and father.

'Please tell them you saw me. Tell Mum and Dad to start again. This is how it is now. Tell them I'm at peace.'

Michael had woken with tears on his face, the sheets wound round him like a shroud.

Felicity touched his shoulder. He hadn't heard her come in. In the shadows of the unlit room on the still morning of Christmas Day, her cheeks were flushed, her sleeves pushed up to show her smooth, pale arms, her olive skin faded by the winter light. Michael didn't need to touch her to know she was glowing with warmth, but he wanted to.

'Hot?' He watched as she opened the small window. She smiled back at him, fanning herself. 'You call this winter, I call this baking. I'm hardly wearing anything.'

'Sounds good,' said Michael. 'Sounds sexy.'

She laughed. 'Silly. I'm pregnant not sexy.'

'You're pregnant and sexy,' he insisted.

'Come and look at Christmas on the sea,' she beckoned him to the window, and the pearl-grey winter sea with snowflakes billowing across the bay.

Since her pregnancy, Felicity had become the most efficient self-heating system, and warmth followed her everywhere. She rarely needed a coat, which as she pointed out, was just as well. Nothing buttoned up over the bump of the baby. Michael gave her his huge fisherman's jumper, and she wore it on top of all her clothes. It was her outer layer for Midnight Mass on Christmas Eve, and she'd put it on again this morning to walk with Michael back to the church.

They laid black hellebores by the wooden cross for her brother Christopher. 'And for Johnnie too,' Felicity had squeezed his hand as they knelt beside Christopher's memorial.

They laid white ones on her parents' grave. 'It's called the Christmas Rose,' Felicity placed them in a small blue jug, squat against the grey of the slate headstone. 'It was my mother's favourite winter flower. I never liked it much until I decided to draw it, and now I see the point of it.'

Michael looked at the graves, some adorned with fresh flowers for Christmas, but more were bare. He saw a robin land on a bush by the wall, its tiny weight bouncing the twig. Michael shivered, confused. He pulled Felicity up to her feet. 'Come on, let's go home,' he said. 'We need to put some breadcrumbs out for the birds.'

'The birds now! You've been overtaken by the Christmas spirit,' teased Felicity. 'I don't think you've ever noticed the birds before, have you?'

Now, from the window, he watched seagulls soar on the chill December air.

Behind him, Felicity took a record out of a paper sleeve and placed it on the gramophone. 'Listen. This is something I love. It's by Thomas Tallis. It's called *Spem in alium.*'

He raised an eyebrow at her. 'I thought aliums were onions?'

'They are, but not this time, listen. Shhh!'

A single silver voice began to sing. In a rush, Michael stood up from the fire, startled. Even though he knew it was a recording, it surprised him. The voice was immediate, intimate as though someone was singing there alive in the room with them. More voices. A choir soaring. The sound inside Michael's head felt bigger than the space available. He felt he might burst. His thoughts crowded in on silver sound as it swelled. All the losses he had known were here, present with him. In this moment, he knew they would remain with him as long as he lived. Time would close the wounds, but the loss of lives, his brother, of loves and beliefs, the hopes and dreams of a generation, and ultimately his own lost self, had caused scars he would always bear.

Across the room Felicity's red dress became a blur.

The music was overwhelming, insistent in a way Michael had never experienced before. He thought he could drown in it, never come back. Felicity saw his tears before he felt them, and crossed the room to him. Her strength radiated through him, and her arms and warmth enveloped him. Michael thought that they could be one entity with the warm beating heart of the baby safe at their centre.

'I love you, Felicity, I love you. I'll never forget you,' he whispered into her hair.

They sat on the sofa, no gap between them.

Felicity replaced the magnificent sorrow of the choral music with the liquid sound of jazz saxophone, and honeyed notes flowed in and out of Michael's thoughts, smoothing every jagged nerve. She had a blue silk pouch in her hand. 'Here's your Christmas present.' She tucked a strand of hair behind her ear, her eyes bright with excitement. He looked at the pouch, at her, back at it again. He wished he could paint. He wanted to remember her as she was at that moment, beautiful and strong. He untied the cord, excited like a child again, he hadn't expected this. Whatever it was. The moment felt solemn, limitless. He reached slowly into the small silk pocket without taking his eyes off Felicity, and brought out a silver watch. Heavy, but with delicate hands, a worn leather strap, the silver buckle tarnished a little and the glass on the face scratched. A watch that had been worn and loved.

The inscription on the back read: 'CWD. *Time will run back and fetch the age of gold.* TWD'

'It was Christopher's. It's Milton. I mean the words are. My father loved Milton. The watch was his present to Christopher on his eighteenth birthday.' Felicity turned the watch over on her palm. 'They brought it home when he died.'

Michael stroked her hair, 'I can't accept it. You mustn't give me this. It's not for me to take. You'll regret it. You should keep it to protect yourself. You and the baby, I mean.'

He hated himself for bringing a shadow to hover above them, like a bird of prey biding its time.

Felicity shook her head, 'No, I've thought about it. I want you to have it. You sold your watch when you came to Cornwall. This is something from Cornwall for you to have wherever you may find yourself. No matter what.' Her conviction was like a shield, her cheeks pink. 'It should be part of someone's life, not sitting in a drawer in my bedroom. Please.'

She was irresistible. He wondered if this was how every man felt who had ever loved a woman. Surely not. Michael had the sense that this was unique. He couldn't imagine his father feeling like this about his mother, or Esther and Reg in The Ship. How did anyone ever experience love though? And then again, how did they not?

Felicity threw him a mischievous look, and held the watch to his ear. 'Listen! It's ticking like a heartbeat. Like the baby.' She put his hand on the drum of her stomach, and he felt the flickering movement within. 'The baby's in time with it. Punctual already, like you, like a soldier. I expect he or she will be born exactly on time.'

'Not if she, or he, is anything like you,' teased Michael.

Felicity put her finger on his lips, and turned his face to hers. 'I want you to have this because I want you to remember us with every passing moment.' Her sadness was delicate and solemn as a wedding veil between them.

He read the inscription again. 'Time will run back and fetch the age of gold.' He cupped her face in his hands. 'Our age of gold,' he repeated.

He handed her a flat package, the wrapping colourful and intricately drawn.

'Here's yours.' He got up and walked around the room, shy. He hadn't known how much he wanted her to like it until it was in her hands.

'Oh! It's already beautiful, and I haven't seen what's inside. I love this, I could make a design from it.' The brown paper was decorated with little drawings of Felicity, miniature stick portraits of her busy doing all the things she liked. Picking flowers, painting, slicing vegetables in the kitchen, sitting in a chair, reading, with her cat on her knee, stirring dye in a tub, leaning across the screen-printing table, walking on the hill, her scarf flying, and finally, one quick sketch of her hugging Michael, a whirl of stick arms and legs and him with his cap on, a smiling pin man.

Felicity bent her head over the parcel, still not opening it. 'This must have taken for ever. It really could be a design, you know. I can't believe you did this and I didn't see you.' The paper crackled as she carefully undid it, folding the layers, unveiling the rectangular board within. 'Oh Michael,' she said.

He had painted a lighthouse, red and white in a cornfield on chalky cliffs. He had painted it simply but with much detail, secretly stealing time over the past weeks. He had hauled out his memories of childhood and among them found himself back at a place he'd loved. He would share it with Felicity. The lighthouse stood on the cliffs near his own home, and was the place he had held most dear in his childhood. As he painted his memory, he wished with all his heart he could take Felicity and their child there.

She propped the painting on the sofa. 'It's lovely. Like something out of a children's book. Is it real? A real place, I mean?'

He nodded. 'It's Kings Sloley in Norfolk, I played there as a child with my brother. The lighthouse keeper's sons were in both our classes at primary school. Then they moved away, and the next one, Mr Perkins, wouldn't let any of us near the place.'

He peered at his picture. He hadn't thought much about what it would actually look like to someone seeing it for the first time, and he was relieved. It looked all right.

'The Lighthouse was where I first flew a kite, and where I learned to ride a bike. I dream about it sometimes, but it's always distant.' He stopped speaking. That music had got right under his skin. All of this was new. He realised how little he had shared of himself with her, how generously she had shared with him.

Felicity's eyes sparkled. 'I'd love to go there. I'd love to go there with you.'

He squeezed her hand. Opened his mouth to say something eloquent, meaningful, but he couldn't. He dropped her hand, 'Anyway, I thought it might be useful. You need an image for your business, and I was thinking a new name might be the thing. You know, "Lighthouse Fabrics" or "Lighthouse Designs" or something? I can adapt this to make it your insignia, if you like it.'

She hadn't spoken. Oh damn, he'd got it wrong. He'd had a nerve hadn't he? Trying to get involved? Ah well, the picture would look okay hung somewhere in the house. Wouldn't it?

'Don't worry my love,' he said softly. 'You don't have to like it.'

Felicity threw her arms around his shoulders, her smiling kisses engulfing both of them. 'Like it? I love it, I love it. It makes such perfect sense.' But you haven't signed it. Come on.' She let go of him and turned to the inkstand on the desk in the corner. 'Make a mark, Marker,' she said and twirled the canvas to show the back. Michael signed it, scratching his initials on the canvas, circling them. Felicity took it, removed a watercolour of a church seen through foxgloves, and hung it on the wall. 'Lighthouse Fabrics it is,' she said. 'You've given me something to last a lifetime, you know.'

The baby, Christopher John Mohune Delaware, arrived at dawn on a spring morning. Michael and

Felicity had spent the evening before writing his names, changing the order, arguing over where the Mohune should go to sound the most dashing. Michael balled up the paper they had scrawled on and threw it into the bin as the midwife bustled in. Audrey Castleton, Arthur's sister-in-law and the village midwife in attendance. A brisk woman with a firm manner, she helped Michael stay calm.

'It's all right, you know,' she glanced at him as she filled the kettle for the tenth time.

'It is?' Michael stared back, and clenched his fists at his side to stop himself clutching her arm.

'You're boiling the kettle again.' She laughed, 'I'm only making a cup of tea for you and me. There's nothing to worry about, you know.'

Occasionally he found himself laughing at his fears. He was every man. Thousands had been there before him, and thousands were still to come. Men who had been through war and pain, yet found themselves floored at the prospect of someone they loved in discomfort. From the sounds Felicity made, when he entered the room to see her, it was clear that 'discomfort', Audrey's word, was a ridiculous understatement. Felicity's hair was sweaty and lank, and her eyes hollow with exhaustion. It had been a long night. He wondered when he might be hit with a sense of elation at the prospect of new life beginning, but frankly, it seemed terrifying. So when Michael found a pair of sloe dark eyes gazing at him, solemn and lit with surprising gravitas, he wasn't expecting to feel anything. A clawing, soaring, sky high, primordial rush of love swirled and settled in a cavity of his heart that had, little though he'd known, rattled with emptiness. Love expanded, filling the aching emptiness left by Johnnie's death. Michael sat on the bed next to Felicity, staring at the extraordinary new being who had arrived in their midst. They were complete now. And Michael suddenly knew just what his mother and father had lost.

'He's called Kit,' said Michael. 'This is our son, Kit,' and he tucked him in Felicity's arms and the three of them slept.

Kit was an equable soul, and his tiny presence prised open the protective shell of closely guarded intimacy that Michael had built around himself and Felicity. Now there was a living embodiment of their love. Their friends and neighbours breathed a sigh of relief and welcomed Kit into their hearts. In the first weeks of his life, Sheila Spencer visited almost daily, sometimes accompanied by Paul. Sheila brought warm loaves, newly baked; Paul helped Michael put up a lean-to porch on the house to shelter the pram Michael's former landlady Verity had given them. No matter how the rain squalled that spring, baby Kit lay asleep, snugly wrapped and dry, covered by the big navy blue pram hood, dreaming of the sea he didn't yet know.

Felicity, to her own surprise, took motherhood in her stride, though her focus changed. Now she worked intensely for shorter stretches of time, and she brought her life into her designs, so whatever she was doing, she would look for the shape or form of it and transcribe it onto paper and then to a screen. She and Michael spent summer hours with Kit kicking his legs on a blanket spread on the grass, and Felicity drew the wild flowers, dissecting speedwells and buttercups, forget-me-nots and purple loosestrife, ladies smocks and the vivid pink flowers of the wild sweet pea to find the forms for her designs.

Kit's arrival opened another channel in Felicity's creative vision. Sketches of everything flowed from her: spoons and bars of soap, sea birds and even a line of kitchen chairs dancing along the border of a wavy stripe. Sometimes Verity offered to take the baby for a walk. She wasn't the only one to give Felicity help. Michael, raised on a rural farm with few neighbours, had not realised how a community looks after its own. It wasn't uncommon for Michael on his way back from the workshop to see his baby son sailing down the hill towards the harbour in his pram, pushed by Esther from the pub. Or, when Michael stopped by the grocers in Love Lane, he might find Kit's pram again, and Kit, propped on a cushion, regally accepting all attention from housewives queuing with their ration books, while Verity bustled with pride and love for this baby.

September came. Felicity and he had talked so much about what would happen when he went, it had almost lost its significance, but since Kit arrived, Michael felt every beat of his heart bringing the moment closer. He could no longer let his mother suffer his loss as well as Johnnie's. The baby was flourishing, Felicity was well, happy, engrossed in her son and her work, and Michael knew that the life he loved was becoming too real. Soon it would be all he knew, he was ready to lose himself, to dive into the fathoms of love and never leave. It was becoming more difficult every day.

Walking to the workshop, he took a detour early one morning up to the top of the hill. A skein of geese, their silhouettes soft indigo against the sky, flew over him, the rhythmic scraping of their cry like a bow pulled across a violin. The light changed imperceptibly as the days drew in, and low rays poured onto the sea, tinting the familiar view sepia. At high tide, the ocean glimmered like a glass pane, and it seemed fuller than Michael had ever seen it before. It wasn't yet eight o'clock and the day was warm already. He'd left Felicity dressing Kit in their bedroom. Michael lit a cigarette, and smoked it hard so the ember burned bright and looked back at the cottage. It contained everything he held dear. He wondered where he would find the heart to take with him.

Later that morning he returned home to find the baby lying on a rug in the garden kicking his legs beside Felicity. Her skirt, a newly finished design, was decorated with ripples of migrating geese in blue, grey and purple flying across the fabric. It felt significant to Michael that it mirrored what he'd seen up on the hill. Her hair tangled loosely down her back, her arms were tanned from the summer outside, and she drew quickly, covering pages of a sketchbook with line drawings, while Kit played beside her. Michael took a snapshot in his head. A memory. A piece of his heart to take with him.

He knelt beside her. 'Come on, we'll go for a picnic. Let's get our things now, and swim at the cove before the tide turns.'

She put her pencil down. 'What about work? I'm so behind, I—'

Michael pulled her to her feet. 'We'll leave work behind for today.'

Felicity's eyes widened, and he saw tears rushing into them, but she nodded and stood up. 'Let's go,' she said.

Michael had booked a ticket on the sleeper from Penzance that night. Earlier, he bathed Kit in the china washstand in the bedroom. His hand cradled the baby's head and he leaned close, storing memories of his son, whispering lines of his favourite poems in a mad belief that Kit might one day remember them. Michael studied Kit's eyelashes as they swept his cheeks, the dimples banded across his tiny hands, his inverted baby version of knuckles. Kit's tiny grasp, surprisingly firm, wrapped the full might of his baby strength around Michael's forefinger. His skin was soft, slippery in the water, smooth as marble, flawless. His legs kicking delight, constantly moving, his mouth pursed to blow bubbles of concentration. He was extraordinary, Michael thought. He'd read once about an experiment where an athlete mirrored every movement of a tiny baby over the course of one day.

It had floored the athlete. Kit, he thought proudly, would run rings around any of them. Kit crowed with laughter then looked surprised, he had made a new noise, and startled himself. For a moment it seemed he might cry, but he righted himself, and his eyebrows, finely drawn above eyes dark as obsidian, rose to an arch. Michael tickled his tummy and he laughed some more. Kit was exhausted by the time Michael had fed him his bottle and put him, warm, milky and almost asleep, in his cradle. Saying a silent goodbye, Michael breathed in the soft sweet smell of his son and prayed never to forget.

The Indian summer was at its golden height. Michael fastened the strap of the wristwatch Felicity had given him. *'Time will run back and fetch the age of gold'*. This was his age of gold. He was in it right now, and he could not fool himself that it would come again. He stood on the threshold of the house, Felicity was in her studio. He would go to her in a moment, and then he would leave for the station. He shut his eyes, the better to experience the scents of the evening, the salt on the air, cut with a hint of woodsmoke and the waft of dry grass. He could hear the gulls in the harbour, the clatter of dishes in a house nearby, and the sharp lilt of children playing on the beach below.

Michael found Felicity emptying a rag bag, scraps of fabric tumbled around her on the doorstep where she sat, and she had begun to fold cloth pieces into piles. 'Order out of chaos,' she said, her voice sharp, and bright. She was keeping busy. That's what she'd said she would do when he left. 'I've got all this to untangle,' she waved at a basket holding a nest of coloured thread. 'It'll take me a while.'

Michael sat down next to her on the step, and dropped a kiss on her bare arm. 'Kit's asleep,' he said.

The smell of bacon frying drifted up from the village, and in the shade, the air had the cool edge of autumn.

She nodded. 'He's tired after today, all the sea air on our picnic.' She was calm. Michael was afraid that if she cried, he wouldn't be able to leave. He pulled her towards him in a tight hug. She yielded against him, her cheek on his shoulder. 'Time for the train, are you sure you want to come to the station?'

She lifted her face and darted her eyes to his, then away, but he caught the sheen of unshed tears. 'Of course I'm coming. Verity's come to sit with Kit, she's in the kitchen. Let's go.'

As they walked out of the gate Michael turned and looked back. Already it wasn't his life any more. The open casement, the red checked curtain fabric at the kitchen window, the hydrangea climbing up to the sill of Felicity's room, all were simply abstract shapes now he was leaving them. He turned to face the road ahead, holding hands with Felicity, and he tried as hard as he could not to cling to her fingers.

Saying goodbye to Felicity was like a nightmare. He was somewhere far away when he kissed her, her face blurred, smeared with tears. She wasn't crying, he realised, they were his tears. He floated above his own body, through their last farewell, and as if from a great height, he saw himself pull away from her and step up on to the train as the whistle blew. It was a nightmare that could have no end. He leaned out of the window, trying to say something. What on earth was he trying to say? She shook her head, walking down the platform, her eyes locked on to his as the train began to move. He was shouting something, but no sound came out of his mouth and the engine gathered speed. Suddenly there was no gaze between them. Only distance. All he could see was the shape of her, her outline delicate, hard to make out, everything so blurred. Her figure flickered in the gloom of the station. She was waving, blowing him a kiss, she smiled, her handkerchief balled in her hand. His eyes smarted, he dashed a hand across them, and she wasn't there. Gone. Out of his life with one breath. Darkness fell inside him. A flame had been extinguished. The train curved away, the setting sun reflected off the sea and bouncing through the row of carriage windows. The glass panes, the passengers within, glowed like facets on an amber necklace until the sun slowly slid beneath the horizon.

It was some time before he looked inside the basket Felicity had given him. The train was quiet. Michael shared the carriage with one elderly man who, having glared at him for a bristling couple of seconds, announced pugnaciously that he would get off at Exeter. Then he shook out his newspaper with a crack and held it up in front of his face. The pages fluttered like a trapped moth until Michael stood up and closed the window, but the man didn't speak again. Michael was left to his thoughts. They were desolate. Opening the basket, he decided, was the last act that connected him to Felicity, and he wanted to savour the moment.

Once his companion had gone, the carriage was his alone, and he was ready for the final act of parting. The train hurtled through St Erth and Liskeard, St Germans and Saltash and out of Cornwall, as Michael spread the picnic on the seat next to him. There was bread and a piece of cheese, apples, a pork pie wrapped in a napkin, and a bottle of beer. He ate slowly, the taste of the bread, the smooth earthy beer they always drank on picnics was evocative of home. Home? No. A place in his past. Felicity and Kit would go on being there. Michael saw black through the window and thought that an abyss lay outside the train carriage as it thundered through the night. He put the picnic tin back in the basket, and noticed that at the bottom was a cushion. Made by Felicity. Every stitch was hers, the green and blue seahorse fabric was the same as the curtains in their bedroom in Mousehole. He pulled it out of the basket, and buried his face in it, it smelled of her. He shut his eyes and breathed as much of her into himself as he could. It would be nice to lie on, and with this thought he turned the cushion over on the seat beside him. The other side was embroidered with an intricate picture of a lighthouse. His lighthouse. Red and white in the landscape he knew so well and which she had never seen except in his painting. Scattered like daisies in the grass at the bottom of the picture, the words, *'light of my life'.* The carriage had been empty since the elderly man had departed at Exeter. Michael lay down, tucked the cushion under his head, and slept.

Returning home was every bit as difficult as he had imagined. Norfolk had changed as much as he had. The scars of war were raw, and Michael found himself close to tears much of the first days. He didn't have any part of himself spare with which to miss Felicity as he sat on the bus through the dereliction of Norwich's bombed streets. Even though clearing up was underway, even though there were busy shops and the glimpse of the market with its striped stalls and colour, Michael was wrenched by what he saw. On the familiar journey towards the coast, he was disturbed by the quantities of debris, sheets of corrugated iron that lay in fields next to rolls of rusting barbed wire. It was worse than Cornwall because in his mind it still looked as it had before the war. He had not anticipated the scars of those five years would still be raw. Buildings sagged, exhausted, surrounded by long grass, the windows like staring eyes, blank and baleful in their neglected state. Others were neat and clean. He noticed a cottage where a woman swept the step, a brown hen pecking contentedly behind her. He saw a spaniel lying flat in the sun on a lawn next to the long shadow of a great cedar tree. He walked the final leg of the journey.

It was a whole day since he'd left Mousehole, and it felt like several lifetimes since he'd last walked in the gate and up the path to his parents' house. His journey was over. His only certainty, his one conviction, was that he was here to stay. He didn't know anything else, and he couldn't bear to think, because every thought turned like a magnet seeking its pole, to Felicity. It was late afternoon when he finally walked into the kitchen at Green Farm House and picked his mother up in his arms. His heart slipped a beat, there was so little of her. She was as light as a shuttlecock, he could have held her up for an age, and he did, spinning round with her in the kitchen, with Badger, the collie dog, barking and the door wide open to the yard. Michael didn't want to put her down. He didn't want to see that his mother, like Badger, was stiff now, and his father, whom he could see walking up to the house through the yard, was bent and slow. He didn't want to stand alone in the kitchen with her and experience for himself Johnnie's absence.

He pulled a chair back and placed his flushed, teary-eyed mother in it. 'I'll find Dad,' he said and burst out into the fresh air, a fighting strength and purpose in his step as he strode to meet his father. He was a man, not a boy any more. He was strong. He had made himself strong while he was away, and he could work now as hard as Johnnie had ever done. He would have to. He was here to take his place, in the midst of his shattered family, and be big enough to carry Johnnie's memory as well. He had to do it, and he could. Everything would be well.

'It's good to see your face again,' Michael's father reached up to put his hand on his son's shoulder, touching his cheek with the back of the other. Michael's father's skin was rough and hard, like rock. The older man's face had sunk in the years Michael hadn't seen him. Hardship had knocked hollows under his eyes and graven age in fissures on his face and hands, but his ribcage was as flimsy as a dandelion clock when Michael embraced him, and he wanted to button up his jacket to stop the wind taking his father away in fragments.

He had been back a month before he got in touch with her. Janey was waiting for him at the King's Head in Blythe. He saw her, a fair head bent over a book at the end of the smoky room, no hat. She looked vulnerable somehow, and he caught his breath. It was as if time had frozen since they last met, and he had stepped sideways to a different universe. Approaching her, he took in the shadow of her hair falling across her cheek as she read, the movement of her wrist as she turned the page, and his throat was dry and tight. She was both familiar and a stranger.

'Janey.' His voice came out strained.

'Oh.' She jumped up, caught her knuckle on the table edge and dropped the book. They both crouched to pick it up, he saw the glitter of her ring. Michael pressed her fingers as he returned the book, and she smiled her thanks. Her green coat was adorned with a small silver brooch shaped like a horseshoe.

She saw him looking at it. 'Your mother gave me this, do you remember?'

He nodded, although, in truth, he didn't know

what he remembered and what he imagined any more. Tea arrived, the waitress sniffing as she dumped a heavy tray between them.

'The sandwiches don't have crusts,' she announced without preamble.

Janey giggled. Michael froze, stole a look at her as she moved the cups on the table. She was graceful. Everything about her was light: her colouring, her soft hair like sunlight streaked across sand, her clothing, her movements. She was, he thought, a gentle soul. He'd like to salute that. Come to think of it, that was the answer. He needed a brandy, he looked at his watch. Four o'clock. What the hell. 'Shall we have a drink instead?'

Janey poured tea. 'Go ahead,' she said coolly.

He opened his mouth to pretend that tea was fine, and saw she was trying not to laugh. He shrugged and called the waitress. He had no idea what he was doing, no plans, and no one to turn to. He had come back. His mother had told him Janey would want to see him, and he was here. Janey had kicked a shoe off. She glanced at him, and perhaps hoping he wouldn't notice, slid a hand down to scratch her instep.

He grinned at her. 'Itchy feet?'

Laughter lit up her face. 'Always. The places I keep meaning to go—' She flicked a glance at him, friendly, uncomplicated. Her nose had a charming tilt to it, insouciant, happy-go-lucky. He owed her some form of certainty. A flutter of hope moved in his chest. She owed him nothing.

'You look different,' she said. By now they had

drunk a cup of tea each, and a Horse's Neck. Janey didn't believe him when he asked the barman for this phenomenon.

'What is it?'

'It's brandy and ginger ale,' Michael explained. 'It's a failsafe when you're nervous.' He hadn't meant to say that. He didn't look at her. The glass was placed in front of him, a curve of lemon peel see-sawing on the rim. He flicked it. 'That's the horse, you see, leaning in for a tipple.'

Janey's peal of laughter turned the heads of two men at the bar.

'I want one,' she said. 'It sounds like something from the movies.'

Her tea went cold as she drank it, chattering, animated, rushing out comments on her favourite films, the books she'd read, the stories she'd come across. She was easy company. Michael ordered another round of drinks.

He raised his glass to her. 'We've both changed,' he said.

She nodded. A flush had crept into her cheeks. 'You're bigger. No, that's not quite it, there's just more of you. You're more visible. You've got life all over you now.' She frowned, bit her lip. 'Sorry, I shouldn't say—'

He interrupted, her, leaning to touch her knee. 'No. Yes, yes you should. Say anything to me. Please.'

She trembled and moved her leg fractionally away. Her ring clinked the side of the glass as she finished her second drink. She took a deep breath, and shifted to face him, holding his gaze.

The room fell away around them.

'Michael. I have something to say. I've been thinking, and I know – well I don't really know actually, but I think.' Confusion and the hot room and the brandy added a shine to her eyes, roses to her cheeks. He nodded, even though he didn't know either. She twisted her ring, it was on her middle finger and hung loose, but her hands couldn't be still, so she moved it round and round as words rushed out. Without thinking, Michael reached out and rested his hands on top of hers, stilling them, pressing them together.

She looked down at their joined hands, and back at his face. 'I want you to know that I won't ask you anything, ever. I don't know what you've done or who or where you've been. And it isn't for me to know. If you want to tell me, please do, but for my part, there's no need.'

She finished speaking, and they sat a while longer in the bar.

CHAPTER 12

Kit hadn't moved for some time. He had been lying dozing on the sofa as the sun had travelled from one side of the window to the other, and absorbing its rays. The lighthouse cushion was warm against his cheek, and smelled of wool and also of some floral fragrance. Probably Dora's perfume. Dora. His sister. He buried his face in it again, searching for some essence of Michael. There was a faint mustiness that made him think of mothballs, and of the cupboards he had emptied in his mother's house, but he knew he would be fooling himself to say that it actually had anything to do with Michael, he had died more than thirty years ago.

It was midsummer, swallows flickered around the Lighthouse, darting to their nests beneath the eaves. Kit locked the front door, placing his gothic key under a watering can in the shed. Luisa and Luca were coming by this morning to drop off some furniture for his tenants who were moving in next week. He'd decided to leave the cushion, and the picture, with Dora. She would look after them, she would be the keeper of the flame for him.

Kit sauntered down through the field towards the sea. He liked the fact that he could leave the key there. He didn't have to give it to a solicitor or anything like that. Luisa had suggested it.

Luisa. God almighty. Luisa. He dragged his hands through his hair. He was in shock, he hadn't been able to speak to her, he didn't know what to say. Tom was his brother. Never having had a brother before didn't stop him understanding what a massive betrayal it could have been. He didn't want to think about the texts, the dancing, the magic he'd shared with Luisa. While it was going on, he'd fooled himself that he was just making a new friend, but it wasn't true. Madness. Not just married, but married to his own brother. His brother. Christ, that in itself was enough to deal with. A whole new family for a man who's spent a lifetime as an only child. Big stuff.

Kit scrambled down the path towards the sea. Shingle undulated like a frozen wave, and beyond it the surface of the sea was smooth and inviting. Why not swim? It would clear his head. Purge him. His mind roamed around the new characters he had in his life. He couldn't deal with the next generation yet, it was his siblings he had to come to terms with first. They were good people. Welcoming and kind. He liked them. This morning he'd met his sister Bella on Skype. If Dora looked like the photographs he had seen of Janey, and Tom was said to be like their father, then Bella, born just three years after Michael had returned to his family and therefore nearer Kit in age than Tom, also looked like Michael and, oddly, like Kit himself.

Kit skimmed a pebble and it bounced five times before sinking. He'd been groggy when the call came through, a Skype session at seven in the morning was not his idea of an easy introduction, but Bella launched straight in.

'Hi Kit. Hey bro!' she grinned. 'I guess you weren't expecting me, but Luisa and I were chatting and she told me all about you. I had to get in touch. I've wanted to for years. You know who I am, right?'

'What? Christ, yes, of course. Bella. How are you?' Kit had been asleep, and had taken a moment to come to his senses. Bella caught him on the hop, and he had to struggle to meet her cheerfulness. She'd talked to Luisa. What might she have said about him?

'Morning Bella.' He hauled himself out of bed and moved to start up his laptop to see Bella more clearly, then changed his mind.

'Just give me a minute to get dressed,' he said to the small image on the phone screen.

She raised a beer bottle in greeting and her bracelets clattered on the glass. 'Welcome to the family. Cheers.' She poured the beer into a glass. 'Don't worry,' she added, 'remember the time difference. This is a sundowner, not a drink problem.'

Kit's laughter was muffled as he pulled his shirt on. 'I'm not worried. It looks good to me at breakfast time in England I can tell you. Where are you?'

'Tuamarina. New Zealand wine country. I don't know what the others have told you about me, but I'm their sister.'

'And mine now too.' Kit pulled on his shoes and went down the stairs, holding his phone in front of him.

'I'm going to make coffee, and you're coming with me. Did you say you've wanted to get in touch for years, or was I dreaming?'

Bella hooted with laughter. 'Hang on there, you're the oldest, so I'm someone's little sister at last,' she said. 'Feels good too, you look like a decent-enough guy.'

Usually taciturn until his first cup of coffee, Kit was surprised to find himself making an effort with her. 'It feels nice to me too. I never imagined having siblings.'

Bella adjusted her screen. 'Okay,' she said, 'I don't know how much you know about our father, but I'm guessing, from what Luisa said, that it's not much, and it doesn't surprise me. He kept things separate, and I don't think he told anyone except me about you.'

Kit tensed throughout his body, he was surprised by how much emotion he carried. 'He told you about me? When? What did he say?' He thought he might cry, but instead he sneezed.

'Bless you.' Bella lit a cigarette. 'I don't know if it was because I'm the eldest – well, apart from you – but he talked about his brother, how he blocked everything out. Couldn't face his death at all. All that came out when he visited me here, and then he talked about you.'

Kit fumbled with the coffee, his eyes never leaving Bella's face. He wondered if she was alone at her house in the middle of some giant New Zealand valley surrounded by zillions of sheep. Sheep again. Obviously a family failing. She was married, Tom had told him that much, with grown-up children. With her silver jewellery and mass of grey-streaked hair, she looked like a Red Indian chieftainess, harnessing the wind and the sun to serve her outback farm. Hard to imagine her living a domestic life back here in Norfolk.

'He must've found it hard keeping all that to himself,' he said.

'He said it had been, but he had my mother to think of, and us growing up. He said the more he loved us, the more he thought of you.'

Bella's voice had a New Zealand twang Kit liked, he could listen to her for hours. It would be great, he thought, to meet her and her family. His family now.

Kit gulped a glass of water, and pinched the bridge of his nose. Bella's expression was kind.

'This is all a shock, I can imagine,' she said. 'It is for me and I left home a long time ago.'

Kit gave her a shaky smile. 'Go on, I want to know all I can about him,' he said.

'I don't suppose Dad would ever have told me if I hadn't removed myself so far from Blythe, and Mum and everything he wanted to protect. Anyway, he came out on his own. It was the year after Drew and I got married. Dad said he wanted to help us build the wine store. He loved making stuff with his hands.

You know, with wood and saws and so forth. I didn't realise at the time, but he knew he wasn't well. He had a bad heart, probably from all the stuff that happened in the war.'

Kit was surprised to find his chest was tight with emotion. 'I knew he made things. He was part of the group that built the Newlyn Studios after the war. My mother always said he built the structure for her life. Her work, I suppose is what she meant.'

Bella had brushed away imaginary ash from the front of her shirt, and said gently, 'He told me about your mother. And about you.'

The sea hissed hypnotically. Kit lay down on the shore and stretched out on the sand. It was damp, and moulded to his shoulders and legs while the salty tang of ozone curled around him. His thoughts ran back to the conversation. A surreal way to meet your sister, on a small screen while you sit in a lighthouse drinking coffee at the other end of the day from her, and she on her verandah with a beer. He wanted to make sense of everything she had told him. She'd said one night in New Zealand all those years ago, Michael had opened up.

Bella explained. 'I think it might have been why he came to see us, you know. All the way across the world on his own, it must've been a helluva big deal. He said he'd been trying to come to terms with the fact that his brother had died and he didn't, and that it haunted him. He said he wouldn't ask me to keep his secret, but that whatever I decided to do, I must remember it wasn't his story alone. He gave me a watch, and I think it should really be yours.' She unbuckled it from her wrist and held it up for Kit's scrutiny.

'Mine? Why?'

'I don't know if you can read it, but it's engraved on the back. "To CWD. *Time will run back and fetch the age of gold.* TWD".'

Kit frowned. 'You mean Michael had it? I wonder if my mother gave it to him. CWD is Christopher William Delaware, her brother. He died in the war.'

'I think you should have it back,' said Bella. 'I kind of feel that's what Dad wanted.'

Kit sat down, propped his chin on his hands. 'Dad. I can't believe there was a real man behind all the stuff I'm hearing, it's hard to take on board. When he gave it to you, who did you tell?'

'No one. Except Drew, my husband.' She paused, a shadow fell across her face. 'It never felt like any of it was mine to tell.' She sighed. 'Are you all right with all this? You know, the new family and all?'

'Yes. Of course. It's just a lot to absorb,' said Kit.

Bella twisted her hair over one shoulder and moved her laptop screen as the sun cut lower in the Tuamarina sky. She explained to Kit how Michael had talked to her about his time in Cornwall, how happy he had been there, how meeting Felicity had saved him. How even so, he had always known he would return to Norfolk, and that having a baby had made that more urgent.

'It was because he loved you so much,' said Bella,

her gaze steady, her eyes a flash of jet in the shadows.

'He understood how much his parents needed him.' Michael had told her he had not known what he was doing when he arrived in Britain after the war. He didn't know where he was going when he took the train to Cornwall, he just knew he couldn't go home, he couldn't face his parents without Johnnie. When he did come back to Norfolk, he hadn't expected to find Janey waiting for him. That she was, he'd said, was more than he deserved.

'He told me about the Lighthouse, and I couldn't believe it. I was actually really angry.' Bella had opened a second bottle of beer, her accent was becoming more Antipodean. The sun had set and her face glowed blue from the lit computer screen. Kit had abandoned his coffee and poured himself a slug of whisky. Eight in the morning and drinking. Thank God no one could see him. Except Bella, who, he thought, wouldn't be fazed by anything.

'Angry? Why?'

'I don't know now. None of it matters in the bigger scheme of things, but I was young, Drew and I were newly married. I guess I had ideals about being honest. I didn't think it was right of him to keep something as big as that from Mum.'

Kit was angry too. How could his own mother have kept him in the dark? It was his story too, and he had never been told. Had his father ever wanted to get in touch with him? Had he tried? What kind of man was Michael? And what kind of man did that make him? The whisky hit the back of his throat and he grimaced, it was all a bit hard core, frankly. He was out of his depth. 'So what happened exactly?'

Bella blew a smoke ring. 'About five years after Dad came back to Norfolk, the Lighthouse came up for sale. I was a baby, and Dad was running the farm himself and taking night classes to become a teacher. He did become an art teacher in the end, I don't know if you knew that?'

'There's such a lot I don't know,' said Kit. 'But go on. Tell me about the Lighthouse.'

Back in the present, on the beach, Kit wanted to relive the conversation with Bella before he forgot it. He squinted into the sun and rolled over on to his side on the sand and looked up at the cliffs and the sky. The tang of the sea on his lips reminded him of home. Suddenly, appearing as if from nowhere, there it was, keening crazily beneath fast moving cloud, the bottom half sliced from view by the bulk of the cliff, his Lighthouse. His very own Lighthouse. He hadn't really stopped to think before, but it was an incredible thing to be given.

Bella said Michael used money his mother had left him to buy the Lighthouse. 'He was sad about you. I was born by then, and I guess that as he watched me grow, he realised what he was missing with you.' She was looking into a distance Kit couldn't see, but she turned to glance at him, and as she did, the screen froze. She was still talking, but her face was caught in that moment, and the pixelated squares showed her kindness graphically. Kit's heart swooped with sudden recognition of his connection to her.

'I would hate to have a child I never saw,' she added as the screen unfroze again. 'Anyway, he wanted to give you something, so that you would know you mattered. He said the Lighthouse was a kind of emblem for your mother. He bought it in her name, for her to keep in trust until she was ready to share it with you. At first it seemed crazy, but then he said it made perfect sense. He said he wished he had known you.'

'Did you stay angry with him?' Kit couldn't imagine having a father at all, let alone one who revealed a whole secret past.

Bella shrugged. 'I don't know. I didn't tell the others though. There never seemed to be the right time, and I couldn't see what good it would do.'

'I wonder if he and my mother kept in touch?'

'They did, or it seemed that way from how he spoke about her . . .'

Bella broke off to smile at someone who had entered the room. 'Hey there, love, come and meet my new brother!'

A face dropped down over the top of the screen, silver stubble, a worn red cap, narrowed eyes used to gazing at the sun. 'Hey,' said Drew, and wandered off again. His voice rumbled, and Bella called out to him, 'I won't be long, get a beer my love.'

'Better go.' Kit felt confused, and a little overwhelmed. He'd had enough for now. Bella had rampaged into his house and woken him up. He'd met her husband, seen her porch all those miles away in New Zealand, had a virtual sundowner with her that was a sun-upper for him, and now she was going to have dinner and spend her evening as usual and he was alone with a new past. That was just the sort of thing that families did to one another all the time. He mustered a grin. She was kind, he reminded himself, she was taking trouble to look at the past with him, and now she was his sister.

'Isn't it odd that we're connected?' he said. 'I mean we were before but we didn't know. I mean I didn't know. Now the distance is only geography. Thank you for telling me all this, I appreciate it.'

'It's all a long time ago,' said Bella. 'And as Mum and Dad are both not around, and your Mum has died, it isn't going to hurt anyone. I reckon we all gain by having family. I'm gonna send you this watch, though, through the post.' She tapped at the face, back on her wrist now, and blew a kiss at the screen.

'Thank you, I'd really like that.' As he spoke, Kit realised how much he meant it. 'You're right. Let's talk again soon, I've enjoyed meeting you.'

Bella blew him a kiss, and teased, 'Me too. I'm glad you're gorgeous, you look like a big brother should. We want to get you over here and hear all about your life before us, too. Let's have another Skype soon. Bye, Kit, bye bro.' She'd turned her camera off and Kit was left feeling dazed, staring at his own reflection in the screen.

*　　*　　*

He got up off the sand and dusted himself down. To swim or not to swim? A shout from the cliffs behind and a dog he recognised as Grayson hurtled towards him then round in a great circle. Sand sprayed like flames at its heels. Tom had arrived.

'Hey, Kit, we've got something for you. Luca's up at the Lighthouse.' He slapped Kit jovially on the arm, grinning. 'I hope it doesn't backfire.'

'Oh?' Apprehension coloured Kit's response. 'Haven't we all had enough of surprises for one lifetime?' He and Tom were at the tide's reach now, Grayson had slowed to a trot and moved along the beach like a shadow, his brindle markings scarcely visible against the camouflage of wet pebbles dark as pewter. 'D'you fancy a swim? I thought I'd go in.'

Tom threw a stone, his action fluid. 'Oh well, one more surprise after all we've dealt with is nothing. I came down here to get you to come back up there, but what the hell. Luca can wait. Luisa's been on at me to embrace all these bloody revelations. I guess a swim could be a bit of a baptism.'

Kit had already taken off his shirt and barefoot, clad in just his shorts, dipped a tentative foot in the water. Cold gripped his toes like a clamp. 'Christ, it's certainly not a baptism of fire,' he said, hopping out again, splashing drops of the icy sea spray up his legs where they burned.

'More like the bloody Arctic,' agreed Tom. 'Any towels?'

'Towels? I wish,' Kit was regretting the invitation.

There was a keen breeze, running like a razor over his skin, and he didn't much relish the steely tone which coloured the water. Alone he might have thought better of swimming. A bracing walk would be plenty. He heard himself answering Tom, 'I guess we'll just have to drip.' Crazy. Perhaps this was some sort of torture he felt he needed to go through as an act of contrition to Tom. He only hoped it worked. Goose-bumps walked over him like ants.

'Here goes then,' Tom dropped his clothes in a heap next to Kit's and, wearing his shorts, plunged in and dived under a wave. He emerged, throwing his head back, and struck off through foaming surf. There was no way out except to shoot himself or follow. Stripping to his boxer shorts, Kit took a deep breath. Head under, and the rush of cold water was like a depth charge. And another. And another. Suddenly, a gasping moment later, it was as if they'd turned down the volume in an action movie, the blistering cold biting feeling ceased, and his limbs became lithe and supple. He was alive and kicking, and the sea was a silken bath.

Tom drifted towards him. 'Hard to beat once you're in.'

'It's my summer ritual back home,' said Kit, 'even if it's raining. But we have the Gulf Stream in Corn-wall, and it's usually quite warm, I haven't been in here until now. Wasn't sure about the North Sea.'

'Must be good for you,' Tom had a flush of goose pimples on his arms, 'I must say, I don't usually bother, but the kids love it.'

'My mother was very keen on it.' Now they had been in for a few minutes Kit was relaxing. He loved the silky pull of the tide, the sensation of flying through the water as he swam a few strokes on the current. 'She carried on swimming every day until a few months before she died. Said it did wonders for the organs.'

Tom groaned. 'Not sure I believe that. Mine feel like I've beaten them into submission. This is a bit macho for me you know, if you weren't here I'd be out by now.'

'If I wasn't here,' mused Kit, 'I don't know about you, but this whole business— My – our father, I'm relieved more than anything else. It's as if I've been heading towards this point all my life.'

'I know what you mean,' said Tom. 'I feel I've been an idiot. Taken so much as read, you know. But actually, this makes sense of things I never questioned, and should have. Like how come Dad, a Norfolk farmer's son, was so caught up in the idea of the post-war art scene? He had books and books about the artists down in Cornwall. You know, Ivon Hitchins, Lanyon, Hepworth and Nicholson and Naum Gabo, and he was always trying to find ways to get them into his teaching legitimately. I mean, I've got a lot of respect for them myself, but I understand his passion now, because he lived among them. With you.'

Kit shot him a questioning look, but Tom was drifting, staring up at a blob of cloud as it trailed through the sky like a forgotten thought bubble in a cartoon.

He didn't appear resentful. Perhaps there was no reason why he should? Dora had been kind too. She was clear that she wanted him in her life. Maddie's new uncle, her new brother. She was already planning to visit him at Christmas when she had decided to take Maddie to see Aaron's sister in Bristol. Kit had offered to go with her, and the grateful look she had thrown him gave him the warmest sense of what being a brother could be like. Bella too. The watch that had belonged to his uncle. All of them were so welcoming and inclusive. He had never imagined that siblings could enhance his life. He'd never thought about siblings at all, come to that.

He took a deep breath and duck dived underwater. It was green and murky near the seabed, clear on top. Kit swam under Tom as he floated like a cut-out, his body straight and strong. On the bottom, small fish streaked about, tails twirling tiny drifts of sand as they hid under fronds of seaweed. He swam through a warm patch of water and rolled over and over like a seal. Delicious, luxurious warmth, who could ask for more?

Surfacing, he saw Tom's back propelled by strong shoulders, powering a burst of butterfly stroke towards the shore. Kit was impressed, he could no more do that than fly. He met Tom in the shallows. Neither of them made a move to get out.

'What was he really like?' Kit hadn't realised how very much he had yearned to know this until the question was out. Asking Felicity had never felt right. There was his stepfather for a start, and he'd always imagined that it would be painful for Felicity to be reminded of Michael. Stupid, really, as having Kit in the house was a living, walking, talking ever-present prompt to the past.

Tom kicked up a foaming trail of bubbles. 'I've never really thought what he was like, he was just Dad. He used to read to me at bed time when I was little. I remember he read *Moonfleet*, when I was about eight. It was his favourite book, so I wanted it to be mine, but I was pretty terrified. Mum said I was a bit young for it.'

'My middle name is Mohune,' said Kit.

'Is that so? Mine's John. I always thought it was after my uncle but maybe mine was after John Trenchard.'

'I'm John Mohune as well you know,' said Kit. 'Christopher John Mohune.'

'Christ, we're the same person,' Tom laughed.

'No,' said Kit, straight-faced, 'one of us has to be Captain John Blackbeard Mohune, with his stolen diamond. Come on, we should get out. Didn't you say Luca's waiting for us?'

Striding out of the sea behind Tom, Kit looked up and down the shoreline. There was no one else there. In front of them grasses sprouted from the cliff, quivering with a breath of wind and tickling the vivid spray of poppies. Kit shook himself as he picked up his shirt and dragged it across his wet skin. 'I'm touched by the welcome your family's given me, you know. You've been so kind, I thought I'd be frozen out.'

Tom finished rubbing his hair with his shirt.

He didn't look at Kit when he spoke. 'It's funny,' he said, 'if I'd been told this would happen, I would've thought I'd be livid, but here you are,' he turned, walking backwards in the sand, meeting Kit's gaze. 'I think the weight of time is stacked towards me at both ends of this story.'

He blinked hard, Kit looked away. 'What d'you mean?'

'There's less than ten years between us, but I had a whole lot more of Dad in my life than you did,' said Tom, flicking the sand with his dangling shirt sleeve. He looked embarrassed.

Kit gave a crack of laughter, which annoyingly came out as more of a croak. 'Christ, yes. I'm old all right, I feel it now, I can tell you. What's the thing Bella said to me, something from Milton. Your dad – our dad I mean – loved it. "The age of gold", or something. D'you know?'

'Of course, "*Time will run back and fetch the age of gold*".' Tom shook his shirt out before putting it on. 'He had a few favourite things like that he'd bring out for us, checking we'd learned them, you know, always the teacher.'

'Was he?' asked Kit. 'Always the teacher?'

Tom nodded, eyes narrowed. 'He loved poetry, painting, all that sort of thing. Not your average Norfolk farmer.'

'They must have loved one another, him and my mother,' said Kit. 'I mean the message she sent him sewn on that cushion was "light of my life", wasn't it?'

Tom sighed, 'I feel protective of my mother, but as Luisa says, what do we know of any of it? It was all a long time ago, we're looking at it from a distance and from a different perspective.'

'Time will run back and fetch the age of gold,' said Kit.

'Well remembered!'

Kit laughed. 'It's the blood of the teacher in my veins,' he said.

They walked in step with one another up the beach.

'When exactly are you off?' Tom slung his shoes, laces tied together, over his shoulder.

Kit began to climb the narrow cliff path. 'The tenants move in next week, so I'll leave in a couple of days. I want to make sure that it's shipshape so it doesn't cause a lot of grief for me to deal with from the other end of the country.'

'How long is it let for?'

'A year. I've got a lot going on with the business at the moment, and I just wanted the Lighthouse to be occupied while I decide what to do about it.'

'Well, if you need anything done, Luisa and I would be happy to help.'

Kit was touched by the genuine kindness of Tom's offer.

'I think, if it wasn't for you guys being here, I would put the Lighthouse on the market, but as it is, it feels like some day this could be a new chapter.'

'I hope so,' said Tom. Catching sight of Luca sitting on the roof of the Land Rover, he cupped a hand to his mouth and shouted. 'Sorry son, we got waylaid.'

Luca jumped down and ambled towards them. He looked unphased. 'Swimming? You, Dad? That's cool.'

'It was cool all right. Icy would be more accurate,' laughed Kit.

Tom had walked around to the other side of the Land Rover and opened the passenger's door. 'Okay, here we go,' he cleared his throat ostentatiously. Kit turned to look at him, as a ball of exuberance, ears, legs and a pink tongue hurtled out of the car.

'It's a puppy,' said Tom.

'So I see,' said Kit. 'Whose puppy?' He groaned. 'Actually, I think I can guess.'

The wall, part flint, part old red brick and crumbling plaster, was all that remained of the oldest outhouses at Green Farm House. A lawn ran across the former cattle-shed floors, and honeysuckle scrambled up the rough red and grey mottled surface. This small walled garden was sheltered and peaceful, protected by its aspect, and adorned with remnants of its past. A metal cartwheel had been embedded in the earth, and where it had leaned through all weathers, it had sunk into the wall like a fossil. An iron water pump stood at the other end near the house, with a cracked china bowl under the spout for the drips. The roof of the house sloped down to head height, a deep brow over the windows looking on to the garden, and in the wide expanse a few black pan tiles made a random display.

Kit tried to imagine Michael here, up a ladder, making the walls good, pulling down the derelict sheds, stopping the rot, or in the house, at his desk, sorting the farm accounts, preparing for his teaching. He thought of him inside, in the sitting room by the fire, settled in the old blue armchair, the lighthouse cushion supporting his back. Michael had done his best, there was no doubt. It was hard, Kit thought, to live a life where people didn't get hurt.

Kit dragged a bench alongside the table and pulled the cloth straight. He finished laying the table for Luisa, marvelling as he did at how frequently these days he sat down to eat with more than half a dozen people. This would be the last time. It was his final evening in Norfolk, he would leave tomorrow morning at dawn. He wandered back towards the house. Luisa was on the doorstep, carrying a concoction she'd just got out of the freezer. She looked as though she was about to step out into the garden. Then something fell off her ice-cream creation, and she gave a yelp of frustration, shrugged at him and went back into the house. By the time he entered, the whole family was milling about. Dora had rescued the creation by scooping it into mounds and pouring rivers of liqueur over it. Luisa was in the midst of her family, and she made sure she didn't catch his eye. He didn't see why she should forgive him, but he hoped she would one day. Kit poured himself a drink, and went back out to the garden. A life lived without hurting people sounded good on paper, but was it possible?

Tis better to have loved and lost
Than never to have loved at all

And by the same token then, it was better to have been loved and been lost than never to have been loved at all. Kit didn't want his life to be empty and solitary any more. He wanted to take Norfolk home with him. A shout from the house alerted him, he spun round in time to see the puppy galloping towards him, with a lump of butter not melting in its mouth. In time he would understand how lucky he was that he'd been given the dog, he thought.

CHAPTER 13

The long grass squelched. The rain had stopped, and all sound seemed to be magnified in the gold fish bowl of the dripping day. A family whizzed past the gate on bicycles, and the piping voices of the children reminded Luisa that she had offered to have Maddie for the night. Was it tonight or tomorrow? She must call Dora. Maddie would love the ice-cream van. They could go and see her friends in it. When it worked.

Luisa heard Tom before she saw him. Metallic hammering, a pause, the soft bark of a saw. In the shed, Tom and the ice-cream van seemed to be glaring at one another in some sort of stand-off. The impression was fair of Tom, he was lost in scowling thought, brandishing a metal pipe and a piece of wood. He'd been frowning ever since Kit left. He said he missed him. Odd to miss someone he'd only just met, but on the other hand, all the years of not knowing he had a brother were wasted in a way, and it made sense to want to catch up.

Luisa had suggested a trip to visit Kit in Cornwall. They could go when Ellie started at university. She was going to Exeter, it would be so easy. Tom was more enthusiastic than she'd expected, and when he suggested staying with Kit, she had to bite her tongue to stop herself reacting. She wanted to shout, 'Are you mad? There could be nothing more embarrassing than the three of us staying in his house together' but instead she counted to five and said, 'Don't you think it might be a bit much for him to have us staying? There are lovely B&B places around there, why don't I look for one?'

The van's frown came from its oddly splayed wind-screen wipers and the saturnine appearance of two bright blue cones welded to the roof.

Luisa reached to touch one, enjoying the solid shape, smooth to the touch. 'We should repaint these a more realistic colour,' she commented. 'No ice creams are blue. Apart from that crazy Baked Alaska I made.'

Tom grinned. 'The car sponge? I liked it.' He ran his hand along the side of the van. 'There's a lot to do, but it's coming together.' His shirt was covered in oil, his hair had wood shavings in it. He waved the piece of wood towards the back of the van. 'Finally got the door of that cupboard to stop swinging about. It's pretty much all set now. I had the engine on charge overnight, so when you're ready, we can try a virgin run.'

Luisa tried a joke. 'That sounds all wrong for an ice-cream van.'

His laugh was almost heartfelt. 'You're right it does. All right, a test drive. That's more like it.' He opened the door and inclined his head towards the passenger's seat. 'Coming? Tod?' He waved her in with a flourish.

Luisa opened her mouth to protest. She had too much to do, she had food to cook, phone calls to make, work to finish, people to chivvy around the place. Ellie was coming home today and she had to prepare. Then she shut her mouth again. If Kit had asked her, she would've said yes straight away.

'Okay.' She climbed into the cab and shuffled herself on to the passenger seat. The familiar plastic smell, the faint whiff of vanilla, the almost childlike simplicity of the dashboard with its round dial and red needle that never went over 25mph rushed her back to her childhood.

Tom's head bent to the steering wheel as he listened to the engine turn over. Everything in his movements and gestures, the frown that snapped between his eyes when he concentrated, the shape of his hands and how he laid them on the wheel was familiar, and yet she felt that he'd changed. He'd gone a bit native. He had longer hair than usual, his skin had bronzed through the long summer days and his jaw was dark with stubble. She didn't recognise the old plaid shirt he was wearing, frayed at the collar and faded pink and pale green, and seeing him dressed in something unfamiliar gave her a sudden sense of how he appeared to others. Strong, magnetic. As if he heard her thoughts he looked up, dropping the frown of concentration and their eyes met. Her heart flipped over, and Luisa felt colour rush to her cheeks.

She put her hand on his arm. 'Whose is this shirt?' The fabric was soft, she found the button on the sleeve and ran her fingers over it.

Tom put his hand gently over hers. 'Dunno. I found it on top of all the paints we brought back from the Lighthouse, someone must've left it.' He moved her hand onto the pocket, which was spattered with white flecks. 'It's covered in paint.'

The engine revved then died. Tom squeezed Luisa's hand and and got out of the van. 'Hang on, Tod, it won't take a minute.'

She laughed. 'It's been so long already, what's a minute or two now?'

'Exactly,' he agreed, and whistling, opened the bonnet again. A slit of light through the door showing the dripping wet day beyond. Tom leaned over the dusty old van, and Luisa watched him. She didn't move. This was the man Tom could be in the summer holidays, when he left behind all the school rules and filing and marking, and he could tinker around in the shed and lead an untrammelled life. She envied him suddenly. He could be anyone he wanted to be for the summer, and then the autumn would come, and he would be needed back in school in his suit, with all his wisdom and knowledge at his fingertips, ready to inspire, or at least contain, a new cohort of pupils. Tom knew who he was, and that made him attractive.

A spanner clanged to the ground. 'Bastard,' said

Tom. 'It's not working yet. Sorry.' He dived under the bonnet again, muttering to himself.

Luisa climbed out, put a hand on his back. 'I'm going to pick Ellie up now, so I wouldn't have had time to go anywhere today.'

'No?' Tom was preoccupied, his muscles tight beneath her hand as he twisted something in the engine with the spanner.

'So I'll make sure everything's sorted for when she arrives back, and if you could just make sure that Mae lays the table, I'll—'

Suddenly the ice-cream van gurgled into life.

Tom peered up at her from the mouth of the engine. 'Ah. I think it'll work now.' His teeth flashed from an oil-smeared face. A familiar gust of frustration blew through Luisa. He hadn't heard a word she'd said, he was all ears for the engine. She opened her mouth to complain, and a whirl and click heralded the opening chime of the ice-cream-van music. Luisa leaned against the door, weak with laughter, Tom shouted something she couldn't hear over the music, but he looked delighted. He leapt back into the cab and silence fell like a cloak as he switched everything off. 'Back to the drawing board,' he said cheerily, 'but at least we know the sound works.'

Luisa leaned on the door frame. 'D'you remember when we met?' You were so sure you wouldn't ever have anything to do with ice creams or Great Yarmouth or any of that Italian stuff. Now look at you, this van is your baby.'

'Yep, well, let me finish it, and it can be yours too,'

he was walking away, but he stopped, turned, and came back. 'I'm looking forward to seeing Ellie too,' he said, and he brushed the back of his fingers against her cheek. 'See you later. Safe journey.'

The International Arrivals Terminal at the airport ought to look a lot more exciting. Bunting, cheerful music, obviously an ice-cream van. Luisa watched, cocooned in happy anticipation, staring vaguely at the stream of faces passing through. She heard the excitement of reunited couples rushing to collide and kiss, the shriek of an overjoyed child swooped up in the midst of a family, or the hesitant greetings of travel-weary individuals by families or friends or just a taxi driver, both sides uncertain how to respond to this freighted moment. The moment, enormous as it was for some people, was swamped by the airlessness of the grey space. A bunch of flowers, bold pink and orange gerberas nodded next to her, folded in a burly man's grasp. The polished floor in front of the doors to customs was an empty runway for the next arrivals. Passengers emerged, eyes glazed with tiredness, leaning on heaped trolleys, dragging bulky wheeled cases, staggering with rucksacks. Approaching the welcome committee, they looked blankly for someone familiar, or a sheet of paper bearing their name. Something to connect with. Ellie would appear through those automatic doors in a moment, and when she came through, Luisa would have her family back.

She fished her phone out of her bag. No message. There wouldn't be any more messages now. Kit had no need to get in touch with her. In a parents' evening talk on drugs at the school last term, the speaker had explained how quickly a habit can form. Just three days, he said, and then you're hooked. How long to walk away from it again?

It was four months since she'd taken Ellie to the airport. None of them had any idea Kit existed then. Luisa had no reason to look beyond the walls of Green Farm House except to wish she could follow her daughter to India to protect her. Luisa scrolled to a photo on her phone she'd taken of Ellie the day she left. She was standing on the escalator up to Departures, awkward with her rucksack on her back, but giving her mum the thumbs up and making a funny face. She was like a firework crackling with excitement. She was ready to go. Ellie had jigged on the spot as she was about to go through. Luisa had completely run out of things to say except 'Don't go' and she was managing to keep that one to herself. She settled for clucking, adjusting the yellow nylon money belt Dora had given Ellie, folding straps into keepers, checking the buckles.

'Don't get excited and throw this away. I know it's not cool, but it's useful,' she cautioned. 'Just make sure you keep important things safe. And . . . and . . .' A wave of emotion rushed up and she stopped, pressed her fingers into her eyes. She mustn't cry. She mustn't.

Ellie swooped on her, rucksack and all.

'Aw, Mum,' she smelled of insect repellent. Luisa had sprayed it onto everything the night before. The smell caught in Luisa's throat and distilled a moment of nostalgia, the citron smell reminding her of summer evenings, all the family together having supper outside with a flare flickering, and the midge-repelling candles lit.

Ellie had given Luisa a tissue. 'Here, Mum, have one of these. You gave me so many, all my pockets are stuffed. I'll be fine you know, and I'll keep in touch. You'll have adventures back home too, and you won't even notice I'm gone soon.'

Well, she'd been right about that, hadn't she? It struck Luisa that perhaps none of this would have happened if Ellie hadn't gone away.

An announcement gurgled through the tannoy and an electric trolley beeped past them. Ellie had kept the yellow money belt, and it had become a joke. She sent occasional pictures of herself modelling it, worn with her bikini on a beach, across her body, military style on the banks of the Ganges River. The last that was seen of it was when Ellie posted a photograph of a pair of grinning small boys holding a football, with it spread out on the ground in front of them, 'Goal post for football.' It was as crisp and new as the day Dora had given it to her.

Luisa looked at her watch. Ellie would appear any minute. Would she be taller? Thinner? She might look the same as she did before, but be a different person inside? Luisa had never been away on her own for longer than a school exchange trip. She had found it almost impossible to believe Ellie, her baby, was in India. Even though Tom's clock always told her the time there, and she'd seen her on Skype, she'd never got over her conviction that Ellie was really at school, or asleep in her room, or away on a Duke of Edinburgh camping trip. That she was on another continent, with a babble of languages Luisa had never heard in her ears, breathing scents of pungent spices she was unfamiliar with, was implausible.

It seemed to Luisa like yesterday that Ellie, aged fourteen, went with a schoolfriend on her first day trip to London. Now she had crossed continents on train journeys lasting days, to arrive at a coastline or a mountain range far away, in time to see the new moon rise the wrong way up. Luisa had missed so much of Ellie's life she could never catch up on. No amount of saying, 'So you arrived at the airport, and then what happened?' would give her even the smallest idea of the full story. Ellie was her own person, her own woman. She had a life her family could not share, and that was only going to happen more and more. Luisa knew that before the whole incident with Kit, this would have upset her, now she accepted it. And so she should, after all she had a lot that had happened at home that she wouldn't be telling Ellie either. Or anyone for that matter.

The white arrivals doors swung open as a new trickle of passengers came through. A slight Indonesian woman steered her trolley with one hand, her other arm supporting a sleeping toddler on her shoulder, while another child bounced on the heap of cases and bundles tied with thin green rope. A man with a moustache ducked under the barrier and engulfed them. The baby woke and sputtered crossly. Happiness poured out of the man like sunshine, and he caught the baby up, surprising it into silence. 'Well, well, well! Well, well, well! Here I am. Here you are. We're together now.' The woman reached up for the startled child, the man kissed her and a quick smile flew between them.

'Mum. *Mum* – I'm here!' Luisa turned in confusion. A hit of patchouli oil and incense, like Mae's joss sticks in her bedroom wafted towards her. Was it Ellie? Where? How had she missed her for God's sake? A tall girl staggering beneath a huge rucksack rushed up and past, staring into the distance. Someone else's daughter. The parents had pushed through the crowd to her and she lurched between them, trying to hug them both. The family walked away, her father attempting without success to swing the rucksack onto his back. Luisa wondered if they had any surprises cooking in their family. Like Kit? Since he'd left for Cornwall again, life had hardly paused. Ellie had suddenly decided to return early, and that had thrown everything into a whirl of excitement that had not yet slowed down. Luisa had never even had a moment with Kit to say – what? Really there was nothing to say. Or not to him. Plenty to tell Ellie.

A new uncle. She would tell her on the way home, it was Luisa's only opportunity to take part in the story of Kit. Her part in it was just a jokey story about the sheep at the Lighthouse. The rest was buried.

Only Luisa knew how it had altered her. The frisson of attraction, the possibility of passion, had changed something inside her. She walked taller, and there was some subtle shift in the way she interacted with others. Luisa didn't any longer feel the need to run after everyone in her life. Sometimes she could simply stand still and let them come to her. Magnetism. She'd found a core of magnetism within her.

Ellie could hear about everything else. The story of Kit and Tom. It was wonderful that Tom was so genuinely pleased. Dora was the same. None of them seemed to mind being shifted down the family into new positions, though a lot of that was surely down to Kit and his charm. Luisa tried to imagine such a thing happening in her family. No chance of it working out there. It would be pumped up testosterone all the way to the pub and a fight of some sort. Anyway, there hadn't been time for any of that, there hadn't been time for anything at all, and now Kit had gone back to his life in Cornwall. Their secret *momento di passione*, their frisson, their whatever it had been, was gone. Delicious, bittersweet, melt in the mouth and transient as her finest ice cream. It had no staying power. And she had no place in her life for anything like that, no time.

'I'm coming back, Mum, I'll be home on Thursday. I've booked the flight, come and get me please Mumma' had been Ellie's message, ripping her right out of her fantasy life and back to earth in the thump of a heartbeat. She hardly had time to plan and create the welcome feast, she certainly didn't have time to think about a crazy infatuation. Rose ice cream. Lovely delicate, sophisticated, quintessentially English yet also Indian – many roses being from the subcontinent originally. Utterly romantic. Perfect to welcome Ellie, a recipe for the future. Luisa pulled out all the stops to make it irresistible. She infused the petals of her favourite rose varieties, pounding them in the pestle. She searched the Internet for the right rose *absolute* essence. She hid the receipt for that, because drop for drop it probably cost more than Tom's favourite single malt whisky, but it was worth it, the flavour was sublime. Then finally, late last night, she'd stirred in her precious rosehip syrup made last autumn. At last her ingredients submitted, and rolled together to become something both delicate and voluptuous with the scent of a magic spell. It was ready. She was ready. Ellie was coming home.

'Hey, Mum! It's me!'

Unbelievable, but she hadn't even seen Ellie appear. After all that. She threw her arms round her daughter, and almost cried, it was so familiar to embrace her. 'Ellie! I didn't see you. Oh, look, you've grown.'

'Hey, Mum.' Contentment, inner peace, beauty, shiny hair, henna tattoos on her wrist, whatever India offered, Ellie seemed to have it in spadeloads now. Luisa hesitated for a microsecond. Her daughter had grown up. It wasn't her automatic right to grab her and hug her any more. Their eyes met, laughter burst from them both and they rocked together. Luisa registered subtle changes: a different weight of the ribcage she held against her own, a new strength in the way Ellie held herself, a softer edge to her voice, an indefinable sense of being relaxed, easy in her own skin. Ellie had grown. She was taller than Luisa, her face thinner too. Tiny plaits framed clear eyes, shining, happy with no hint of redness or exhaustion from the flight. About her hung a sultry, evocative, provocative scent, more subtle than patchouli, but delicious, like amber. Until she saw her daughter return, Luisa hadn't understood what going away like this meant. Much had been lost in translation. The Skype sessions had not prepared her for the raw, radiant, physical reality of Ellie all grown up. Luisa didn't know how to behave except as a mother, and Ellie looked as though she was past the mothering stage.

'God, it's very strange to be somewhere so muted,' said Ellie, pulling her bag up on to her shoulder. 'Every scrap of India seems to be a different colour, they don't do minimal in any way at all.' She coiled a huge crimson shawl around her neck and pulled her hair over it, bracelets tinkling. She was glamorous, Luisa noticed heads turning as they walked out of the airport building. Pride tangled with excitement, a pang of regret for the end of her childhood, and Luisa's tears spilled over.

She wiped them away quickly, but Ellie caught her hand. 'Mum! I knew you'd cry, Mae and I discussed it. Come on, we've got to get home. I need to see everyone. Did you come in the ice-cream van? Is it done? I thought I could work through the rest of the summer in it and earn some money for uni.'

Luisa laughed. 'The van? I can't believe you even remember I have a van. It's still not mended, of course, but Dad says—'

Ellie was jumping with excitement now. 'I know, Dad will fix it. He always says that. Oh I can't wait to see them all. Why didn't Mae come with you? My phone's out of battery, can we call her and Luca in the car? Mum, I want to know everything about home. It's so long to be away, what's happened?'

Luisa laughed. 'Let's get in the car and I'll tell you everything.'

Ellie sat with her feet up on the dashboard, gulping the water from the bottle Luisa passed to her, a flow of chatter passing between them as if she had never been away. Luisa drove with a smile sealed on her lips. Ellie couldn't know the thousand tiny ways she had changed, or the countless gestures and intonations that showed she was still the same Ellie she'd always been. They turned on to the motorway, and Ellie took her mother's iPod and put on an Otis Redding song, 'These Arms of Mine'.

Luisa was surprised. 'Is this not a bit old-fashioned for you? I always thought my favourites were too slow for you lot,' she teased.

Ellie shook her head and put her hand out for her mother's. 'No. I heard this in a bar that night just before I called you, and it made me so homesick I decided then and there to come back,' she said.

They listened to the bittersweet song in silence. It was so easy to be happy, Luisa thought, this was it. Simple stuff, but who could ever ask for more?

Ellie turned to her. 'Mum what's the special ice cream for tonight? You did make one, didn't you? Like we always have for birthdays and everything?'

Luisa smiled. 'It's a surprise,' she said.

ACKNOWLEDGEMENTS

I owe the most enormous debt of gratitude to my editor, Alexandra Pringle, for giving me time to find my way around this story, and I don't know how to thank her. All I know is that *From a Distance* would not be the book it has become without Alexandra's wisdom and faith, or her team's many talents and limitless enthusiasm.

I also thank Gillian Stern for becoming my characters' best friend and champion, as well as mine, and for getting right under their skins to edit this book, and Justine Taylor for a comet-like copy edit, blazing a trail through what was by then a somewhat battered final draft.

Thanks too, to the venerable fabric designer Pat Albeck for sharing her expert knowledge of the process of silk screen printing and to my fellow novelist Louisa Young for reading an early draft and asking the questions that set my sights on a very particular horizon.

To Roman for helping me research, to James for putting up with me, and to all the rest of my beloved family and dear friends for consistent understanding and support as I headed back for yet another edit, yet another draft, yet another dive away from them and into the world I was creating. Thank you.

My final thanks are to Louise and Graham Banks for allowing me to dedicate this book to the memory of Sam, their son, whose wild and wonderful musical taste I have borrowed.

ALSO AVAILABLE BY RAFFAELLA BARKER

COME AND TELL ME SOME LIES

Gabriella lives in a damp, ramshackle, book-strewn farmhouse in Norfolk with her tempestuous poet father and unconventional mother. Alongside her ever expanding set of siblings and half-siblings, numerous pets and her father's rag-tag admirers, Gabriella navigates a chaotic childhood of wild bohemian parties and fluctuating levels of poverty. Longing to be normal, Gabriella enrols in a strict day school, only to find herself balancing two very different lives. Struggling to keep the eccentricities of her family contained, her failure to achieve conformity amongst her peers is endearing, and absolute.

Come and Tell Me Some Lies is Raffaella Barker's enchanting first novel – a humorous, bittersweet tale of a girl who longs to be normal, and a family that can't help be anything but.

'A gentle, charming account of a family of cosmopolitan sophistication living in a rural shambles'
EVENING STANDARD

HENS DANCING

When Venetia Summers's husband runs off with his masseuse, the bohemian idyll she has strived to create for her young family suddenly loses some of its rosy hue. From her tumble-down cottage in Norfolk she struggles to keep up with the chaos caused by her two boys, her splendid baby daughter and the hordes of animals, relatives and would-be artists that live in her home. From juggling errant cockerels, jam-making frenzies and Warhammers, to unexpected romance, Bloody Marys and forays into fashion design, *Hens Dancing* is like a rural *Bridget Jones's Diary* as it charts a year in Venetia's madcap household.

'A positive hymn to provincial living, it is an entertaining celebration of family life with all its highs, lows and eccentricities'
THE TIMES

BLOOMSBURY

SUMMERTIME

After one year of being 'buffered from single-motherhood' by her boyfriend, David, Venetia Summers suddenly finds her life unravelling as he is sent to the Brazilian jungle and she is left alone in Norfolk. As chaos reigns in her home and her three children run wilder than ever she finds her life further complicated by a bad-mouthed green parrot, a burgeoning fashion career designing demented cardigans and her brother's outrageous wedding. As emails languish unanswered, phone lines cut out and her long-distance relationship proves both vexing and bewildering, life and love take some very unexpected turns.

'Very, very funny'
INDEPENDENT

GREEN GRASS

Laura Sale has grown tired of her life. Her daily routine of dividing her time between pandering to the demands of her challenging conceptual artist husband, Inigo, and those of their thirteen-year-old twins Dolly and Fred, has taken its toll. She longs to remember what makes her happy. A chance encounter with Guy, her first love, is the catalyst she needs, and she swaps North London for the rural idyll she grew up in. In her new Norfolk home Laura finds herself confronting old ghosts, ferrets, an ungracious goat and a collapsing relationship. As she starts to savour the space she has craved, and takes control of her destiny, Laura finds it lit with possibility.

'She writes beautifully . . . Combining with apparent ease, emotion and admirable precision'
INDEPENDENT ON SUNDAY

ORDER BY PHONE: +44 (0)1256 302 699; BY EMAIL: DIRECT@MACMILLAN.CO.UK
DELIVERY IS USUALLY 3–5 WORKING DAYS. FREE POSTAGE AND PACKAGING FOR ORDERS OVER £20.
ONLINE: WWW.BLOOMSBURY.COM/BOOKSHOP
PRICES AND AVAILABILITY SUBJECT TO CHANGE WITHOUT NOTICE.

WWW.BLOOMSBURY.COM/RAFFAELLABARKER

B L O O M S B U R Y